FORCES OF NATURE

THE HEART BROTHERS: AMANZI

NEICY P

Contains explicit language & adult themes suitable for ages 16+ only.

"AYE! AYE! AYE!" MY GIRLS CHEERED ME ON. I WAS IN THE circle twirling my hips to the Wobble song.

"We did it, Bitches!" I hollered.

"Yes, we did, and it is about to go down on this cruise ship. Dick was the furthest thing from my mind last semester. Now that we got that fiya ass degree, I'm ready to get plucked, fucked, and sucked sideways. You heard me," Kara said.

"Girl, I hear you," I told her.

"Fuck that. I want to get white girl wasted!" Brianna yelled.

"One more drink and yo ass will be there," Val laughed.

The turn-up was for real. We had been so deep into the books these last four years that we deserved this much-needed break. The University of Tampa didn't owe me anything, and I didn't owe shit to them. I was ready to start my career as an Aquarium Marine Freshwater Technician Biologist in Florida. It wasn't my dream job, but I had to start somewhere after receiving my bachelor's in marine biology. I ranked number two in my class, receiving job offers from all over the world. I thought about places away from my home state, but Florida had everything that I needed. I had family, friends, a job, and most of all, the water. That aqua water saved me from many hot summers in Tampa and dull moments around groups that couldn't hold my attention. I would drift off into a place where my heart desired, which was the water. The beach was the only place I didn't have to daydream. My friends went there to grab the attention of the boys with their small bathing suits and provocative behavior.

Not me. I went there to get lost and fantasize about me enjoying the underwater life with creatures I created in my head. I always wondered what it was like living below the surface. That was one reason I wanted to be a marine biologist. I needed to explore what was beyond humanity and bring it forward. I was tired of being cheated out of engaging in the different parts of life. I experienced it once before and vowed to get a better understanding once I got older.

I remembered my father surprising my mother and me with a small getaway in Cocoa Beach, Florida. My mother wasn't too happy with Dad picking her up from work early. She complained most of the ride about how they needed her, and we needed the money. Daddy wasn't hearing that. He wanted to spend a couple of days with his favorite ladies. Once he told Mom that, she kinda got quiet and enjoyed the glorious view. I kept the window down, letting in the freshwater smell. I stared into the Atlantic Ocean, wanting to know all its secrets. The colors of the sunset made me gasp as if it was my first time seeing it. The orange mixed in with the blue gave me Dreamwork vibes. I leaned on the door with my hands tucked under my chin, waiting for the movie to start. And it did. Dolphins started flipping out of the water, going deeper into the ocean. I wanted to draw my parents to what I was seeing, but I didn't. This view and scene were for my eyes only.

When we arrived at the beach rental condos, Dad grabbed the bags while Mom viewed our room. Being so close to the water, I was anxious in the parking lot that was connected to a wooden ramp and stairs that led you down to the beach.

"I know you are not thinking what I think you're thinking?"

Mom said behind me. I didn't look at her. I inhaled with my eyes closed, feeling more at home than in any other place.

"I won't step a foot on the sand. Can I just walk the ramp, please?" I begged her. Mom leaned forward and wrapped her arms around my shoulders. Her face was pressed against mine, smiling as if she knew that it would have been pure torture if she told me no.

"You have five minutes," she answered. I didn't waste another second debating about it. I ran to the ramp and stopped at the first step. A wave washed up against the sand, greeting me. I smiled softly and called it beautiful. A slight chill ran up my spine, causing me to shiver.

"Are you cold little one?" the man appeared out of nowhere and asked me. He was extremely tall, with eyes bright enough to see through the night. He had a head full of dreads that fell over his face and down his body, making it hard for me to get a good look at him. His skin looked wet, as if he had just gotten out of the water. That was funny because I didn't see anyone coming from that direction. Something inside of me wanted to touch the water that was running down his arm. I swallowed down the envy I had of this man before I expressed it on my face.

"A little," I answered. Although my parents gave me the speech about not talking to strangers, this man seemed familiar to me. I looked back to see where my parents were and turned to the strange man when I didn't spot them.

He glanced out into the water and shook his head. "Well, I can say that it is not the water that sends that chill over you. Most people think when night falls, the temperature of the water drops."

"I know that already," I frowned.

The stranger smirked and folded his arm. "You do? How so?"

"The specific heat capacity of the ocean is greater than land or the atmosphere.

That means it will stay at a specific temperature and not quickly change. The volume of the ocean contributes to its retaining heat, as only a much smaller volume of land can maintain heat. Meaning, it will take the water to cool off a lot longer than twelve hours of darkness," I schooled him.

The man laughed and clapped his hands, enjoying my intellectual comeback. "That is amazing. School has taught you this?"

"No. My science class hasn't gotten that far yet. I have been reading about the oceans, seas, lakes, ponds, and other massive bodies of water forever. I love it," I announced proudly.

"Really? Love is a strong word for a young girl like yourself. Are you sure you are not exaggerating?" He doubted.

It was my turn to shake my head. "No. I'm not," I replied. My father called out to me near the entrance of the resort. I turned away from the man and the water, feeling a slow ache building around my heart. I looked over my shoulder and watched the waves get violent. The man stood and stared out into the water, amazed at what he thought was out of control.

"The chill did come from the water. It had nothing to do with the water's temperature dropping, though," I spoke. My statement forced the man to seek the answer to the riddle as he turned around to face me. "It was because the water loves me as I love it," I finished.

The man sighed and backed up toward the water. The smirk on his face revealed much more than it should have.

"You may be right," he said to me and held his arms out. The water stopped moving altogether. His eyes stayed on mine as the wave rose behind him. "This can be for your eyes only," he whispered, falling and dissolving into the water as if he was never there. My hands were over my mouth, watching the wave move backward into the ocean. Telling people about dolphins and whales swimming near the beach was believable. Bringing up a man falling into the water and floating a way like a giant wave would have them thinking that I was crazy. I kept that secret and my eyes open for any other unexpected things to happen. I heard his voice many times after that. Our conversations were brief, but they were amazing.

I asked him his name once before and he told me he had many. I wanted to be special. I didn't want to call him something that everyone did. He must've known that and asked what I wanted to call him. The name escaped the brain of my heart. *"Sol. I want to call you my Sol. Is that okay?"* I wondered what he thought.

"That is more than fine," he answered. That was what he was. He had to be for the way he made me feel. My obsession with these creatures was sickening. It was another reason I went into my field. I felt it was my duty to find out what and who he was.

I worked hard up to the years of my graduation, securing spots with teams of people ready to work with me during my summer internships at the Aquarium. They saw how passionate a worker I was and what I was willing to do to improve the company and build the skills I was developing. The company gave me a massive start-up bonus to secure a place ten miles away from the job. With the rest of the money, I paid my parents' house off and bought a car. With the advantages that were given to me at Tampa University, I knew I wasn't going to get in anywhere else. As much as I wanted to join my girls at their HBCUs, I couldn't leave the water. We stayed in touch and celebrated our success together, as we promised.

"Out of all people, you need to get fucked up. You graduated top of your class in a program that doesn't have many beautiful black women. Let's toast it up for Liya!" Kara acknowledged. The girls hooted and hollered, drawing attention to us. People started congratulating me and passing me money.

"Thanks, guys," I got a little emotional. The road to this wasn't a joke. My parents were the most supportive duo I have ever witnessed. Anything that I needed or wanted was granted to me with no complaints. When I received my full scholarship, they went to the dealership and purchase me a new 2019 Volkswagen GLI. I wasn't as acceptive of the gift. I knew they had a mortgage to pay with other bills. It was another note and added car insurance that they couldn't afford. Dad told me that my exceptional way of finishing high school with them not having to pay for college was all the reason for my gift. They would have gone broke to secure my future. For that, I owed them everything. Dad told me I didn't have to pay back shit because it was their job. A lot of parents didn't think like that. I was truly blessed to have them in my corner and promised to give them the world.

"Oh, cry-baby ass. Drink this and let's live it up. We are about to be on this boat for six more days," Val announced.

"This is about to be the best six days of my life," I beamed.

"Yeah, and it can start with him," Brianna pointed to a guy who was staring in our direction. He was shorter than the usual guys I was attracted to with medium brown skin and short fade. From the looks of it, he was working with something that I knew I could handle. He nodded his head my way, and I wasn't feeling it at all.

"No, ma'am. I need my man ducking to enter a room," I insisted.

"You are not taking him home to meet your parents. Get yo shit licked and move on to the next," Val said.

"Nope," I stuck with my answer and started dancing with drunk ass Kara. She had her hand up in the air with her drink splashing all over the place. "Kara," I said, reaching for her drink.

"Damnit, Adaliya. I'm sorry. Can you give me another one?" she asked. I laughed and shook my head.

"Yeah, I gotcha," I told her and walked to the bar to get her ass a bottle of water. I didn't mind the turn-up, but it was too early for her to be this drunk. I wanted my girl to go all night long with the group. I tossed the empty cup in the garbage and got the bartender's attention.

"Can I have four bottles of water, please?" I ordered. The bartender nodded and went to retrieve my drinks. I turned around to face the open water; looking out to it made me feel free. I could thank my father for the love that I had for it. He used to take me fishing all the time. My mother found it boring, but I loved hearing the waves clash into the boat and the smell of the salt water. I walked near the railing and closed my eyes, using my other senses to create different sites just as beautiful as the one before me. I smiled when I couldn't come up with anything and opened my eyes. "You're beautiful," I told the water. It was so... sexy to me. Just like the man that I fantasized about. I always wanted to be closer to him. I twirled the gleaming ring on my finger every time my mind thought of Sol. After our first meeting, I ran out to the beach with a cup and took some water from where the man had disappeared. Dad brought me a sterling silver mermaid ring. The fin circled an empty ball that sat in the center. He wanted to put faucet water in my shit. I looked at him like he was delusional. I told him I was going to find my unique gem, and I did. The water sparkled like any other diamond. I upgraded it when I got older to make it fit my now-adult finger. People thought it was an interesting engagement ring and asked about my fiancé. I couldn't tell them about him. He was still my own kept secret.

"Ma'am," the bartender called me. I turned around and saw him holding up my bottles of water. I went to retrieve it when the ship bumped into something ahead of us. I stumbled back, trying to reach out for someone to stop what I knew was going to be the ending. My back hit the railing, forcing me to flip backward and over. The fall felt longer than it looked. I braced myself for the impact and hard dive my body was about to endure. I took a deep breath before crashing under the water with my hands extended. I curled my body, making a U-turn. I glanced up and kicked my way back up to the surface with ease. My head peeked above the water calmly. I eased out the last bit of air that I had been holding and inhaled more. A minute ago, the small waves that I admired rushed forward and pushed me toward the ship. I tried to scream for help, but the water flowed through my nose and mouth. I came back up, coughing and blowing my nose.

"Liya! Liya!" I heard my friends calling out my name. I tried to swim against the waves to get away from the boat.

"I'm here," I yelled frantically.

"Hey, stop this muthafucka!" Kara yelled. The siren went off, and the ship looked like it was trying to stop. I thought of myself as a great swimmer, but I couldn't keep up with this ocean. I trod into the water, hoping that they would try to rescue me.

"Hold on, Liya!" Brianna hollered.

"Okay," I told her. I was petrified. As much as I loved the water, being out in the opening was not on my bucket list. I didn't want to think about the shit out here and how I couldn't protect myself. I kept calm as possible and stayed in that one spot. Consuming that alcohol wasn't helping my stamina much in this situation.

"You got this, Adaliya. You got this," I encouraged myself. I swam forward in the ship's direction and stopped when I felt something brush against my leg. "No. No. No," I was on the verge of panicking. I didn't want to, but I looked down to see if something was in the water. I only saw my legs kicking frantically. I felt something on my back and turned around quickly.

"Oh my God," I chanted over and over. The touch felt cold and slimy. My mind started racing through all the underwater creatures I studied while growing up and in school. I didn't have to think any longer. I felt something cold wrap around my ankle and tug me down. I went under fast, seeing that there were no other fish in sight. I kicked at the thing that was attached to my leg while flapping my arms. The grip got tighter, almost breaking my shit. I cringed and released some of the air from my nose. I didn't let the pain slow down my fight. I had to get the fuck out of here if I wanted to live.

"Please, stay with me," the voice sang.

For a moment, just a split second, I thought it was him.

I glanced down at my attacker and saw this creature that looked human but wasn't human. It had violet eyes and pale skin, with seaweed as hair. It had a face of an adolescent. I was so caught up in his looks that I didn't realize how deep I was dragged under. I gazed back up to the surface and knew that I had to get loose if I wanted to make it to the top. I started kicking at the thing again. The baby face creature opened its mouth and flashed me its sharp teeth. It snarled and pulled me down deeper. I screamed at the sight, losing the air that I had preserved to reach the surface. I tried to battle and swim-up, but it was too strong. I closed my eyes tightly, trying to reach out to the object of my fixation.

He didn't answer.

I didn't feel him.

I was alone.

The water rushed through my lungs as I choked. I glanced up one last time before succumbing to the water that I used to love.

"You are a good son," Mother told Landon.

"You are a wise Mother. Thank you," Landon replied.

"You are very welcome," Mother answered. "Now come, children. The sun will set soon."

I didn't want to indulge in her favorite activity like shit was okay. She had admitted to killing Qala's mate. I saw how crazy Landon got when Mother did it to him. Qala would not be all-forgiving like Landon. I didn't blame him. I got ready to stand up when my heartbeat skipped. That only happened when there was trouble in my water. I closed my eyes and searched for the problem. I knew Qala wasn't in the water tearing my shit up. Landon may have been the oldest, but I was something different to deal with. I had more to lose than a couple of creatures created by Mother. I saw an invisible boulder crashing into a cruise ship. It staggered for a second yet stayed on course. I found that strange, seeing that I wasn't the one to create that barrier. My leaders wouldn't dare do such a thing without my consent. I felt the splash and her presence in the water that she loves too well. She got to the surface but was pulled down deep into the ocean by one of my younglings.

"Come on, man," Skye told me. I became too stunned to move. Landon noticed it and moved to the table.

"Manzi," he whispered. I looked up, and the violet in my eyes got darker.

"I gotta go," I said, and stood to my feet.

"Manzi, what's wrong? Talk to us," Landon told me. I didn't speak; I shot a glare to Mother before disappearing out of the room. I heard them asking her what was wrong with me and the silly ass apology.

I didn't want to hear that. I knew that this shit had better be reversible without her help. If I had to rely on Mother and she did me the same way she did Landon, I planned on bringing the water to the castle. I arrived in the sky, falling into the ocean like a giant funnel. I heard the people on the ship screaming *look*. I wasn't worried about who saw me. I needed to get to her. I placed my hands in front of me while staring into her dead eyes. The dive was hard and created a wave underneath the water. The sea creatures knew their king had arrived and was pissed. They all swarmed away as I got closer to the woman still being pulled down to one of the sectors. I grabbed her arm, stopping her from going any further. The youngling looked up at me and growled. His fierce eyes got mournful when he noticed who he was up against. I bared my teeth and hissed at him.

"GO HOME!" I yelled. The youngling released the woman and swam away. I pulled the woman up to me and felt the coldness of her body. I teleported to a small island called the Maldives off the Indiana Ocean. It was the lowest country in the world, threatened by the rise of sea level. I created a small straw home that had one room and a bathroom. There was a king-size bed on hardwood floors. It was the only thing that I needed there at the time. I placed the woman on the bed and kneeled next to her. The water that she consumed made her face and body swell that quick. I rested my hands on the wounds that the youngling made on her ankles, then rested my mouth over hers. I inhaled and pulled the water from her lungs while healing the bruises. The glow of my eyes reflected from the face that was becoming her own again. I pulled back and waited for her to open her eyes and acknowledge me as she did every time she looked into the water.

"Come on," my impatient ass was about to blow. The woman didn't make me wait longer. She jumped up, gasping for air as if she was still underwater. She grabbed her ankles, fighting off the sheet that was over it. I pulled it off her and tossed it to the floor.

"Where am I?" she frantically spoke while looking around the room.

"Don't worry. You're safe," I said coolly to my beauty. The woman's eyes got wider hearing my voice and scanned my face. I saw the fear of amazement taking over her expression. It was as if she was delighted to see me but scared at the same time.

"Am I dead? I feel like I'm dead. Refreshed," she asked with tears in her eyes. "Is this heaven?"

I released a heavy sigh, thankful that I could deliver the good news. "No, you are not dead. I found you near the shore and brought you here so that you can rest until you get better," I assured her with a lie. The woman closed her eyes and surrendered to the emotions of her near-death experience. She started crying and shaking. I tugged her body toward mine and wrapped my arms around her.

"It's okay. You are okay now. I have a ship that is on its way here to retrieve us. I will ride back to the states with you. Just you and I," I consoled. She pulled back, shaking her head.

"No. I almost died. I felt the water rushing through my mouth and I-I couldn't breathe. I co-couldn't ca-ca-call for help. Heee di-didn't come for me," she tried to talk through her heavy breathing.

"Calm down." I rubbed her arms. "Look," I gazed down at her. The woman stared into my eyes and jumped out of my arms, falling to the floor. She got to her feet and pressed her body to the wall. I was truly confused by her actions. Usually, people relaxed when they stared into my eyes.

"Noooo!" she yelled.

"Wait. I just want to help you." I stood and moved in her direction.

"No, the water! Please keep me away from the water," she begged.

My heart stopped completely. I knew she didn't say that. The woman that I have waited years to mature and take where her heart desired the most was afraid of me. This wasn't real and far from fucking funny. The fear in her eyes told it all. My body deflated when she said I didn't come for her. I always did when she was in distress. It killed me to know that she was waiting on me to save her. I felt defeated standing there. A feeling that I have never thought I would cross when dealing with my mate.

"Hey, what's going on?" Egypt's soothing voice entered the room.

"I don't want to go in the water. Please," she begged Egypt, afraid to move in my direction.

"It's okay," Egypt said as she walked cautiously to her.

"No, it's not. It's not fine," the woman hyperventilated. Skye brushed past me and stood in front of her. He blew the cool air into her face, forcing her to sleep. She collapsed in Egypt's arms with tears running down her face.

"What is going on?" Skye asked. The water outside rose like my temper. I felt the waves getting thicker and more aggressive, almost reaching the doorstep of my home. My tattoos glowed, filling my circle with the color of the purest water. I felt the length of my hair growing as I turned around with an agenda. I didn't know what was worse; witnessing my mate dying or watching her live from a far, fearing what I was. I knew her stubborn lying ass had something to do with this. It had her name written all over it. I was sure that she would be ready for me once I arrived, but it didn't matter.

"Manzi! Manzi, look. Your mate. She is alive and well. She didn't die. She is fine. There is no need for you to go up there with all that mess," Skye tried to reason with me.

"It doesn't matter," I whispered.

"What the hell you mean it doesn't matter? She is alive. You saved her," he said.

"BUT SHE FEARS ME!" I roared out. I saw her body quiver from the thunder of my voice. I took a deep breath and released it before explaining what my brothers didn't know. "That stunt helped her develop the fear of water. She hates me, Skye. She can't even look at me without cringing."

Landon walked over to me, shaking his head. "We can work with this, Manzi. We can help her get over this fear. Don't give up on her."

"How? It feels like she's still dead to me." My voice was laced with misery. My brothers saw the pain on my face and wished they had the healing powers to make me better. But I knew what a temporary relief could be. My body brightened with anticipation. I knew she was looking down, scanning over what she had done like some fucking puppeteer. "Make sure she gets back to Tampa. Her name is Adaliya." I turned and walked away, placing my mate in the hands of my brothers and sister. Landon frowned, wanting to know how I knew her name. I wasn't around humans as often as they wanted me to. She was a secret that I thought I could keep. Skye said nothing after seeing me stalk her and knew that it was something serious.

"I will go with him. You make sure that Adaliya gets home," Skye told Landon. I didn't know what he thought he was about to do. But I was about to be a category five hurricane in Mother's shit. She had fucked up significantly. I teleported up to the glasshouse to have an unpleasant talk with my mother. Skye was on my ass, ready to hold me back from the outburst that was building in my soul once we arrived in the room she was in.

"Before you address me, Son, know that I had nothing to do

with that," Mother said as I approached her, watching the sunrise over the northern states in her live picture room.

"You really want me to believe that? After you told Egypt about the many mates you allowed to die," I replied harshly. Skye skipped his ass in my path with his wings out, trying to create a barricade between us.

"Oh, stop it already. I have learned my lesson. I treat you all accordingly, as situations and personalities are different. Landon understands my methods now, but you didn't and won't because you don't display the same emotions as he does. I wouldn't dare try that trick on you, Amanzi. You aren't the compromising type," Mother spoke.

"But you will find another way to do your bidden," I insinuated.

Mother turned around with her pearly white hair in a bun. Her eyes gleamed as they glared at me. "My bidden? Boy, every bad thing that happens on Earth isn't my fault. You will have to look deeper within your own roots to figure this one out."

She stood with her white wine in her hand, shaking her head. I allowed her to walk past me, and she grunted as if I had a choice. I knew my mother's power, but it didn't stop me from speaking my peace. I didn't understand what she was talking about because my roots came from her. Everything that I became began with Mother Nature.

"Mother, can you elaborate, please? What happened out there looked like nature taking its course?" Skye asked for both of our confused minds. Mother raised her eyebrows and placed her glass on the table. She put her hands on the back of her glass chair and directed her words toward me.

"I have told you that the strength and wisdom of a person are embedded into the roots of their soul. You liked that. You liked it so much that you started building your family of ocean people from the ground or, should I say, the seabed up. I wasn't telling you not to help Landon because I wanted him to figure it out on his own or punish him. I told you that so YOU could protect your territory better. You wanted to show me how much you agreed with Landon's attitude and left the Mogosens to do your job. They may have certain abilities, Amanzi, but they couldn't keep the troubles out of the water. You were distracted, and he got in. Now, weave out what you call children to find, which one has grown from a bad seed. Your lack of not taking advice from your brothers or me is going to cost you," Mother explained.

I thought for sure that she was going to be cryptic like the rest. Mother was striking me with that straightforward shit. I glanced at Skye, who was in disbelief that someone had got in my water without me noticing. I had to have been out of it not to catch Qala around my shit.

"When did this happen?" I asked my mother.

"The time Landon called you to help with Egypt. He knew you were going to do whatever to save your brother from falling back into that dark place. Your Mosogens tried to fight him off, but they failed. That is why you can't find Jonah and Semaj that were guarding the water near the Tampa shore," she replied.

"Fuck!" I cursed loudly. I felt nothing during that time. I released most of my energy, trying to save Egypt. I was at my most vulnerable state and that nigga capitalized on it.

"Do you know who it is?" Skye probed.

"Of course, she does. But she isn't going to tell me because it is against the universe," I sarcastically said. A lot of this shit could have been prevented if she had told us everything from the jump. I wasn't too keen on puzzles and shit. I was willing to destroy all the mogosens and younglings that I created to ensure the cleansing of the water. Most of the mogosens were great warriors and leaders who raised the younglings to be the same. I knew they would suggest the same thing if I had told my first creations Femi and Dafari of these matters. I remembered raising them together. They knew what loyalty meant to me since they were younglings. Now that they are leaders of two of the sections, their control over the water has increased.

"The last time I tried to tell you about your people, Great Creator Amanzi, you told me to let you be. I can't see what I haven't created. You gave Qala an idea and of course, he is running with it." She picked up her wineglass and sipped out of it before walking over to Skye. "This is me, letting you be. Come on, son. It seems as if your brothers are going to be very busy. How about keeping your mother company, huh?" Mother looped her arms around Skye's and led him to where her piano was.

"I know I can't be much help to you underwater. But if you need me, call me," Skye stated before walking out with Mother.

"Thanks," I mumbled and glanced down, watching one of my many sections from where I stood. It was quiet, as it has been since my new sister-in-law gained her abilities. I thought nothing of it since Qala took another L. He rarely came back-to-back with his plots. I assumed he was tired of the wait, knowing that we got stronger with time. I threw my head back and closed my eyes. I inhaled profoundly, feeling the water filling my lungs like air. I exhaled with bubbles traveling to the surface of the Caribbean Sea. As my feet sunk into the seabed, my eyes opened and adjusted to the light rays that forced the human inside lens to bend to focus. I saw everything as if I was on the land. My hair grew into the long seaweeds that flowed behind me. Seagrass draped over my body like a royalty robe. My tattoos of water waves surrounded the center, one that I shared with my brother. It was an upside-down pyramid in the middle of double rings. The three circles around it displayed my brothers and our territory. The massive circle in the center shined the brightest when I was under the water. I stood in my element, and it reacted as if Landon and Skye would be in their territory.

I walked in the middle of two ridges that led to one city that became an underwater feature. Port Royal, known as "Sin City," was the lost city sunk in the Caribbean Sea due to a massive 7.7

earthquake in 1692. There were buildings and ruined pirate ships rooted into the seafloor. My people grew accustomed to what was given to us by the woman that disagreed with their existence. Skye told me that this was more of a gift to me, but I have never known Mother to be that generous. That's why I couldn't believe that she didn't have a hand in the bullshit that was going on.

As I got closer, the Mosogens were gliding around, doing their assigned duties and speaking with each other in a different language that we only shared. The tattoos on their bodies brighten the bottom of the sea. We had leaders, guards, soldiers, pickers, teachers, and piyas that were born with a purpose to contribute to their sections. Jonah and Semaj were amongst the piyas group. They were the ones that protected the water from the land. They were just like me at first. They didn't want to be around the humans and their bullshit. But they blended in well, receiving the stamp of approval from Landon. Jonah and Semaj have just started land duty with their leader Lenmon. He told me he would reach out to me when he got in touch with them and hadn't yet. I was going to pay a visit to him once I got things under control in the water.

My brothers and I were unsure of Qala's abilities. He showed tremendous strength holding Egypt down to inject her with that bullshit he created in that fucked up lab. That meant I had to stay on my toes and expect the unexpected. I had skipped out several times to help Landon with his situation. I didn't know if that was Qala's way of getting me out of the picture so that he could infiltrate my garden. I was not too fond of that, and damage control was in full effect.

My people were planted in the seabed around the places we called home by the season. Our seasons were aligned with the seasons on the land. In the first week of the season, they were pulled from the ground by experienced pickers once they flourished into what we called the younglings. The younglings were brought to me for job assignments. They were then placed under their teachers to learn the obligations of their set sections. Once they have proven themselves, the younglings would evolve into their adulthood, called Mosogens.

There was much for me to protect. I needed to plant younglings after every seasonal meeting. If the leaders of the sections found the mosogens worthy, they would brand them and prepare a celebration. On their first day of duty, they would receive their weapons made of titanium and ice. It was the most brutal combination of materials that would cause major damage.

My thoughts cleared when I came upon the stone pergola walkway leading up to the opening of Port Royal. The statue of the lion with his foot on a ball sat on the left. An eagle's figure with emerald eyes sat high on top of a podium on the right of the closed gate. Kamau and Amber were two of my sternest guards who stood at the entrance of the city. They were created after Dafari and Femi. It would take more than Qala's army to get through them. They were both over seven feet tall with slender bodies. Amber's yellow kelp hair was decorated with purple corals. Her skin was pale as all the others with purple eyes. Kamau had seaweed hair that was kept short. The guard's brand was of tridents laid out to create the shape of the sun. Kamau and Amber's brands were marked on their chest. Amber's bow and arrow were attached to her back. Kamau was wearing gloves that encased two sharp rigged swords.

They noticed me walking toward them and poked out their chest proudly as they always did. "Father," they greeted me.

I bowed my head and addressed them. "I'm confused about a situation that needed my interference. One of the younglings got loose and attacked a human female. Can any of you tell me how this happened?"

"No, Father. We were unaware of any impromptu activities in our section," Kamau answered first.

"Bring the youngling to me. Tell the messengers that I need

to see them all now," I ordered. All branded mosogens were connected. The guards didn't have to travel far or leave their posts to get the message out. Amber nodded her head and closed her eyes to communicate with the guards that circle the sections.

"It's done, Father," Amber noted and stepped aside for me to enter the gate that I rose over my cities, preventing human scientists from entering. The towns were also protected by the electric magnetic field that coated the seabed. The ones that survived the entry got sick and nearly died once they reached the surface. It had been decades since the humans had tried again.

I traveled down the pathway and through the stone arch to the stairs. All movement from my people stopped as one soldier spotted me at the entryway.

"Father!" Oni yelled. Everyone turned to me and kneeled. My facial expression wasn't welcoming. They felt my energy when I arrived in the water. As I descended the stairs, big deep waves at the top crashed against the shores. I was pissed and needed to get the snake out of my water. Because fucking with my children, was going to cost them their life. Fucking with my mate was going to cost them their souls.

Dafari and Femi showed up with concerned looks on their faces. As a real father, they never knew how many problems affected me. When Landon lost Nelor, I gave Dafari and Femi strict instructions. Dafari went to the land to help Lenmon guard the water against the creatures that tried to get in, while Femi took over it when I was away. I didn't tell them why, nor did I tell them the danger that we were in. I didn't have to because we had never been attacked like that. After Landon's hiatus from being the land king, it shook some shit in my territory. I couldn't get around or pretend that we were safe. I had to inform the leaders of what was going on and what they needed to look out for. Once Landon returned to his job, I regained control, with Femi and Dafari going back to their sections to check on our people.

I glided past them and through the sections, mugging

everyone because I didn't know who to trust. My two leaders followed me and warned the rest to stay back until they found out what was happening. Three of my messengers fell in line with them without saying a word.

Out of all the sunken cities, this one had a unique look to it. The boats were outdated with pirates' signatures on them. The cracked wood allowed the younglings to swim through them like a playground when they were done with their training. I didn't want them to feel as if I was a strict ruler, which I was to ensure the safety of my people. I allowed them to enjoy their youngling state with a bit of fun. The buildings were used as homes, giving the Mosogens a place to relax away from their jobs. The need to destroy all that shit was overwhelming. My hands closed into a tight fist as the ground shook, threatening their pleasures to crumble. The other leaders swam from where the meeting was being held to see why the atmosphere changed. I ignored their looks and entered the circle of stone rocks. I went to the middle where my throne awaited and sat as the others stood, anticipating the news that turned my mood sour.

"A boulder appeared out of nowhere, causing the cruise ship to stammer. It wasn't a strong one to cause the damage that would have sunk it, but it was noticeable to me," I started.

"None of us dare to cause pain to the humans, Father," Dafari stepped forward and spoke up for his brothers and sisters.

"Maybe no one in this room. But I have seen the things that Qala could do if he got a sample of our blood. I think he manipulated one of our own. It would have been the only way for the enemy to enter my water without being detected. I was told that this had happened when I went to help my brother. Go back three seasons of picking and find out who hasn't developed the same as the others. I don't think that this was the first act that this person had performed. Look back at some smaller events that occurred when I was away. I could speak with Jonah about his last encounter with Qala's men, but he is nowhere to be found.

He or Semaj. I was told that they were harmed by Qala when he tried to succeed with his plan," I replied.

"Do you know when this happened?" Femi frowned and repeated the question I asked my mother.

"This happened two seasons ago. Jonah was guarding the area as well."

"Yes, Father," Nsia answered. She was the only female leader in the group. Nsai nodded to the guard of her section, giving them the order to retrieve her guard, Jonah.

"What else do we need to look out for?" Femi wanted to know.

"It will be hard to say since the enemy had time to adapt to our ways of living. The only thing I could say is to watch out and report strange behavior," I answered in the best way possible. Dafari nodded, but he noticed something else in my eyes. As much as I wanted to focus on Qala and his schemes, my heart was troubled. I couldn't stop thinking of the woman who almost got killed behind his bullshit. Dafari tilted his head and threw caution to the left as he approached me. He and Femi were the only ones that had the heart to do this now. The others sat back and watched on.

"Is there anything else, Father, that troubles you so?" Dafari asked.

"Your brothers are missing," I told him.

"We are sure that they are fine, Father. But that is not what Dafari was referring to. Is there something else bothering you?"

My bright eyes flashed with fury. "The enemy has entered my water without me knowing. The enemy has been amongst my people for sixteen fucking quarters without me knowing. The enemy found my weakness without me knowing. Shouldn't that be all, Dafari?" I growled.

"It should be, but it is not," Femi responded instead. "There is something else that is bothering you. We can feel it."

Before I could respond, Kamau and Amber walked in with

the youngling that I caught outside his sector. I recognized him from a couple of seasons ago. He was the only youngling that hadn't transitioned over into a full mosogens after seasons of living. He was small, with dots on his face and pale skin. His hair was to his shoulders and his eyes were violet, different from the others but the same as mine. Sipho moved forward, recognizing the youngling as his group mate. The frown on his face showed how displeased he was seeing him here. The youngling didn't make eye contact with anyone. He kept his head down and floated to the center of the room.

"Zuri," I called out his name with no room for the bull or shy shit. To my surprise, he looked up at me and took a deep breath.

"Yes, Father," his voice was light and innocent.

"Do you want to tell me why you were out of your section today, attacking a human?" I spoke. Sipho gasped. His tattoos and branded mark glowed. I knew if I weren't in his presence, Zuri would have been punished. The other leaders shook their heads at the disobedience shown by him. In all the years that my people had been here, nothing like this had happened before. I wasn't sure what was going on, but I needed to get to the bottom of this. Zuri nodded his head, prepping himself to answer my question.

"I just wanted someone to play with, Father. All the other younglings think I am a mistake and don't have a purpose. They call me weird, and no one wants to be my friend. I didn't try to hurt her. I just wanted to have someone of my own so that I wouldn't get sad when they don't want to be bothered with me." Zuri's childlike answer turned the frowns of the leaders right-side up. I motioned for Sipho to move forward and stand next to Zuri. Zuri shifted to his left, giving Sipho the much-needed room to stand in front of me.

"You allow this type of shit to go on in your sector?" I hissed.

"No, Father. This is my first-time hearing about this," Sipho replied and glanced down at Zuri.

"Now that you know...." I encouraged his statement.

"I will make sure that it doesn't happen again. I promise you," Sipho said. Dafari's eyes went into a slant, not believing Sipho's sorry ass excuse. I was wondering why he had to lie when something else occurred to me.

"I'm curious, Sipho. How is it you didn't feel your youngling leave the section?" I questioned.

"I don't know, Father," he gave me his unintelligent answer. I was ready to scold him for it, but Amber jumped in and saved him.

"We contacted the guards at Sipho's sector. They didn't detect a lost youngling either. Kaflia stumbled upon him on her way back with her hunting group. She didn't want the youngling to be in the open water alone without supervision, so she brought him back here. Kamu nor I could get a read on him."

"That is strange," I noted and stood to my feet. I rested my hand on Zuri's head and felt the connection to him instantly. He was one of my healthiest creations. I didn't understand what was wrong with him and had an idea why the younglings were calling him weird. "Sipho. I want you to bring Zuri to the healers for a check-up. Once he is done, report his findings to me but send him home." I said and directed my last statement to him. "I don't want you to take any other detours. Do you understand me?"

"Yes, Father," Zuri spoke and bowed his head. Sipho threw a nod towards the entrance. Zuri glided ahead of him slowly.

"Would you like for us to retrieve the healers for you, Father?" Nsia wondered.

"No, I am fine. There will be no planting until the enemy is found. Tell the pickers to leave the others grounded," I tried walking away.

"Father," Valin finally stepped in. He was one of my quiet ones. When he spoke, I knew it was worth stopping and listening to. I paused and turned in his direction. "Why is your heart so heavy?"

We already had enough on our plate. I couldn't allow them to fill their thoughts with problems that they couldn't solve. But the look on their faces had me yearning for that comfort that my brothers gave me effortlessly. I wanted to say that their support was enough, but it wasn't. The water was my home. Skye nor Landon couldn't come down to help me with this issue so that I could focus on mate. The only ones I had to rely on were circling me, gravitating to the bright circle on my chest. I shook that needy feeling off and covered my hurt with determination. They saw the change and backed away from what they thought was going to be a loud outburst. I addressed them all with a few words.

"I said that I am fine. Do what I say," I demanded. They all nodded and started the hunt for the enemy that would die an improper death.

THOSE STUPID MUTHAFUCKERS THOUGHT THEY DESTROYED everything in the lab. What they didn't know was that I was the key to all that was happening. I might've used Landon's blood to create those creatures on the land only because his blood was pure of those creatures. It wasn't mangled up with the nonsense I had in me. That was the reason my blood transformed them into the mindless beasts that they were fighting. I thought I could do better with the DNA of Amanzi's creatures. His mogosens were products of the water he thought only was controlled by him. I could manipulate water. I didn't understand why Mother Nature told him he ruled it. Giving them niggas false hope was a trap altogether.

They didn't know the history of Mother Nature and Qalaneive. Of course, they knew her side, which was a bunch of bullshit and half-ass. I would've tried to reason with Landon or Skye. Landon was now a no-go, since his mother gave him a mate to help him with his duties. He felt all grateful and wanted to show his gratitude by being loyal to the land once again. Skye was just faithful all the way around. I believed if I had approached him, Skye would have spat fire on me. That would have made me fuck him up, and I wasn't ready to do that yet. The only one that

I knew I could get through to was Amanzi. I saw how he behaved with the mention of Mother Nature. I didn't know why their relationship was like that, but I would capitalize on it.

To do that, I had to isolate him from the others. Keep him where he thought he was safe while I worked my magic—the true magic of the water.

"I think we need another scientist. There is no way I can do this on my own," Dr. Uganja interrupted my thoughts. "They salvaged nothing from the old lab, and the brothers have confiscated Dr. Feeble's notes. We don't know if they are aware of what we are trying to do."

"I don't care what they know. They won't be able to stop me," I responded, standing to my feet. We were at my condo in Atlanta, Georgia. I knew they thought I traveled to cause problems all over the world. Like Mother Nature, I could do things sitting still. Plus, the view of the city that I love was hard to leave, amongst some other things. The spacious area didn't have any furniture but the chair that I sat in. Dr. Uganja was on the floor with shards of papers that were collected from the old lab. I didn't know what he was searching for. We were already on Phase 3 of our plan and didn't need anything else moving forward. I walked to the large bay window and leaned on the frame. "You are doing just fine by yourself, Dr. Uganja. I'm not comfortable allowing any of your other colleagues on this project. The last one got in over his head and almost got you killed."

"I think sending him after that woman pushed my friend over. Shemar was a good man and a great biologist. We never had problems before with him focusing on the goal," Dr. Uganji replied. He was adamant about painting his sick-ass friend in an excellent light. His delusional thoughts had me questioning his ability to finish what I hired him to do.

"His goal was to watch the descendant of the sun god. I didn't order him to approach her, talk to her, ask her out, fuck her, or offer a relationship that he couldn't give. Dr. Feeble thought that going above and beyond was going to be helpful. As we saw, it wasn't and got him killed along with Nelor," I expressed.

Dr. Uganja frowned with confusion. "I thought you said your mate was killed."

My fist bald, thinking at the mention of her unfortunate demise. I closed my eyes and inhaled before my anger ran over. "I did. But I am connected to everything to which they are connected. I have love for Nelor like I have love for Egypt, Adaliya, and Olivia."

"How is that?" He probed, getting closer. I peeked at him over my shoulder to stop him from moving or talking any further. I wasn't too trustworthy about giving him any more information about who I was. Dr. Uganja swallowed the big lump in his throat, wishing he could take his questions back. I made the shit very clear for the near future.

"That is none of your concern," I addressed and turned back around.

Dr. Uganja raised his hands in surrender, letting me know he wouldn't push that issue, but his mouth opened to inquire about something else. "If you are telling me that, how do you know Ali won't do the same thing that Dr. Feeble did? He could have been tempted toward Egypt because of your blood."

"That may be true, but no one told him to inject the serum into himself. Everything that happened to Dr. Feeble was his fault and his fault alone," I replied.

"Plus, I'm a pure breed. I know how to control urges that are bad for me," Ali appeared and added. I knew he teleported out of the water. Ali was wet, wearing green knit pants and no shirt. He was truly created to be in the water with a long torso and legs. His body was toned and structured to perfection. Ali's purple eyes made him look more exotic. Dr. Uganja stared at Ali walking through the condo. He wasn't on board with me creating another creature until we had everything under control. I wasn't waiting. I wanted them niggas to feel me painfully.

"That is what you are saying now. If you see her, the mating urge will take over and push you to mate her," Dr. Uganja continued. Ali frowned, not wanting to repeat himself.

"He won't," I assured Dr. Uganja and turned my attention to Ali. "How is everything?"

Ali grunted and rubbed his hand across his short, untamed hair. "Everything is well. I didn't expect him to react so quickly. He went to meet up with his brothers and that bitch they call Mother."

"Amanzi feels everything that happens in the water. That is why it is imperative for you to blend in. I don't want him to find out who you are too early. It will put a rift into our plans," I responded.

Ali walked over to stand next to me. "I felt him. When he fell into the water from the sky, I felt the power that he had. That shit made me look for shelter. How is it possible for me to fight him if I'm no match for him?"

"I didn't intend to make you Amanzi's equal or fight him. You are there to wound his heart by destroying what he loves. That will weaken him long enough to put him where I need him to be," I told him.

"I know that with time, I can be what you need to finish him and those brothers off. I can be the king of the water," Ali thought.

"That is not your fight," I said with a glare. Ali didn't argue. He bowed his head in acceptance. "Good. Make sure the activity in the water stays consistent. Dr. Uganja. I want you to focus on that search. I'm sure that he will be around when he finds out that his daughter lived and is mated to a family that he loathes."

"For us to do that, we will have to leave Atlanta. We have already exhausted all of our resources here. We need to move forward," was all that he could get out of his mouth. I flashed in front of him and snatched his ass off his feet. My many faces changed, wanting to greet the stupid shit out of his mouth.

"We are not leaving Atlanta! Ever!" I growled at him. My hand grew bigger around his neck. Dr. Uganja pulled at my fingers as his eyes rolled to the back of his head. If I had the patience to look for another scientist, I would've killed his dumb ass right here. "Blink if you understand me, muthafucker," I told him. Because letting him go to nod, his head wasn't happening. Dr. Uganja blinked his eyes profusely. I tossed him away from me and turned around. I heard his body hit the floor with grunts and the crack of his bone. I return to the view of the city, thinking about what my meeting will be like with the so-called Water King. Hopefully, he would listen before attacking. I would hate for Mother Nature to lose her baby.

"How the fuck do you not know the answer to that? Cologne. Say cologne, bitch!" Daddy screamed at the television. He was big mad at the black family that had the chance to go to the next round. My parents and I were watching Family Feud on a Thursday night. That was something I enjoyed doing in my spare time. I was a true homebody. My friends had to bribe me to get out of the house practically. They got caught up in our game show ritual several times and chilled with us, forgetting their plans.

My parents owned a single-family home that held three bedrooms. I yearned for a sibling, but my parents were thankful for me. The family room was the place where we mostly spent our time. The room was big enough to add another living room set. The entertainment system was between the two casement windows. The transparent net curtains blended well with the old furniture that had been in here since I was nine. The significant change that I agreed with was the removal of that dingy ass grey carpet. Mom replaced that with grey wood floors with white trimming on the boards. It was a peaceful room that was filled with family love.

"We are going to go with money clip, Steve," the woman announced.

My Dad threw his arms up and picked his plate up from the tray. "That's a stupid bitch. Black people get on these shows and embarrass the fuck out of us. Nobody ain't buying no nigga with no money a fucking money clip. Watch the white folks get it," he ranted and walked to the kitchen with his plate.

"Look at ole boy face at the end. He knows that shit is wrong too," Mom laughed and shook her head.

"Look at Steve. He wants to curse their asses out so bad," I noted.

"He should. They wrong for that dumb shit with only seventy-eight points," Dad hollered. We were all serious about our game shows as if we were playing them. No matter how many times I told my dad that those people couldn't hear him, he insisted on screaming louder. I knew that we would have done worse than the people on television. That shit looked easy from here, but we all knew that under pressure, we would have been hollering out stupid shit too.

"How is work, baby?" Mom asked me.

"Work is good. I met so many wonderful people whose drive is on the same level as mine. We will start onsite training tomorrow with the veterans of the company. They are willing to put any of us to work once we catch on," I enlightened her.

"That's great, baby. What will they have you doing again?" Mom questioned.

"I will be in the," I paused, noticing something leaking through the cracks of the front door. I sat forward and tilted my head downward to get a better view. "Mom? Do you see that?"

"See what, baby?" Mom didn't pick her head up from the book.

"That, Mom. Look!" I pointed.

"There is nothing there, Liya," Mom responded. Dad walked in with another plate of food, splashing water as he walked back to his seat. I glanced to the kitchen and saw the water coming through there as well.

"Dad! Where is that coming from?" I got frantic and scared.

"Where is what coming from?" Dad's focus was on the television. I wasn't sure if they were playing with me or not, but this seemed severe.

"Dad, maybe you need to change the channel to the news. I think something is going on," my voice elevated as the water came in faster.

"Girl, hush. The fast money round is about to come up," Dad sat down with his feet in the rising water.

"Are you guys serious? There is water rushing in here and you are worried about some television show. We gotta get the fuck out of here," I stood and went cold. My body started shivering. Air was rushing in out of my lungs, preparing for the worse. I jumped back on the sofa and pulled my knees up to my chest.

"Mommy. The water. There is a lot of water coming in," I shuddered.

Mom didn't hear me, and neither did my dad. I didn't know what was going on. I thought that she would have been pissed that the water would destroy the floors that she worked so hard getting. The water rose, and I got woozy. When it got to the cushion, I crawled to the top and pressed myself against the wall. I sat forward quickly, feeling the water drenching my shirt. I gazed up and saw it running down the walls and dripping from the ceiling.

"Oh my god," I stood with my back turned to the water. Something grabbed my ankle, causing me to leap forward and press my back against the wall. The creature's head was sitting above the surface with his clear eyes on me.

"What the fu-," came out of my mouth. Before I could finish, the creature's mouth opened, with water shooting out of it. I threw my hands up to block it from my face. That ice water hit me in my stomach like an uppercut punch from Mike Tyson. I bent down, clutching my stomach, forgetting about protecting my face. The water went into my nose and mouth. I tried spitting that shit out, but it didn't help. The creature floated toward me. It rose above the water and hovered over me. My parents were submerged under, drowning themselves, still watching television. I closed my eyes, shaking my head, knowing what he wanted to do. I moaned out my horror as the water got thicker, flowing out of his mouth. Seconds later, I was engulfed in what I feared the most. I tried closing my mouth. I tried reaching for my mom and dad to pull them from the trance that they were in. I tried to survive this... this... this...

I closed my eyes tightly. I kicked and swung my arms around, hoping that I got out of whatever nightmare I was in. *This can't be real*, I thought.

Water in my house?

Me drowning? Wait. Me drowning? That did happen. I did drown. I died. That thing... that thing... it had my leg. The water? The water!

"No! Noooo! Get off of me! Let me fucking go!" I kicked and screamed, hoping to free myself from this nonsense. I finally found my voice.

"Liya! Liya, wake up! Liya!" I heard my father's stern voice. His hands were clutching my arms, holding me down in the water.

"No, Daddy! Please! Let me go! I don't want to go in the water!" I shrilled.

"You are not in the water, Adaliya. Wake up!" My mom screamed. I opened my eyes and saw my parents standing over me. I frantically moved my father's hands off of me and ran to the center of the room.

"You didn't hear. None of you didn't see the fucking water coming in the door," I pointed to the front door?

"Liya!"

"Noooo! Listen. The water was coming in and you two were

watching Family Feud. You didn't believe me. I kept telling you this, and you just sat there like you wanted to die," I explained.

"Adaliya," Mom called out to me. I knew I was losing my fucking mind. I was pacing the living room floor with a handful of my hair.

"It was the water. It came rushing in," I was mumbling to myself.

"There is no water, Liya. Look," Dad whispered and motioned for me to look around the dry floors. "Water didn't get in here. You are okay, baby girl. Look. It is a beautiful day outside. There is no rain. No water. It's dry like them biscuits your mother cooked the other day," Dad reassured me. Mom glared at him but didn't reply to his statement.

"You were having a bad dream, Liya. We were watching Family Feud last night. You fell asleep before the fast money round and we turned in because we didn't want to bother you," she tried to calm me down herself. I didn't want to believe them, but the dry floors and sunny day outside were evidence. It wasn't slowing my breathing or bringing my anxiety down. Dad snatched my medication from the table and passed them to me.

"Take this, Liya. Come on. Take it," he coerced me.

I grabbed the pills and swallowed them without water. I fell to the floor with my knees pressed to my chest. I tucked my head and rocked until my head stopped spinning. It was like waking up to the same nightmare all over. It was a big fucking reminder of the issues that kept me from reaching my life goals. I didn't know how I was going to recover from this.

I thought I was dead, waking up to the angle of a man. His creamy brown skin and full beard that connected to his fresh mohawk haircut had me mesmerized. The glowing of his tattooed body shined without the sun's help. I knew God sent him to retrieve my soul from the water where I fought for my life. When he told me I wasn't dead in a soothing voice, emotions overcame me. My savior sounded familiar, but the thought of me dying overcame me knowing him and began to ugly cry on his shoulders. He must've thought that I was crazy after running away from him. I could have sworn I saw the ocean in his eyes. Any other time, I would have enjoyed it and begged him to continue staring at me. But all I could think of was the rush of the water taking up the air that I needed to survive in my lungs. I felt like I was drowning looking at him. He had tattoos of water waves around the center artwork that looked as if it was floating. I was too scared to be amazed at what I was seeing. I awakened once again, clutching at the woman that entered the room. I asked the same questions about my whereabouts. They told me it was his favorite place. I didn't know who they were implying to and didn't bother asking questions. I told them I wanted to go home. The woman helped me out of bed and smiled at me.

"Whatever you want, sis," she replied. The guy collected my parents' information from me to contact them. I knew that my friends somehow got in touch with them and told them what had happened. I couldn't relieve the moments, explaining to them how I ended up here. Egypt did the honors by telling them I was safe and on my way home by plane.

The couple, Landon and Egypt, escorted me to the airport. I thought they were going to leave me there, yet they didn't. We boarded the plane and took our seats in the middle aisle. Landon sat on one end with Egypt next to him and me next to her. There was an open seat next to me, which I hoped stayed empty. I was so jumpy and nervous that it was embarrassing. Egypt conversed with me and held my hand for nineteen hours to keep me calm. I didn't want to fall asleep and wake up screaming about some nightmare, scaring the people on the plane. But after talking for hours and the motion on the plane, I couldn't help resting my eyes for a moment. Egypt encouraged me to do so.

"Everything will be alright. Trust us," Landon leaned forward and spoke.

Damn. It was hard not to believe whatever came out of his

mouth. He was fine as fuck. I wasn't gay, but Egypt could have gotten it on a drunk night. They were both fascinating creatures with emerald, green eyes. I had never seen a black person with those color eyes before. The couple captured the attention of all the attendants and passengers on the plane. Something about them made you want to bow down to their feet as if they were a god and goddess. What made it even more interesting was the guy that took up the seat next to me. He flashed a smile in my direction and looked down at Landon.

"How did everything go?" Landon questioned the man.

"He didn't break anything as you did. He listened and found out that it wasn't his mother's fault. She thinks Qala had something to do with it," the man answered and glanced down at me. "How are you feeling, sis?"

"I'm. I think I'm okay. Who are you?" I wondered.

"My name is Skye. And they were right. You don't have anything to worry about. Get you some rest," he answered with the touch of his hand. It felt cool on my hot skin. His eyes were a pale blue, close to white. I looked over at Landon and had to ask.

"You guys are brothers?"

"Yes. I'm the oldest. Skye is the middle child, and we have a younger brother name Amanzi," Landon responded.

"Amanzi," I whispered the name that meant more to me than anything. Landon and Skye's eyes brightened. Egypt tilted her head and brushed my hair behind my ear.

"His name sounds natural coming from your mouth. Do you know him?" she wondered.

I shook my head. "No. But the name Amanzi means something to me," I hesitated. I inhaled and sat back in my seat. I gripped the armrest tightly as my mind traveled to where I didn't want to be. My breathing picked up, and I felt myself getting lightheaded. "Water," I rasped.

"You mean something to him as well. With time, you will love the water again. It will embrace you like the queen he needs,"

Skye explained cryptically. I frowned and turned to Egypt. She shushed me and patted her hand across my clammy forehead.

"She needs to rest, Skye. Peacefully," Egypt requested.

"No problem," Skye whispered and leaned into my face. His cool breath smelled like fresh air, untouched. I took in the air and felt my eyes getting heavy.

"Don't worry. We won't let him give up on you. That is a promise," Landon said as I felt my body relax and prepare for a long nap.

I was in and out of consciousness throughout the rest of the ride home. The conversations that they were having were hard to follow. I heard something about some mogosens, younglings, someone shifting into an animal. It sounded like a script from a movie. I remembered Skye vaguely waking me when we landed.

"She is still exhausted," Egypt told him.

"We can grab a wheelchair for her," one attendant suggested.

"There is no need," Skye told them. I felt myself being lifted in big arms. My arms went around his neck instantly.

"Follow me," Landon's strong voice spoke. "Excuse me," he said once. Everyone moved out of our way and allowed us off the plane first. My mother's frantic voice shrilled through the airport, forcing my head from Skye's shoulder.

"Mommy," I whispered. She rushed over to me with my father by her side. In Skye's arms, I could look down at their concerned faces. Mom reached up and touched my face with her shaky hand.

"Baby. I was so worried about you. Are you okay? Did you get hurt? Where did they find you?" Mom let loose with the questions.

"Hi, ma'am. My name is Egypt. This is my fiancé Landon and his brother Skye. My other brother-in-law, Amanzi, was the one that found Adaliya on an island off the Indian Ocean. We were out there on vacation. She seemed out of it at first, but calmed down on our way here. Amanzi is a doctor. He examined her and made sure she didn't suffer any physical injuries. She checked out fine, but he recommended she sees a psychiatrist due to the psychological damage the accident caused," she described.

"What psychological damages? Liya, what is this woman talking about?" My father jumped in with fear in his eyes.

"That is something that you will have to ask her once you get home. I don't think it's best to get her riled up talking about it in public like this," Landon indicated and pointed to the exit.

"I can carry her to the car for you, sir," Skye insisted. Dad wanted to object. He didn't like what he was hearing, and it had him on pause. Mom brushed her hands up and down his arm, clutching his hand at the end.

"Come on, sweetheart," Mom coerced father to move his feet. Father nodded and led us to the car that was parked in front of the busy airport. Dad unlocked the back of his 2019 black 1500 RAM truck. It wasn't sitting on rims or chrome, like all the other decked-out vehicles. My father was a simple man that loved the simple things in life. It took little to make him or my mother happy or upset, especially when the matters were about me. Skye placed me in the car with my mother getting in on the other side. She reached for a blanket and threw it over me. Mom cradled my head in her lap.

"See you soon, sis," Skye uttered and moved out of the way for Egypt and Landon to say their goodbyes.

"We will continue our vacation here in Tampa. Here is my card if you need anything," Egypt said and squeezed my fingers. Landon repeated what Skye said and closed the door.

"Sis? What is all that about?" Mom asked me. I shrugged my shoulders and closed my eyes. Dad talked with them a little longer before pulling off. He told my mother that I needed to speak to someone about my accident. I was scheduled to go three days after returning but got rushed to the hospital after my first encounter with dehydration. They kept me overnight to make sure that I was stable enough to walk out there on my own. I went to the doctor the next day for her to tell me some shit that I already knew. She told me I wasn't ready to hear how to cure my phobia without passing out. I told her I was ready and did precisely what she said I was going to do. Dr. Allen placed a glass of water on the table in front of me. The movement of it had me fainting on the floor.

"I know she wants to get better quickly. There are some steps that she can't afford to skip. Adaliya will have to take the long road of recovery," Dr. Allen expressed to my parents.

"How much time are we talking about?" My mother questioned.

Dr. Allen shrugged and sighed before answering her question. "For however long it takes. The traumatic experience that your daughter went through will affect Adaliya for the rest of her life. Doctors wouldn't place a time cap on when she should get better because everyone deals with trauma differently. Adaliya showing up here shows how she is willing to move past this, but her mind isn't. She has to be equipped here to get through what she encountered," Dr. Allen told them, pointing to her head.

I didn't want to believe her and encouraged my mother to bring me to another doctor. They gave me the same ole shit, which had me back unconscious. Dad thought it would be best for me to take it easy for a while. That was almost a month ago. Now, I woke up from nightmares, screaming and juddering. Dr. Allen told my parents that I was going to need medication to help me with my anxiety. I hated relying on this shit, seeing that the side effects were hearing voices. It was the same one that I heard before the accident. The voice came more and more. I called myself, ignoring him since he wasn't there for me when I needed him the most. I was ready to tell the doctor about it and then thought differently. If they knew I was hearing voices and shit, they would have kept me for real. Things were already changing around me due to this crap.

I moved back in with my parents and slept on their couch in

a room. It was the most boring view ever. Grass, dirt, and other houses were all I saw when I looked out the window. I couldn't walk into any other room because there was water everywhere. We had a pool in the back of the house. There was a large pond over the fence that circled my bedroom and bathroom. Of course, they blocked the scenic view with dark-out curtains, yet me knowing what was on the other side was worse than me seeing it.

I definitely wasn't going to submerge myself in the tub full of water or have it pouring over my body. I would have collapsed for sure with no regard for walking into a bathroom again. My father would give me a wet towel to take a nice hoe bath nightly. I wasn't drinking or allowing anything down my throat that wasn't chewable. I explained that to the doctor, and she told me it was normal to feel that way.

I knew it wasn't normal for me. I was supposed to be out there working my dream job and swimming around with the other biologist. I knew it had to be the devil fucking up my shit, but it was hard trying to regain the confidence that it took so long to gather and resurface better than ever.

"Are you okay, now?" Dad squatted in front of me and spoke. Without picking my head up, I nodded while taking in deep breaths.

"Okay. Let's get you off the floor." Dad tucked his hands under my arms and lifted me. Mom had the broom in her hand, sweeping up the glass vase I broke. I frowned and reached for the broom.

"I can do that, Mom."

"No, I got this. I don't want you to cut your feet. Just go and get yourself together. I'll fold everything up for you," she replied. I felt terrible in so many ways. They worked so hard to get me out of the house and prepare me to live on my own. Here I was, wearing out their couch, breaking their shit, putting them on a fucked-up babysitting schedule, and redecorating their house with dark colors. I was sucking the life out of the home that brought me so many good memories as a child.

I turned around with my shoulders down, feeling helpless. Dad patted me on the back for comfort and directed me to the dining area. He went to get some items out of the bathroom. I wasn't able to stand over the sink to brush my teeth and wash my face. Dad brought me the toothpaste and toothbrush with a cup and a warm towel. I sat at the dining room table, completing my new morning ritual. After everything was removed from the living room, I went back to the couch and chilled.

I was petrified to flick through the channels or go through my phone. I looked up water so much, that random shit about water popped up on it. That was why I started using my parent's phone or the house phone they had to get for me. Thank God they knew how to hook that shit up because I was lost. I believed the young tech was too. Once we got it working, I called the girls and gave them the new number, which was a bust. We created a group chat a long time ago. We texted to keep in touch with each other since we were in class and worked a lot.

I would receive the text as a voicemail. A couple of days ago, the girls were going crazy in the chat about something. My phone chimed for almost two hours strong, nonstop. I was tempted to see what the hell they were talking about, yet my nerves got the best of me. When I checked the voicemail, it was Courtney telling us about her engagement with Greyson. She was going on and on about the way he did it. The girls congratulated her and set up a meet and greet amongst her bridal party. I didn't think that I wanted to go. It had nothing to do with my phobia. Courtney was a bitch to heart. She didn't come on the cruise with us because she thought the ship wasn't safe enough. Kara facetimed and told her about my accident. Courtney rolled her eyes and mumbled *I told you so* like the shit was okay to say. Kara hung the phone up in her face and carried on with her day. I knew a lot of people were wondering why we were friends with her. And, like we always said, there was one in each group. Courtney was always like that since middle school. We grew to love her and ignored the bullshit that came out of her mouth.

"Here. These are some clothes you can put on for today. I know you don't want nobody seeing you in that," Mom sat some clothes on the side of me. I peeked down at them and frowned a bit.

"I'm not going anywhere," I responded.

"I know," she rolled her eyes with that. "Some people are coming to see you today." Before I could ask who, someone was knocking on the door, Mom turned to answer it, while Dad stood in the doorway waiting for the entry of our new guest. I leaned over myself, trying to get a glimpse as the door opened.

"Good morning Ms. Adele," Val's loud ass voice rung the room. That alone placed a huge smile on my face. I got up and ran to the door, knowing that the others were behind her. Kara cleared the threshold with her arms open and ready. I went into them and clutched onto my friend. Val covered my back while Brianna wrapped her arms around all three of us from the side.

"Girl, we miss yo big head ass," Brianna teared up a bit.

"I miss you guys, too," I said and pulled out of the group hug to look at them. "What are you guys doing here?

"We came to hang with you since you are all antisocial and shit," Kara replied. Courtney cleared her throat behind her and waved her hand to the side. Kara rolled her eyes and moved out of her way. I swear she was doing too much in her tight bodycon dress and six-inch heels. Val dismissed her easily and strolled into the living room.

"Oh, Adaliya. How have you been?" she swung her arms around my shoulder, embraced me in an awkward hug, and pulled back with a sympathetic look on her face. "I knew it was dangerous to get on that ship. Next time, you guys need to listen to me. I'm sure that Greyson's family wouldn't have minded if we occupied their house on the lake," she said smoothly. I visibly shook and stepped away from her.

"Courtney, seriously. Why would you even say that shit?" Kara scolded her and grabbed my hand. Courtney gasped, raising her hand to her chest.

"Oh my God. I'm so sorry, Adaliya. I meant nothing by it. I meant that we should have gone to the blank house instead of the cruise ship. That's all," she tried to explain.

"I know what you meant, Courtney and it's okay. I knew you didn't mean anything by it," I told her over my shoulder.

"That bitch meant it," Brianna mumbled under her breath.

"Do you know any other words to describe me, Brianna? Don't show how much of a waste college could be to someone," Courtney replied, walking into the room.

"Girl, fuck you. If it weren't for the checks that your daddy was giving to your professors, yo ass would have been working for the WASTE development," Brianna snapped.

"Whoa! Guys, what's going on? I thought you guys came here to chill," I sat between Val and Kara. Courtney was sitting across from Brianna in one recliner.

"Don't worry about them two. They had been going at it since we met up," Kara explained.

"But, why, though?" I questioned.

"Because," Brianna sat up to clarify the situation. "She didn't want to come here. She wanted to see bridesmaids and wedding dresses. We already told her no, but her selective hearing ass set up an appointment with an event planner at the same time we planned on coming here. The bitch is selfish."

"I didn't think that we needed to be here this early. We all know that Adaliya isn't a morning person. We could have run a few errands before coming here," Courtney tried to defend herself.

"If you have some other stuff to do, Courtney, I won't be mad. You can go," I instructed her.

"Are you sure?" Courtney pulled her purse strap over her shoulder.

"Sit your boujee ass down," Val answered for me. "If you were in this situation, Liya would have been here for you."

"We all were there for you when your parents got a divorce. As a matter of fact, Liya slept by your house for almost a week to keep you company. The shit you are doing right now is bogus," Brianna explained further. Courtney nodded her head with a sad smile on her face.

"You're right. I'm sorry, Adaliya," she apologized.

"Don't worry about it, Court. I know you mean well," I replied and sighed. I gave the other girls my attention and smiled. "So... what have y'all been up to? How are the new jobs? Tell me, please. I want to know it all," I expressed.

"You already know about my stupid ass boss. I think he knows I am going to out-shine him with my ideas. That's why he keeps throwing my shit to the side like I'm one of those regulars," Kara went off.

"I told you not to go with that company. You know that they have all white men on the board and wouldn't take advice from your black ass. You should have followed your first mind and started your own shit. That way, muthafuckers can't tell you how to run it," Brianna replied.

"I know, Bri. But I wanted to work under people who have been in the game for years and gather enough experience to branch off. Smart assholes run the company. I got to figure out a way to get their attention," she whispered with a sigh. Kara graduated from Howard University with a bachelor's degree in architecture. The girl had mad skills in creating and designing rooms, houses, and buildings. I didn't know how gifted Kara was until she sketched out a tree house for her backyard. Her father, Mr. McDonogh, saw it and purchased everything she needed. Kara stayed up many nights building that shit by herself. Mr. McDonogh didn't have to worry about it being out of compliance because he took Kara to work with him during the summer. He told her she was one of the best workers he had ever had. Everybody thought he was only telling her that because she was his daughter. When she sketched and designed their new home, people started asking for her services. We knew she was going to blow up with Currency Inc. It was the same company that hired her father. Mr. McDonogh told her what she was going to go through, yet she continued with her plans.

"Stick with it, Kara. They won't be able to hold you down any longer once those designs hit the websites," I encouraged.

"You are not lying. I can't wait to get my money right. Kara is going to be the first person I call," Val told us.

"You know how many people asked me about that design?" Kara asked.

"It doesn't matter! They can't have it," Val sang.

"Well, how soon will it take for you to get the money," Courtney asked her.

"Apple sent me a contract about the software I developed for the special needs group that needs help with electronic devices. I have Marrisa looking over the paperwork right now," she boasted.

"Wow! That is amazing, Val. You have been working on that project for years," Kara retorted.

"Hard work pays off," Brianna said and shot a glare at Courtney.

Courtney squinted her eyes and folded her arms. "Why are you looking at me like that? I have worked hard for what I accomplished thus far."

"You did work hard. Shit, you had to stay in shape to run after that nigga the whole four years. You should've joined the Olympics for a twelve-hundred-meter run," Brianna chimed in.

"Here they go," Kara sat back and watched the girls go at it again. This was something that they did on the regular. We tried to intervene before, but they were both strong-minded women with a lot to say. Brianna went off and joined the Airforce right out of school. She continued her education while serving and became a young officer. We thought that would warn Courtney of her mouth, knowing that Brianna could take her ass out without breaking a sweat. Brianna told us that there were other ways to hurt Courtney, and she didn't mind doing it at all.

"Y'all know we didn't come over here for that right," Kara tried to stop them. They talked over her as if she said nothing. I used to love it when they did this. Not because of the foolery that Brianna would say and have us all laughing. It gave me the time to drift. I felt myself venturing off into that particular place and stopped. I shook my head and kept my attention on what was going on in the room. Courtney was waving her finger at Brianna, trying to get her point across. Brianna shut her up by doing that ghetto clapping that Courtney despised. Val opened her mouth to speak, and I swore I heard the waves crashing. I sat up from the couch and pinched myself. The girls heard about the episodes I had with my parents. I wasn't trying to let them see me that way. I cleared my throat softly and smiled when Val glanced at me.

"They are crazy," she noted.

"Oh, I know," I responded quickly. I started tapping my feet, crooning a song and all types of other shit to keep my mind from drifting to the place where my heart yearned to be. I thought I was doing well until the flash of Kara's ring fucked me up. It was the same color as the man's eyes that rescued me from the shore.

"Hey, are you alright?" Kara noticed my uneven breathing. I didn't answer. I jumped up and ran into the hallway closet, stumbling over shoes. I closed the door and collapsed on the floor.

"Adaliya!" I heard Val call out my name while passing up the closet door.

"Where did she go?" Brianna wondered.

Dad's voice came through the heavy haze and told them I needed to lie down after taking my medicine.

"I told you we should have come around three," Courtney insisted.

"Shut the fuck up," Kara was tired of her shit.

"You guys could pass back later. Go on and take care of your business. Liya will call when she is ready for company," Mom suggested.

"Alright. Just tell her we love her and can't wait to get our girl back," Kara replied.

"We love you, Liya!" Brianna shouted out. I sat back and leaned my head against the wall.

"I love you, too," I whispered with tears threatening to roll down my face. I planned on sitting my stupid ass in that closet alone until his voice came through.

"Everything is going to be alright, beautiful," he whispered near my ear. A small whimper left my mouth as I gave in to him for the first time.

"How? I can't stop thinking about it," I replied.

"And I can't stop thinking of you," he replied before his arms wrapped around my shoulders. "I never meant to hurt you. Your Sol, love you so much."

"And I love you more. Please don't leave me. I don't want to be alone right now," I requested.

His arms tightened around me. Sol pressed his lips to my temple and rested his head on top of mine. "You were never alone, Luna."

"But you left me. You left me to die," my tears spilled over.

"You were mistaken. You will never die alone, Luna. The world that you want to know will fall with you," he explained. I shook my head and tried to sit up. His hold confined me there to continue listening to what he had to say. "You aren't meant to die in the water. That is your home. It is where you will live with me and our children." I paused with a small smile. My anxiety left without any other help from the meds. I relaxed in his arms and sighed with the relief of him being there for me at that moment.

"Tell me about our children," I mumbled.

"Well, we have Dafari, Femi, Valin and Trinity. They are some of our first creations," he started. I listened as my delusional thoughts conquered the problematic moment that almost drove me over.

I hated going against my brothers, but I knew it. Mom told Amanzi best. He wanted to show her how much control she didn't have over him by creating a family outside of us. None of us couldn't see or talk to the mosogens unless we had Amanzi's permission. I didn't know how he expected any of us to help him with those stipulations.

After leaving Mother's home, I rushed over to Adaliya's house to watch over her while Amanzi took care of his business. I walked by the open window several times and peeked in at her. She looked miserable—nothing like the woman I've seen on the rooftop in New Orleans or Cabo. Adaliya had been on Amanzi's radar for a long time. I witnessed Amanzi on land plenty of times watching over Adaliya. He stayed in the shadows, not wanting to seem like he was stalking her. Whenever she was near any water, he was there. I remembered flying over New Orleans to visit Landon when he was living on the streets in Atlanta. My brothers clowned me a lot about not teleporting to my destinations. Teleporting took away the scenic view of some of the most beautiful places. The New Orleans Superdome and the Smoothie King center always displayed beautiful lights that flashed over the mid-city area of New Orleans. While admiring the view, a flash of something caught my attention. I changed direction to move towards the new, unfamiliar attraction. I was more than surprised to see Amanzi in water form, staring down into the rooftop pool of the NOPSI Hotel in the Quarters. His violet eyes were flashing down into the bright water. I passed this area plenty of times and have never seen this pool water this way. I was ready to ask him about it until I noticed a woman swimming in the pool. Her body moved against the water perfectly. Anyone would have thought that she was an experienced swimmer. The only one that displayed that type of performance was the man that I was standing next to.

"She is amazing," I whispered to him.

Amanzi smiled, staring down at the woman. "Extraordinary is what she is."

"You want to challenge her or something? If so, my money is on her," I clowned. Amanzi didn't respond. He just stood there and watched the young lady go back and forth in the water. I became a bit worried, realizing that she didn't come up for air yet. She didn't look like she was struggling to breathe, either. "Hey, you don't think doing this may affect her somehow? You know some humans don't do well taking in our energy like that," I warned him.

"I didn't give her anything," Amanzi's quick reply was.

"Manzi? There is no way that she could stay underwater like that without your help. I mean, it had been almost twenty minutes now. If you keep this up, she may get injured. Pull her up," I suggested.

"It's not me, Skye. She is a natural. Always had been," he took a step closer to the pool and squatted. He moved his hand against the water and small waves appeared. The woman stopped stroking and flipped over onto her back. She started floating underwater with ease. Her eyes opened and I could've sworn that they were the same color as Amanzi's favorite water.

"What the hell?" I spoke. My tone didn't break Amanzi out

of the reverie that he was currently in. He continued to lust over the way the water caressed the woman's body. It wrapped around her legs, opening them wider. She inhaled a good amount of that water through her nose. It came out of her mouth like aspiration of cool air. I was amazed.

Amanzi closed his eyes and tilted his head with a moan that caused the woman to gasp. Her arms stretched out with her hands grabbing onto something that wasn't visible to my eyes. The waves moved in sync with Amanzi's hand. The woman's head went back, sealing her eyes tightly as she succumbed to whatever was happening to her.

"Liya," Amanzi said her name softly. Hearing her name, the woman opened her now normal eyes and shot out of the water. I flipped off the building while Amanzi merged into the pool. Liya brushed the water from her face and looked around.

"Hello! Is anyone there?" she yelled. "Hello." Liya was spooked by what she knew she heard. She swam to the stairs to exit the pool.

"Don't go," I heard Amanzi say. Liya turned around to look into the water again. It seemed as if she knew his voice. She receded into the water and paused when the door to the hotel opened.

"How long are you going to be out here? You said that you were only going to take an hour. It has been three. I fell asleep on your ass and everything," a lady told her.

"I'm sorry, Kara. I didn't know I was out here that long," she mumbled and slowly stepped out of the water. "What time is it?"

"It's time for our ass to go and have fun with the rest of the group. They are waiting for us in the lobby. Let's go," her friend told her and waited with the door open. Liya didn't look ready to go. She wanted to go back into the water. She stared at it for another minute before grabbing her robe and leaving.

"That was too close," I noted. Amanzi stepped out of the pool wearing a pair of dark denim jeans and a navy button-down. His two-karat diamond earring was crystal clear and shiny. I shook my head and smiled.

"So, my little brother is a stalker now. You already got it bad, having the water do that shit to her while I'm standing right here. I feel violated somehow," I expressed.

"Nobody asked you to stay and watch. You could've kept going, but you stayed," Amanzi spoke.

"What are you doing, Amanzi? Landon is already gone over the death of Nelor. I don't need you to freak out on Mother too if she does something to your mate," I warned him.

Amanzi glanced back at me with cold eyes. I knew that telling him that would piss him off, but he had to hear it. We were going through a lot at the time, and I needed him to focus on getting Landon back on track. We didn't need any other distractions.

"She is not a fucking distraction," he responded to my thoughts and teleported in front of me. "And, if your mother knows what's best for her, she will leave that one alone. I won't negotiate or damage the piano she so calls love. I will bring her entire world down."

I didn't talk him down because Amanzi was always true to his word. I hoped Mother wasn't crazy enough to test that fool. Landon and I both talked to Amanzi about his attitude towards the humans and our mother. Landon didn't agree with half of the decisions Mother made. After he straightened things out with her, we thought we were all back on board with our duties.

Now, this.

We told him he was creating ways for Qala to get to him without problems by having more vulnerable weaknesses. Of course, he had a lot of ground to cover. Hell, so did Landon and me. We connected well with the animals around the world to help us with our territory. Amanzi thought that the underwater creatures weren't enough and now he had to pay for it. He wasn't going to do it alone, though. Landon and Egypt haven't left

Florida at all. They wanted to make sure that Qala didn't attempt kidnapping Liya the same way that he did Egypt. Liya wasn't going to make it easy for anyone to capture her. She never left the house, which made it easier for us to protect her. I wanted to knock on her door and sit with her, but I didn't want to freak her out by saying the wrong shit. If I triggered anything that made her think of the water, Amanzi would have drowned me. For a man that loves the sky, water was definitely not something I wanted to fuck with.

I circled the subdivision and stopped when I reached the front of her house. I tried not to be too obvious with my stakeout. Egypt told me she usually watched her at night. The daytime wasn't as bad as the nightmares she endured kept her up.

"I thought it was forbidden for the Heart brothers to fornicate with the likes of the humans," Egypt's long-lost father approached and said to me. He looked in the window at Liya and smiled. "She is beautiful."

"Watch it, Nesbate. That is my brother's mate that you are thirsting over," I growled. Out of all the gods, I hated him the most. Nesbate was a fruition god. Mom explained to Egypt how her father was trying to create a family for himself by chasing and impregnating women worldwide. The sad part about that shit was he never took care of them. I was surprised when Mother didn't tell Egypt about Nesbate being able to prevent his offspring's deaths. He didn't find them worthy enough to carry on his bloodline or name. I was sure that Landon didn't know these things. If so, he wouldn't push Egypt to meet his punk ass.

"Well," he cleared his throat before continuing. "I know it is not Landon's mate. From what I heard; he had mated with my daughter. You all know the consequences of mating with a God's daughter without notifying their living parents."

"No, we didn't know and didn't care. You never claimed Egypt as yours until 'you heard' of her mating with my brother. She is a grown woman who made her mind up to become

Landon's partner of his soul and land. There is nothing you can do about that," I informed him.

"That's what you think?" Nesbate responded with some hostility in his throat.

"Nigga, that's what I know. Egypt is one of us now. The only thing that she needs from you is the history of her people. Your chance at being a father passed a long time ago. Don't get your feelings hurt, fucking with my brother. As you know, we ride hard for the ones that we love," I reminded.

"Is that a threat, Skye?" he wanted to know.

"Call it whatever you want?" I dismissed his ass and walked away from him before I made a scene.

"I will call it this. I will see my daughter and give her the truth about the Mother you love so much. Then we will see if she wants to be a part of your family," he yelled behind me. I turned around, wanting him to see the seriousness on my face.

"I don't know about that, Nesbate. You are going to need permission from Landon to see her. After I tell him what your intentions are, he will shut the shit down, asap," I stated and kept it moving. If he knew what was best for him, he would stay away. I didn't think anyone had a chance going up against Landon's Sabretooth. Let alone Egypt's Bastet. But being drowned by Amanzi for staring at Liya was going to be a treat that I would gladly take a front seat to watch.

"We got word on why Cyan didn't make the meeting. It's not good," Dafari told me. We were traveling to the other sections to find the imposter that was amongst us. The Donghai River only had one leader named Lutalo. He trained most of the leaders in the southern sections. I was confident that there weren't any activities going on in his area. I needed him to be aware of the things that were going on just in case I needed him in another section.

"Whatever you need Father. I am at your disposal," Lutalo said. He gave me a firm handshake and looked behind me where the others stood. "Look after him."

The water has been quiet for some days and that had me worried. Dafari and Femi understood. They didn't let me out of their sight. My first-born healer, Trinity heard what was going on and made it her business to travel with us. I knew I couldn't change her mind. I had thousands of daughters, but my first one never allowed me to talk my emotions down. When she arrived in the room at the site of Port Royale, she folded her slim arms over her small body and frowned. Dafari and Femi took a step back and allowed her to approach me. The fury in my eyes didn't warn her away. Trinity stood in front of me with her hands out for me to take.

"I can't do this with you right now," I told her.

"There is always time for healing," she responded and dared me to turn her down again with her furious glare.

"Father, it wouldn't hurt, you know," Femi interject quietly with his head down. I dismissed everyone and stormed out of the room. Trinity trailed behind me with her two brothers. She walked around to block me from moving forward.

"How do you preach do's and don'ts's but don't abide by them yourself? You wouldn't allow any of us to go into the field like this. I feel your pain, Father. Let me heal you," Trinity insisted.

My children didn't understand the type of pain that I was feeling. When I planted them, I ensured natural feelings in their DNA. Happy, sad, scared, and angry were a few emotions that they could feel. They also felt love, yet it wasn't the love I had for Adaliya. It was the same love I experience with my brothers and mother. The heartache I was experiencing wasn't something that any of them could heal because I never felt it before until now. I was consumed with emotions that were interfering with other shit and it was fucking them all up.

Trinity laid her hand on my chest and closed her eyes.

"Trinity," I called out her name and grabbed her wrist. Her eyes popped open with tremendous sadness in them. Femi and Dafari were alarmed at the sight and stepped next to their sister.

"What is it, Trinity? Is Father, okay? What's wrong?" Dafari questioned. Trinity stared into my eyes and shook her head.

"I don't know," she explained with a frown on her face. *"I don't know."*

"What do you mean?" Femi asked.

"I. Don't. Know. It's like... he is sad but in more pain than I ever felt. What is this?" Trinity wanted to know.

"I don't have time to explain this to any of you. We have to get to the other sections." I walked around the three of them and

began barking orders. From then on, they haven't left my side. Trinity's uncertainty pushed her to recruit Valin to be my third guard.

"I am the King of the water. I don't need all my leaders following behind me. They need to get to their sections and make sure that the threat isn't near," I told her.

"Like all kings, you need to be protected from the enemy as well. You have selected strong guards for our sections. We trust them with our lives and others. IF you were to die, Father, we will be no more. I am not leaving your side and that is final," Valin spoke and walked ahead of me, protecting my front. Dafari was behind me with Femi on my right. Trinity was on my left closer to my heart. I had the strongest diamond shield in the world.

"Let's go," I told Dafari. I motioned them to get closer to depart from Dunghai River. I closed my eyes, and we appeared at the front gate of Cyan's section. It was guarded by six guards, who all looked overworked. They were standing there like statues, as if they were sleeping with their eyes open. I took a step forward, yet Valin held his hand out and went to inspect the awkward scene. He pulled out his spiked machete that had ice crystals all around the handle. Valin floated towards the front, ready for whatever.

"Guards!" Valin called out. Nemendi's head snapped in Valin's direction. He sneered and drew an iced chain from his waist. Nemendi swung it at Valin. Valin blocked the chain with his machete, pulling and kicking Nemendi in the chest. Nemendi fell into Flanelle, causing him to awake from his paralysis. Flanelle shot a glare our way and tossed flying knives at us. Dafari jumped in front of me and held up his glass shield. The knives slid across and dropped to the seabed. Another guard flew over the shield towards me. I placed my hand up and froze him where he was.

"That is enough," I mumbled. Their dazed eyes opened wider as they began to see again. Valin had his weapon pressed against Nemendi's neck while he was on the ground. Nemendi closed his eyes and opened them again. He looked confused at the whole scene that he didn't know took place.

"Valin? What are you doing here?" he spoke and turned to see me. "Father? Father!" Nemendi tried to get loose of Valin's hold.

"Don't move," Valin ordered. Flanelle and Pit step forward with the rest of the guards.

"Father, what is going on?" Flanelle asked.

"You attacked us. You threw your knives at our father," Dafari scoffed.

"I would never do such a thing," Flanelle tried to defend himself. I placed my hand on Dafari to defuse the situation and pointed up. Damon was above us frozen with his bow and arrow pointed directly at me. Flanelle glanced back at his brothers, not believing what he was seeing.

"That is impossible," he gasped. Nemendi dropped his head to the ground, surrendering to Valin.

"What's going on?" he repeated, tiredly that time.

"That is what we came to find out," I waved my hand for Trinity to check on him.

"We were guarding the gates as Cyann asked us to," Flanelle answered.

"For how long you guys have been like that?" Trinity kneeled and inspected Nemendi. She placed her hand over his face to check his breathing.

"Two seasons," he mumbled.

"Two seasons! What do you mean? Like, the whole season. No breaks or anything," Femi interfered and questioned.

"Yes. We will let Cyann explain it to you," Nemendi replied.

"Trinity, get with the other healers and examine them further. It seems as if Qala has touched this place somehow," I instructed and entered the gates to the lost city of Dwarka. Valin retracted his weapon and helped his brother up.

"Everything is going to be alright," he told Nemendi. He didn't look too sure about the words that came out of Valin's mouth. None of them did.

"That is strange. The magnetic field has been weakened," Femi noticed the lighter color surrounding the city.

"He should have reported this. They had been out there for a whole season guarding this city," Dafari stated.

"There has got to be a logical reason on why he didn't," Femi tried to make sense out of it all as he watched the younglings in the groups. He frowned noticing something that wasn't ordinary. "That is Pia. He was assigned as a picker, not a teacher." The group stopped and observed the other activities around the city. There were a lot of things that needed to be addressed. It didn't make any sense with asking any of the others because they weren't going to say anything. It was best if I went straight to their leader.

The seabed was covered in black pebbles. It wasn't as uncomfortable to walk on as it looked. The pebbles were warm and smooth, like Mother's glass house. Like all the other cities underwater, the Mosogens stayed in the buildings and homes that sunk. It was told that Dwarka had sunk due to the rise of sea level and a Tsunami. Some houses were in ruin, but my people didn't need suitable roofs over their heads. They were fine with the roofless homes that bared windows. Privacy wasn't something high on their priority list. We lived, breathed, ate, slept, and fought together. That was why it should have been easy to fish out the intruder. The bond that we had with each other was hard to fake.

I walked over the threshold with my eyes centered on Cyann. He was surrounded by guards, giving them orders.

"It seems as if you have a problem, Cyann," my voice traveled deeply towards the group. A wash of relief came over Cyann's face, hearing the words from my mouth. He brushed past his guards and came straight at me.

"Father," his whisper filled with regret. Cyann kneeled in front of me, head bowed, and his weapon laid across the ground. The guards in the group kneeled along with their leader, praising my presence.

"We have much to discuss I see," I said and reached for his shoulders. I pulled his tense body up and stood him in front of me. Cyann looked as tired as the guards and soldiers around the city.

"Yes, we do. My messengers had been trying to reach out to the others in the water, but we had no such luck. Something is blocking us from communicating with anyone outside of Dwarka," Cyann explained one of the many questions I had.

"When was the last time you were able to communicate," Dafari questioned.

"Six seasons ago. It was happening every once in a while. We didn't pay any mind to it and thought that it had something to do with all the changes that you were making at the top. But we went completely blank a few nights ago. I sent out some guards and hunters to inspect our surroundings. They never came back. I sent another group out there and only one returned. He was mauled up by something that he had never seen. Ninka tried to heal him, but she couldn't. We watched him die." Cyann's eyes got heavy.

"Die! We can't die. There is nothing in this water that can kill us like that," Valin said. Silver streams ran down Cyann's face. He clutched his hands as his attention went to Valin.

"There is now," his haunted voice revealed. My violet eyes were burning with anger. I didn't create my people to be harmed by some sick bitch with a vendetta against my mother. Qala had to know that he went too far.

"Were the others discovered?" I said through clenched teeth.

"Miji said that he found their remaining close to the cliff on the west. I wanted to send more people out there, but I didn't want to chance losing others," Cyann responded.

"You did right. We will go and check on things. For now, gather the people and put them in the main hall of your home," I ordered and turned to leave.

"Father!" Cyann called after me. I glanced over my shoulder and saw that he had his weapons in his hands. "Let me go with you."

"No. I need you here to guard the rest of the people," I replied and stormed off.

"That's why they have Pia teaching. He had to shift everyone around since he lost the others," Defari said.

"I saw that. Most of his teachers were standing as guards in that room," Femi added.

"He said that something killed them. But, how?" Valin wondered.

"If that was the case, I would have felt the activities a long time ago," I fumed and exited the gates. I turned toward the west, already seeing the difference in the atmosphere. I drifted that way with my guards on alert. They had their weapons out prepared to protect me as I surveyed the area. I got to the edge of the cliff and looked down into the deep abyss of the ocean, which my people couldn't enter unless I was present. The darkness offered some answers to me. I didn't know what was down there, but I didn't want to risk my children following behind me. I turned my back to it and saw Dafari frowning at the substance that was on the pebbles. It was silver and shiny specks of dust sprinkled all over the surface. I bent and brushed my finger over it. I brought my fingers to my nose and sniffed. Pain, fear, and defeat were what they felt before dying. I saw the screams of my younglings as they watched their teachers and guards encounter something that I had never seen before.

"Akalya, Michem, Jestin, Cora, and younglings were killed here," I revealed with an ache in my heart. "The others seemed to have been dragged off this cliff and down to the bottom."

"I can't believe this," Trinity wept over the loss of her siblings.

"Don't Trinity," I warned a minute too late. She touched the same spot and relived the group's last events. She gasped and fell into Femi with silver streams running down her face. "Oh, no! Oh, no!"

"What did you see?" a pissed-off Valin demanded. He didn't have to wait long for an answer as a swish blew past us. Valin spun around and faced the direction where it went. He grunted with his spiked machete out. Dafari and Femi stepped on each side of me with their weapons drawn. Dafari's khopesh was long like Femi's two-blade sword. Trinity wiped her tears from her face and pulled out a slick whip. She jerked it once, sending waves that sliced through the water. Her bright eyes were glowing with fury and vengeance. We didn't see anything, looking the way we came from.

"Where is it? Does anyone see it?" Femi growled. I squinted my eyes at the way the water moved as if someone else was controlling it.

That wasn't possible. No one had control over the water like that, I thought.

Whatever it was, got closer and made a detour above us. We spun around at the movement, placing me in front of the group. Femi tried to move in front of me, but I stopped him with my hand up. If the creature didn't fear me and threatened the group that I was with, that meant it was truly out to kill whoever his master wanted dead.

The water curved and swirled around us. It pushed forward, faster in our direction. I heard the growl of the creature before it appeared midway in front of me. It had no eyes or nose but was covered with whiskers that didn't move. Its body was a floating grey blob that blended well with the water. The slimy face looked as if it was melting into its wide mouth. It had dorsal fins in layers on its back and a huge caudal fin that moved from side to side which gave the blob the speed it needed. The black spikes on it were dripping the same shit that coated its face. I tilted my head to the side and measured the length of it to be ninety feet long, weighing almost six hundred pounds. I grunted and brought my hand up, creating a sharp blade of ice directly in front of us. The creature didn't stop or slowed down from the appending attack. I wanted to say that it didn't see me but if it was a creature of the water, it would have felt the danger that it was in. It opened its mouth with a screech and ran into the blade. The sound of Velcro being pulled apart was heard as the blob was split in half. I couldn't warn or tell my children anything about what I was witnessing or hearing. They never had encountered something like this before. Shit, neither had I. Two halves of the blob fell on each side of us, flapping like a fish on dry land.

"Stay back," I told Dafari, who took a step forward to get a good look at the thing. They still had their weapons drawn for any surprises. Once the blob stopped moving, it gave off a sour odor. Trinity quickly covered her nose and started coughing.

"Ugh!" she groaned loudly and stepped behind the group. The others ignored the smell and leaned in to examine the thing that killed their siblings.

"How did it appear like that without us seeing it? I mean, I felt it near, but I couldn't get a good track on it," Valin inquired. Trinity appeared in front of us shaking her head.

"Ninka is the only healer here. She has been swamped with the others that have been feeling the effect of the massive energy drained from the city."

"That is the answer for the weak field," Valin concluded.

"I will strengthen the field. Get everyone together and teleport everyone in groups. Label this a no-go, until we find out where this thing came from," I instructed.

"Yes, father," my group answered and got to work. I waved my hand forward, forcing the water to push the blob off the cliff. I inhaled deeply, knowing that it was only the beginning of whatever was to come.

"*Amanzi,*" my brother's voice rang in the sea. I took one final glance at the hollow space and sighed.

"Coming," I whispered and evaporated into the water. I allow myself to be carried into the current in the sea. The flow of the water was amazing. The speed and strength of it matched my racing heart. It was the most calming area in the water that granted me peace. The current flowed nicely within the sea, transferring into the ocean where Landon was. When I surfaced, Landon was looking down into the dirty water. He came out to the dock on West Shore Blvd in Tampa. The dock was empty of boats and people. I leaped out of the water and landed on side of him. I didn't have to ask him why he was out of his base area. Landon was doing what I would have done for him in this situation. I couldn't lie. My big brother was looking healthier these days. Landon was standing up straight and taller than his usual height. His green eyes were remarkable and matched all the earth tone colors of his beach wear. I cracked myself up, knowing that this dude wasn't going in the water. Landon smiled at my thoughts and nudged me with his shoulders before asking me his question. I didn't think that I have ever seen him that lively before.

"How is everything going?" Landon asked. me

"I don't know yet. I just encountered something that wasn't created by me or Mother near one of my sections. It killed a dozen of my people, leaving only traces of dust for us," I confessed. Landon stood straight up with a frown on his face. His green eyes got darker, and a growl released from his lips.

"Muthafucker," he hissed and looked at me. "I'm sorry about that man. Is there anything that we can do?"

I shook my head and leaned on the wooden rail. "No," I mumbled and thought of the blob once again.

"What are you thinking so hard about?" Landon wanted to know.

"When Qala created those shifters to attack humans and us, he put some effort into creating them. For some reason, I didn't have to use any real strength to kill this creature," I answered.

"You think he has something else plan?" Landon countered.

"I know he does. Since when Qala gave up on anything," I said and looked out into the water.

Landon shook his head and sighed. He was getting ready to ask the same question that I haven't answered yet. He knew how pissed I get when they asked me shit like this. Yet, it never stopped them from opening up their mouth. "Do you think things would have been a little easier if you wouldn't have created the Mosogens?"

I twisted my head and glared at him. "Don't ask me shit like that Landon."

"I'm just saying. Things would go a lot cooler if you would have incorporated your sea creatures more," Landon suggested.

"I don't tell you how to run your land, Landon," was my only comeback.

"You have once before. I was considerate and change things around to improve my duties to help you guys out," Landon responded. I frowned at that fool.

"You weren't doing your job at all. I mean, you were laying in the gutter waiting for Egypt to bring you breakfast, lunch, and dinner. You cannot compare your situation to mine. Plus, I had to grow more people because of you. So, don't try it," I went off and looked back into the water. The waves were crashing into each other as if it was trying to escape the threat. It knew that it was in danger from something that could cause it more harm than good.

Landon shifted his stance, gathering my attention. This fool cleared his throat several times before he could get what he wanted out. "Yeah, about that. I want to let you know how sorry I am. I put you and Skye in a difficult situation that allowed Qala to slip past your defenses. I wish I could have done things differently, but..." he shrugged his shoulders looking out into my home.

"I wouldn't wish it. If things would have been different, you wouldn't have met Egypt. She brought back the light into your eyes, Landon. I will deal with this ten times over to have my brother back," I confirmed.

"I hear you, Manzi. You shouldn't have to sacrifice the safety of your people for my sanity. I'm sorry," he apologized.

"It's cool. You are making up for it, though," I said. Landon nodded his head.

"Egypt and I both. They talk every night," Landon confessed, leaning on the railing.

"Really? About what?" I got closer to him and asked.

"How she is trying to get back to her regular self. Liya told her she hears the water calling to her. She daydreams about going back there and succumbs to her anxiety. It's like she knows where she belongs and can't find her way home," Landon said.

Hearing that lifted a ton off my back. I was smiling proudly, knowing that there was hope at the end of this nightmare. I tried communicating with her when she felt overwhelmed. I was relieved when she allowed me to hold her in the closet. It felt good to be there for her when she needed me the most. I inhaled the freshwater scent of the ocean and relished in that feeling.

"That's my girl," I whispered. "So, what about you? How have things been going for you and Egypt? I know Tampa isn't the most romantic place for the two newly mated to celebrate their joining," I asked Landon.

"It's amazing, man. Egypt does something to my soul. It connects with her somehow with all the other spirit animals inside of me. They all love her and that alone makes things easier for us to grow with each other. I get ready to ask her a question and she answers it before I could get it out. I don't have to explain myself or go into further details on how I feel about something because she feels it herself. The love that she displays for me is indescribable. When the wolf inside of me saw Nelor as the evil bitch she was, it broke our hearts. We thought she was the one for us. Egypt took our broken hearts and mended that shit with a simple kiss, and I love you. I have never felt so free," Landon expressed. The nigga was glowing like a pregnant woman.

"So, all along, she was right," I said about Mother.

"She was right about Nelor not surviving longer than twenty-five," Landon admitted while thinking of her last moments. Egypt fucked her up, fa real.

"But, what about the other stuff?" I continued.

"Mother has her way of things. Like I told her before, she could have handled things differently. I'm not going to say what she did, didn't strengthen me because it did. Not only as a good mate for Egypt but as a great protector of the land. I hope you will see that one day," Landon answered.

"Mother plays too many games for me. She tells you half of the shit and wants you to figure the rest out like some mystery. I knew it wouldn't be easy but she gotta do better with her communication," I countered.

"That I will agree on. Skye told me about Egypt's father. That nigga told him he was going to give her the background of Mother Nature and it will have her not wanting to be involved with the family. I don't know what that history is all about, but he got me fucked up. I'm not letting her nowhere near his grimy ass," Landon said.

"What the fuck? That's that bullshit right there. I know Mother is hiding something that she doesn't want us to find out. If Qala didn't tell us about her killing his mate, we still wouldn't know that shit," I added.

"That's what gets me, though. How did Qala come about? This fool is talking about his mate and shit. Who is he?" Landon started thinking.

"I don't know. After Mother showed no remorse for her

killing that dude's mate, I would want to tear this muthafucker up too. I was about to when I thought she had something to do with Adaliya," I shook my head, getting pissed at the thought.

"You already know what I almost did. If it wasn't for y'all, I would have fucked her up. Him coming after Egypt and Liya are all the way wrong. How does he know who our mates are?" Landon expressed.

"I don't know about Egypt. But I used to visit Adaliya a lot when I came to the surface. You had me stressed out. I couldn't get my mind right until I saw her. She gets me in a trance so deep, that I forget everything around me, including safety. As much as I want to fault Mother for this, I can't. This was all my fault. I should have been more careful," I admitted.

"Him finding her may not be Mother's fault, but him looking for her is. I don't know what he has in common with Nesbate. He met Skye over at Liya's house. Skye saw him staring at her strangely and stuck around until he knew for sure that she is not targeted by them," Landon revealed something new to me.

My glare deepened as the waves collided against the dock, shifting the stilts that it was standing on. "I will douse that bitch Landon. I don't play with him like that."

"None of us do," Landon growled. "We are going to get this under control. You keep your focus on your people." I shook my head, knowing I needed to be with Adaliya. I knew my brothers were going to do whatever was necessary to protect her, but it wasn't going to be my way. I was ready to tell him that and felt the disturbance in the water. My head snapped down as I looked into the Dafari's eyes. Trinity was clutching her heart as if she was in pain.

"We can protect Liya up here," Landon told me, seeing the trouble in the water as if he was looking through my eyes. I gave him a sharp nod.

"Keep her safe," I demanded and dove into the water in human form. Dafari approached me, ready for war.

"After you left, Valin spotted two more of those creatures around Cyann sections. He thinks that there are more in the no-zone area," Dafari spoke. I didn't waste any time talking. We teleported to the area and came upon two more blobs preparing to attack the entrance. Damon shot out three arrows at the blob. We all watched as it traveled straight through it.

"What the fuck?" I mumbled. Femi swam closer and tried striking it with his ice spear. He twisted it and other spikes shot out. Femi thrust downward with a furious growl toward the belly of the blob. The creature turned to face him and snapped its choppers at him. Femi dodged it barely. He floated to the ground staring up at it.

"How are we supposed to beat it if our weapons can't hurt them?"

"Get everyone to Port Royal," I spoke as the ocean lifted me off my feet. I held out my hand and waited for my weapon of choice. The round ridged blade with sharp edges mimicked a unicorn's horn with the point at the end materialized quickly. The handle was crystal gold with rubies and diamonds encrusted in them. My eyes went dark as the anger of the audacity of this muthafucker to show up here thinking that it was going to be easy to kill my people while I was present.

I didn't like that at all and was planning on making them feel every part of my anger.

"This is the third time that we had to come out here for the same thing, Ma'am. This must stop," the paramedic spoke to my mother. I was in the living room, laying on the couch with an IV of fluids in my arm.

I drifted off with Sol in an uncharted area. We were talking about the home he had ready for me and gave me a visual. It was a magical place that looked like it should have been in a snow globe. The huge castle was dripped in ice and crystalized jewels that gave off different colors around its surrounding. There were no abandoned ships, beheaded statues, or debris in the area. It was clean and pure. The clear water made me feel as if the city was still on the surface, glistening underneath the sun. What was even more beautiful was the waterfall that sat behind the castle. I didn't know how it was possible to have a waterfall underwater.

"Anything's possible," Sol told me.

Not that. As much as I wanted to believe the site that was bestowed upon me, my reality was too real to succumb to my imagination. The city that I yearned to know was exactly the way I pictured it as a child. In total disbelief, I turned to tell Sol that until I saw the creature that pulled me underwater. I yelled and everything was back to normal.

The vision was too vivid and reminded me of why I was sitting on the couch. I reached for a cracker and felt dizzy. I noticed I had been talking to him for hours without drinking anything. I got up with my cup to get ice to help with my dehydration, but it was an epic failure. My father was at the stove, frying chicken for dinner. He spoke to me with his back turned. I didn't answer him back, trying to save my energy to make it to the fridge. That forced my dad to glance back at me. Dad called my name, getting worried now. The small white spots got bigger taking over my vision. I stumbled into the chair, falling face first towards the floor. Dad damn near flipped that hot grease over to get to me. That was the last thing I saw before blacking out once again. When I woke up, my parents and EMT workers were standing over me.

That happened once more plus the three EMT visits. I was sure that they were going to put our number on block and send the police out here the next time because there was going to be the next time.

One of them walked over and squatted in front of me. "How are you feeling?" the man asked with no remorse or care in the world.

"Better," I gave him a short answer and sat up to prove my point.

"Good," he replied for no damn reason and started unhooking the IV. "Because the next time we have to come out here, we are going to take you to the hospital and have you admitted to the psych ward."

"Whoa! Hey, don't threaten my daughter like that. Who the hell do you think you are?" My father stormed in after he heard what was told to me.

"I am a very hard worker, who takes his job very seriously. What your daughter doing is causing harm to herself. If neither of you can't make her sip a glass of water, then it is our job to remove and place her where she can get proper care," he stood and addressed my father.

"It's not like she wants this to happen. She tries her absolute best to stay hydrated by eating ice, which was something you all suggested. This illness is an illness that takes time to heal," Mom stepped in and spoke.

"We know that. But it is time that is being taken away from a gunshot, stabbing, car accident, or other major victims with more serious problems. This," he pointed at me and continued, "is curable without us. Theirs aren't. I suggest you get her the help that she needs, or my partner is right. We will put in our notes of her conditions and request that she gets admitted to the hospital," the woman told him and packed up the rest of their things.

"That's what you think," Dad told them.

"Theron," my mother said his name, attempting to quiet him down.

"Nah, fuck that, Adele. They not going to come up in here and tell me what they are going to do with my child. I don't give a damn how often they gotta come out here. That's their fucking job. If you think that it's going to be easy for any of you to get my daughter out this house to admit her with their nuts, then you lost your damn mind," Dad spat.

"If that's what you think, sir. Because if you put your hands on any of us, you will go to jail and your daughter will still end up with the nuts, as you say. Don't get upset about an option that she may need to take to get better," the woman responded with enough sass for Mom to step in front of Dad.

"That's where you are wrong dear. He won't be going to jail. As crazy as we both will get, you will need to reserve two more beds for us on the fifth floor. Because like he said before, it won't be easy getting her out of here," Mom threatened. The EMTs didn't want that smoke with my parents. They gathered their shit and left quickly.

"They done lost their fucking minds talking to her like that,"

Dad was still ranting. Mom exhaled and placed her hands on her hip.

"As much as I don't want to admit it, Theron. They are right. This can't keep happening," Mom told us both and looked at me. "I know it has only been three weeks, baby. But you haven't made any attempt towards getting better. Your father and I made the living area a suitable place for you to sleep because of the view outside your window. You haven't taken a deceit shower or bath since you been back home. The doctor prescribed you anxiety pills that you only take when you are too far over. You have been ignoring your friends' texts and calls. Your job could be understood for so long before they give your position to someone else. You lounge, eat crackers, bread, or anything else to soak up the wetness in your mouth to end up right back in this situation. I mean, tell us, baby. Do you want to get better?" Mom said softly after reminding me of my daily activities. I knew she was feeling like this for a while.

My mother was the type of woman that snap back after anything. I didn't know where she got that strength from, but homegirl wasn't from this planet. Dad told me after she gave birth, two weeks later she was back at work, saying fuck that maternity leave. She didn't want to lose her position at the Global Warehouse. She was one of the four women shift managers they didn't fuck with. Mom was well respected for her hard work and dedication. She retired with the nickname, *The Bull*. Mom lived up to that name wherever she went. My grandmother died, and she was holding up too well for her siblings' liking. She was smiling and greeting the other family members like they were there for a happier occasion. Aunt Latrika couldn't stand it any longer and tried to approach Mom about her behavior. Mom whispered something to her that made her face pale with dread. She patted Aunt Latrika on the shoulder and kept it moving. I wanted to be that way, but my father told me that there was nothing wrong with a soft woman.

He loved the independence that my mother instilled in me. I had that go-get-it mentally that made me look cocky. I wasn't worried about failing because I wasn't built that way, thanks to my mom. When I fell, Dad was there picking me up. When I cried, Dad told me it was okay to shed some tears and be emotional. Mom didn't like that at all. They had their arguments about it, but it never interfered with the love that they both had for me. Mom taking up for me against the EMTs wasn't a surprise at all. She would have rather me get that type of news from them. Even though my parents wouldn't send me to the crazy floor, Mom was ready to take another drastic measure to get me back on my feet where I belonged. Dad was okay with me being right there with them. Sometimes he would sit in the living room with me and watch old westerns. I got content with being in the space that brought me comfort.

Everything was within arm's reach, and I was afraid to step out of my house, thinking that I was going to fall in a puddle and drown. The shit sounded funny, but the struggle was real. I couldn't say any of this shit to my mother because it wasn't the solution that she wanted to hear. Mom sat next to me, holding my hands for support. I didn't know what to tell her. Fear of disappointed her more kept me silent with my head down.

"Come Adele. Liya had a rough night. Let's come up with some answers tomorrow. We are all tired and need some rest," Dad interfered. Mom glanced up at him and shook her head.

"Okay. Tomorrow we are going to write down a plan of action to get my baby back on her feet. We are not looking for you to be steady. All I want to see is some effort," Mom said before kissing me on my forehead. "Goodnight baby."

Dad leaned down and hugged me. "It's going to be alright Liya." He kissed me on my cheek and retreated to their bedroom. I was left there sitting and wondering what the hell I was going to do. Whenever my father told me that everything was going to be alright, I believed him. For some reason, the words were just words coming from his mouth. I didn't feel the meaning behind it at all because he didn't believe in them himself. I felt myself getting emotional and got pissed. I stood up and tossed the pillow across the living room. I walked into the kitchen to get the nighttime snacks that helped me throughout the night. Peanuts, crackers, and bread were my favorites. I knew eating all this shit was going to make me thirsty. I would wait to get the ice because I didn't want it to melt. I knew I was going to be fine with the full bag of Saline they gave me.

I walked through the cold kitchen to get to the pantry. I didn't understand why my mother had the temperature in Antarctica all day. I tightened my fitted black robe around my shivering body. I swung the pantry door opened and grabbed my snacks. As I was closing it shut, something caught my eye. I tried not to look at it head-on, afraid of what I might see. From my peripheral, it seemed to be a shadow on the wall in our dining room. It was moving in waves. I quickly closed my eyes and turned around. With everything going on, Dad must've forgotten to close the curtains on the patio doors. Like a horror movie, I bolted out of the kitchen and dove onto the couch. My shaky hands reached for the anxiety pills that sat on the end table. I took two and sat back, thinking of the desert. Dry ass land. Fire. Concrete. Anything that wasn't moist was featured in my thoughts. I counted to ten forward and backward.

"You are not helping her, Theron. That soft talking and telling her that things are going to be alright is not preparing her for what is out there," Mom's loud voice said.

"She doesn't need to be out there in the world Adele. Can't you see that? Liya would see a glass of water on the table and freak the fuck out. That is not the way I want to send her out there. I won't push her either. You told them, people, that healing takes time. It has only been three weeks. She still needs more time," Dad argued.

"If you give Liya any more time, she is going to get worse

Theron and it will be harder for her to overcome this. I don't want to lose my baby over some shit that we can help her get over now. I know you see Adaliya as that same little girl that you used to coddle when things seemed to be too hard for her to handle. This is not the case. That young woman graduated ahead of her class, above muthafuckers that didn't think she was going to make it. They made it harder for her and she excelled. This... illness isn't any different. My baby dreamed of swimming in the ocean with all creatures that haven't been discovered yet. If that was MY LIYA, she would have dove back in that water and searched for that thing that almost ruined her life instead of giving up on what she worked so hard for. I know she doesn't want to be like this, yet you are telling her it is okay. It is not okay, and I won't accept that. Not for her," Mom ended their conversation with a valid point.

She was all the way right. I just couldn't get a grasp on things yet. I sighed and grabbed my phone. I went to my favorites and dialed her number. I knew it was late, but I needed her voice of reason.

"No, Egypt, fuck. What are you doing?" I heard Landon's voice in the background.

"I'm sorry, baby. It's Adaliya," Egypt sounded out-breath.

"Sis! Do you really need Egypt at this moment? Like, can you wait for at least another thirty minutes?" Landon said louder for me to hear.

I was ready to hang up anyway, hearing how close Landon seemed like he was before I called. "Landon stop," Egypt replied before I could do anything. Landon sighed loudly.

"No, Egypt. I'm fine. I can give you a call back when you guys finish up," I assured her.

"You are okay, Liya. We finished an hour ago. He was starting up again. Now," she casually responded. "Are you okay?"

I sighed and tried not to give in to my emotions. "No. I had an episode today and my mother sounds fed up with it. I want to get better, but I don't know how crucial these steps are going to be."

"Okay, sis. You know I am here for you. Tell me what you need from us, and you got it," Egypt sounded pump.

"That's the problem. I don't know where to start. I mean, I tried before and failed," I admitted.

"Let's take small steps this time. How about you and I go out for a bit tomorrow? Nowhere fancy. Just a place where we can eat and enjoy a social hour," she suggested.

Thinking of what was on the other side of that door had my heart racing. My mouth was getting watery, and I felt like I was going to faint. Just then, Sol's hand slipped into mine. He squeezed it a little to confirm his presence. I moaned his name and leaned my head against his shoulder.

"Breathe, Liya. Take a deep breath in and release it slowly," Egypt spoke and took in deep breaths with me. I did what she ordered, making sure the air filled my lungs before releasing it. After ten minutes, I felt myself getting over the thought long enough to hear Egypt out. "It's not going to be easy, Liya. Asking for help was a major step, and you did that knowing what it was going to bring. The hardest step will be sticking with your plans and not giving up. You have to know that there is a precious treasure waiting for you at the end of this rainbow."

"Not if it is in the water," I joked about it.

"You know that there were precious jewels tossed in the Caribbeans," Egypt smiling voice jumped through the phone.

"Yeah, I know about that. San Jose galleon lay lost on the ocean floor. The Columbian government almost got their hands on it, but the jewels went missing again the very next day. It was a shame because amongst the treasure lies the diamond of the sea. It is said to be the colors of the water. Like the water-water. The blues, purples, greens, and rarest color of water vantablack is bald up in this rock of a sharp crystal that can cut your fingers off if you hold it wrong," I blabbered.

"Wow. I didn't know that," Egypt laughed out.

"How could you not? It was the jewel that was heard over the world and mentioned over four times a year on the discovery channel."

I heard Landon's laughter through the phone along with Egypt's added outburst. "Who watches the discovery channel like that, Adaliya?" he asked me.

I pulled the phone away from my ear and stared at it in horror. "Everyone at least watches the discovery channel once a week to understand the predators of nature. Wouldn't that excite you!" I replied too enthusiastically.

"We don't need the discovery channel for that," Landon growled. I knew that none of them was looking for me to respond to that. Egypt checked out of our conversation as her moan and cry for pleasure slipped.

"Oh-Oh-Okay. We will talk tomorrow about the outing. Bye. Have a goodnight. I mean enjoy your night. Or, shit. Whatever," I said and hung up. I placed the phone on the table and released a deep sigh. I didn't realize how much I missed talking to the opposite sex until now. Landon sounded like an aggressive lover. I hoped and prayed that it was a trait that ran in the family. His brother was something special... and familiar. I swore I saw him before somewhere. And, his voice. His voice could have melted me in my sane state. It did before. Did it? I wanted to think of him some more, but his eyes messed me up. The way they swirled like one of the hypnosis pendants had me frantic. When Egypt told me he wanted to be with me, I didn't believe her. There wasn't a man on the planet that would deal with the foolishness that I had going on. As much as I hoped for that possibility, I couldn't sike myself out into thinking that I was going to end up with somebody. Let alone, a doctor. He already worked in a stressful environment. He didn't need my problems interfering with that. He. Him. The man. "Arghhhh," I groaned with frustration.

"How the hell am I going to date a man whose name I couldn't say without trembling?"

That was another big issue I had to get over. I shook my head and leaned over and switched the light off. I was thinking twelve steps ahead of the first one. I erased those thoughts from my head and focused on my road to recovery with his family. The covers moved up underneath my chin. A soft kiss brushed up against my cheek.

"I'm sorry, Luna. I will make it up to you. I promise," Sol vowed.

"It's okay. I am going to get better," I stated. I moved around until I got comfortable with my eyes shut tight. "Good night, Sol."

"Good night, Luna. I love you," he said near my ear.

"I love you."

"Are you sure about this?" I asked Adaliya, looking up into the chandelier of LaCroix hotel. The sixteen-floor building sat near the shore of Old Tampa Bay River. I was prepared for her to have the same episode she did when we came out the first time. We went to have lunch at Datz restaurant on S. MacDill Ave. The waitress approached us and sat a pitcher of water on the table. Adaliya jumped up from the table, knocking everything off it. She turned to escape the big mess and ran directly into Skye's chest.

"Whoa! I know the food isn't that bad here," he joked. Adaliya shook her head, on the verge of a panic attack. I went to her and rested my hand on her back.

"This is that next step that we were talking about," I whispered.

"I know. It's just," she breathed out and tried to hold back the tears. A slight breeze brushed past me and settled around Adaliya.

"It's okay. That is why we are here. To help you with the hard parts," Skye answered and spoke with the waitress over her head. "Can we please get another table and a pitcher of water?"

A growl was heard out of nowhere as Adaliya's face ashen at

the thought. I took her hand and turned her to me. "We are not moving backwards," I assured her. I walked with her, behind the waitress that looked extremely afraid to serve us.

I led Adaliya to her seat and the waiter's hand shook as he placed the menu on the table. "Take your time," he mumbled and rushed off. Skye and I talked and got to know Adaliya a little better. In the middle of the conversation, Skye smiled and looked out the picture window that looked out into the river. In a small whisper, he said that she is doing great and will be ready for him sooner than he thought. I knew Amanzi wasn't going to stay away. Landon told me about the creatures that he had been dealing with and the people that he had lost. I thought a hurricane was going to sprout up in the gulf with all the activities that had been going on.

Adaliya did well the rest of the day and asked if we can do the same thing the next day at another spot. We had been doing that for two weeks with her getting stronger and stronger. Each time we went out, Amanzi's presence was sensed. I believed Adaliya felt it every time. I caught her glancing at the water once and blushing at the sight. It was the same action that mates had when they caught each other's eyes. I wanted to call her up on it but didn't want to make it obvious how better she was getting. Coming to this hotel was proof itself. The glass rooftop restaurant gave us nothing but a view of the water. Adaliya shivered when we pulled up. I thought she was going to need a breather, yet she surprised me by grabbing her purse from the backseat. She looked at me with a soft smile and asked was I ready. I nodded my head, proud of the woman that I was accompanying.

"I'm sure. Besides, Courtney wouldn't forgive me if I miss it," Adaliya responded and pointed left. "I think the elevator is this way."

The hotel was massive. There were two check-in points on each side with an information desk in the center. The beige and blue marble floors traveled throughout the hotel. The greenish-blue colored walls were decorated with framed old letters. I got closer, trying to read the one that was hanging over the information desk. Even with my cat's eyes, I couldn't read the smudge writings.

"I don't expect others to understand the amount of love that I have for you. It's how you carry yourself. The way that you move without anyone paying attention. I smell your scent which can only be described as a heartfelt breeze in the early morning before the sun kisses your face. Blissful. I count the days, dreading missing the uninterrupted moments that we have shared. If I had a choice, I would die in you. The smile that you put on my face can't be matched by no other.

It's a letter from Alistar Boar. He was on the 1598 LaCroix ship that got lost at sea. Their bodies were never recovered, nor was the ship. The letters surfaced in the early 1600s and were gifted to Spain's general by the Native Tribes during the Period of Friendship," Adaliya sounded sad about it. I glanced over thinking that she was having a moment and asked her what was wrong. Adaliya shook her head and sighed. "The letters were never meant to be displayed to the public. It doesn't belong here. After the general left the letters behind, a writer by the name of Hesiman took them to a university to study with his colleagues. Professor Arnez Incanus thought it would be a great idea to find out who the letters belonged to. They went all around the world, looking for the woman that was the subject of Alistar's letters. When they didn't find any, they passed the letters on to their students who saw it as an adventure. It took some time, but they found Alistar's family and gave them the letters. His great-great-granddaughter, Beth thought she should share the love that Alistar expressed to his wife with the world. She gave it back to the students, who then gave it to the university. They thought it would be a great idea to display them just as the hotel is doing. It is sad," she mumbled.

I frowned, not understanding what was so sad about it. They

were trying to help. "I'm confused. Why do you think it was so sad?"

"Because. Those letters weren't meant for his wife. Alistar wrote those letters and gave them to his true love. Metaphorically he was speaking about the water. After he wrote those letters, he tossed them into the sea, ocean, or river. That is why he addresses the letter by a different name each time. He was expressing how he felt while he was on the boat with his crew. Those letters weren't supposed to be retrieved. They belong to the water."

I nodded my head and read the inscription that was engraved on the plaque of the desk. "*The memories and thoughts held while boarding the LaCroix.*"

Knowing what I knew now, made me look at the art differently. I didn't bother asking her how she knew about this. Her passion for the history of the water was too strong for her to be wrong. The chiming of the elevator brought us back to the real reason we were there. We left the hanging picture and hurried to the elevator. There were three other people there, going to the same sixteen floor.

"So, what did Landon say about you meeting up with your father? You didn't get a chance to talk about it last night when he got in," Adaliya inquired.

"Girl. He told me something about staying away from my father because he was troubled. I don't know why he thought that was all that needed to be said without any further explanation. I disagreed, and he got all saber-, I mean Landon on me. I tried to ask Skye about it, and he shut me down as well. I don't know what is going on and I hope they know me well enough to know that I don't let stuff go like that," I answered her with as much information that I could without her getting suspicious. I was getting too comfortable around her and spoke out of terms sometimes. It was too much going on and keeping it to myself had been difficult. I talked to Deshawn about it and she damn near growled like one of Landon's animals. She knew what it meant to me to find out where I truly came from. My mother wasn't giving me any information about my other family.

"What kind of trouble do you think your father is in to have Landon and Skye acting like that?" Adaliya followed up with another question.

"I don't know, but I will find out one way or another," I replied and changed the subject. "So, have you been hearing this mystery voice lately?" Adaliya dropped her head and blushed.

"I hear him every day. When I get in one of my moods, he comes to me in a whisper. Our connection somehow is deep, and it feels so real. I just wish that I could put a face with the voice," she said and then looked at me in horror. "I mean, I do still want to meet up with Amanzi."

I dismissed her statement by waving it off. "It is fine, Liya. I am not the type of sister-in-law that runs her mouth. In your mind, what does he look like?" I asked her. When she first told me about the voices she had been hearing, I knew right away who was talking to her. I knew he was going to find a way to make sure he did whatever he needed on his end to make her feel better. He had to know that talking with her was improving his odds.

"He is tall. Handsome. He has long hair that flows majestically in the water. He has these eyes that peer through my soul and a smile that can wake up to every morning. Tattoos of waves of water surrounding an upside-down triangle," she smiled before continuing. "What gets me the most is his intellect. I found myself having multiple orgasms during his conversations alone. If his words can do that to me, I know if he was truly real, he would have my body singing in the ocean."

"Well, damn girl. Doesn't he remind you of someone, though?" I replied. Adaliya stared up at me, trying to figure out what I who talking about. I smiled and bumped her shoulder softly. I was not prepared for that description at all. She, in her own words, described Amanzi. If he was anything like his brother, he didn't need to talk about sex or send images of his dick to arouse Adaliya. All Landon had to do was to tell me how his day went, and I became hot instantly.

We both tried to regain our composure as the door opened to the top floor. I was happy that I wasn't allergic to flowers, or I would have turned around. The rooftop was filled with them and petals leading to the dining area. Adaliya couldn't do anything but shake her head.

"I'm sorry. I forgot to tell you that Courtney could be a little over the top sometimes," she said and walked beside me.

"You think," I countered and glanced around the room. The glass windows were covered with other floral arrangements blocking out the view of the water. The layout was beautiful. The floors were made of glass that overlay the white carpet of the 2200 square ft. room. The round tables that were decorated with white silk sheets and diamonds were aligned in front of a long rectangular table that sat in the front of the room. That table had white, pink, and gold silk cloths with more flowers hanging from the front of them. There were six chairs at the table with the two in the middle looking like thrones.

The people around us were dressed in suits and formal dresses. I was wearing a fitted round-neck purple dress that stopped at my calves. My scarf-printed bandage four-inch gold shoes accented the dress perfectly. Adaliya had on a one-shoulder strap navy blue dress that hugged her breast as the chiffon material dropped over her waist. The flowy dress moved as if she was in the water. I didn't know if she noticed it when she walked out to my car. The wind blew the dress back, showing her curvy figure. She finished the dress off with sparkling cage shoes. Ms. Adele came out the door to hand Adaliya her purse. I sent a mental picture of Adaliya to Landon to send to Amanzi. I knew he needed something to look forward to.

All eyes were on us when we entered the room. Adaliya told me that there were going to be a lot of people there because of Greyson. With that warning, I was still stunned by the number of people that were in attendance. I didn't trust many people after my ordeal with Shemar. My eyes were always open and scanning for potential threats. My radar went up when Adaliya's friend Courtney approached us in a gown that could have been her reception dress. It was a strapless ivory and lace fit and flare dress that had beading across the bodice. The lace was designed as roses and covered the silk completely. Her diamond chandelier earrings touched her bare shoulders. Courtney's makeup was over the top with eyelashes that could've blown her groom away. The sparkling shit that hung on them made me want to laugh. Adaliya stepped in front of me to cover my amusement.

"Hey, Courtney. This place is beautiful," she commented.

"Aww! Thank you, Liya. But what did you expect?" Courtney replied with an arrogant tone.

"Something a little more settle," came out of my mouth before I thought of something else to say. I stepped to Adaliya's side and greeted her friend with a forced smile. Courtney's eyes went up and down my frame, searching for a flaw in my perfection.

When she couldn't find any, she was left with, "if you knew who I was, you would know that I don't do anything settle."

"Clearly," I responded.

"I'm sorry. You are?" Courtney moved forward and asked. Adaliya cleared her throat and made the introductions.

"This is my good friend and conscious therapist, Egypt soon to be Heart. Egypt this is Courtney..."

"The lying scheming trifling ass heifer that wants everybody to praise her and soon to get an annulment within three months of marriage," another woman interrupted and spoke.

Courtney speared her with a look of disappointment. She placed her hand on her hip and shook her head. "I can excuse Liya for not complying with the color scheme I put out for you guys. But the rest of you have no excuse. Briana, Kara, and

Valma, please tell me why you aren't in the dresses I picked for you guys to wear?"

"Who the fuck was wearing hunter green and red to a pastel color event?" Val answered.

"You guys are in the category of the Brecks Red Spider Lilies. Everyone has a category," she mumbled with a smile for the rest of the guests that were passing by.

"Yellow daisies. Lavender carnations. Pink tulips. You have all these bright pretty ass colors at each of these tables. But here it is our Christmas tree-looking asses are all the way in the back with the cousins you are not too fond of," Kara countered.

"Does it matter where you guys are sitting? You were invited. Some can't say that" Courtney sassed and waved over our head. "Please don't ruin my day with your bull," she directed her last comment to Briana. Courtney walked off in the direction of a group that looked and acted like her.

"I don't know why y'all thought that you were going to get through to her. She might as well place pictures of herself around this bitch because that's what this gathering is about. That was why I didn't give that hideous dress a first, second, or third thought," Brianna said to the group.

"If all of you feel this way, why are we here? I definitely wouldn't be in a place that I was lucky to be invited to," I had to know.

"Because we believe that the Courtney we grew up with is in there somewhere," Val said and held her hand out. "Hi, Egypt. Liya told us how much you are helping her to get back to herself. We really appreciate it."

I took her hand in mine and nodded my head. "It is no problem this way. I look at Adaliya as a sister, anyway."

"Good. We can go ahead and trade you in for Courtney. She will be pissed to know that we have another beauty in the group that she will have to compete with," Brianna winked and walked to our table.

"Oh. You guys already know?" I followed behind the group and inquired.

"Child, we knew what Courtney was about for a while. We just don't pay any mind to her bullshit," Kara replied and pulled out her chair from the round table.

"We all ignore it. Everybody but Brianna. That is why they clash all the time," Adaliya informed me.

"I don't see how any of you do it," I admitted.

"Me either," Brianna said and raised her hand to get the waitress's attention. "Can we please get something to drink?"

The waitress gave us a pleasant smile with a tray filled with water. She looked down at the tray and swung it toward her back. The girls and I looked at her crazy. I thought she was entertaining us as she served. Ole' girl did say she was over the top. I started looking for magicians and ponies.

"Hello. I'm Susie and I will be the waitress for this table. I noticed that there were special instructions for this table. Do you guys want something to drink?"

Brianna looked at us around the table and frowned. "I thought that was what I called you over here for."

"Yes, can I have Crown Apple and Coke, please?" Kara ordered.

"Since when you drink brown," Adaliya smirked at her.

"Since I walked in here, having to put up with these people," Kara gestured around the room.

"If that is the case, make that two," Brianna added.

"I'm sorry, ma'am. I was told not to serve liquor at this table. I have juice, soft drinks, and wa.." she paused and looked at Adaliya. Adaliya stared, waiting for her to continue. When she didn't look like she knew what to say.

"Water. You have water," Adaliya surprised the girls at the table with a word that everyone danced around.

The waitress looked down at her tray. I peeked at it and saw that she had a picture of Adaliya on it. "What is that?" I pointed.

"The bride-to-be wanted to make sure that Adaliya was comfortable enough to stay the entire time," she answered. "Would you like some...?" Susie paused again.

Adaliya saved her the trouble and shook her head. "No, thank you. I don't want any water."

Susie sighed and nodded her head with relief. "Okay. I will bring a couple of glasses to the table if it isn't a problem. Whenever you guys figure out what y'all want, let me know." Susie walked off towards the bar.

"What the hell is going on? How the fuck are we restricted from drinking?" Val raged as everyone else was seen having a cocktail or two.

"You remember the last time y'all was drinking. Kara was on the table shaking her ass," Adaliya reminded them.

"It was her twenty-one-birthday party. We all were fucked up," Kara replied.

"That's exactly why you hoes drinking water," Brianna said and glanced over to Adaliya. "I'm proud of you, sis. Getting better enough to come and chill with your friends."

"I'm not in the clear yet, guys," she smirked.

"Don't sell yourself so short. You have been doing great. We went past the beach the other day and she stared at the water the entire time without flinching. That is progress," I chimed in and nudged her.

"That is awesome, Liya. Are you thinking about starting your job soon?" Kara asked.

"I don't know yet. I'm taking it a day at a time. With the support that I am getting from my sister and brothers, I think I will be okay to sit in a couple of meetings," she proudly gloated.

"Hold up. What brothers? We have been your friends for over a decade and haven't met these brothers," Val probed.

"Well, I told you about the guy that found me on the shore. He was vacationing out there with his brothers and sister, which is Egypt. I was so messed up that I kinda freaked him out. But his family told me he talks about me all the time and can't wait to take me out," she confessed more.

We made it our business to talk about Amanzi and how much of a good man he was. She told me how embarrassed she was after their first encounter and didn't want to see him. Skye told Adaliya that her reaction was valid, after dealing with a life and death situation. "*My brother is a forgiving man. Especially when it comes to someone that he is interested in.*" The first part of his statement got glares from me and Landon. Amanzi was still on the fence about his mother and her actions towards Landon. Yet, Adaliya accepted those words and worked on herself.

"Wait a minute, chick. What this dude looks like?" Kara pressed.

"I don't remember him clearly," she responded shyly.

Brianna didn't like that answer. She directed her next comment to me. "Alright, sis. Can we see a picture of your brother please? We need to make sure that our girl is on the right track to salvation." I laughed and pulled out my phone. It was hard getting them together nowadays. When they did, it was always something. I told Landon that he needs to spend time with his brothers more. Even though they were immortal, he would want to cherish the times that he spent with them. Before Amanzi went to help Adaliya, I took a picture of them sitting around their mother. I pulled my phone and passed it to Kara, who was sitting on my right. Brianna was sitting next to her with Val to her right. Kara took one glimpse of the picture and dropped the phone on the table.

"My GOD!" she screeched, catching the other guests' attention from the tables that were around us.

"Let me see," Brianna said and picked up the phone. I could see the instant drool that formed from her mouth. "Tell me who is who, so I won't be embarrassing myself behind another woman's nigga."

"I don't care. All of them fools are fine as fuck. Including the woman in all white. She can get it to," Vall commented. We all chuckled and marveled at the people in the picture.

"The dude standing up, though," Brianna's eyes were glued to Skye.

"That is Skye. He is the only single man in the picture. The one sitting on the love seat is Amanzi," I clarified.

"How can you forget something that looks like this?" Kara turned the phone to Adaliya. She held her hand up, blocking the picture.

"I don't want to see him like that. I want to wait for our second physical interaction, again."

"Girl, I don't think that picture does him any justice. He is sitting down on this one with his legs stretched out to the middle of the floor. He gotta be over six feet. That's yo shit right there," Val added.

"He is six-nine," I confirmed.

"Oh my god! This bitch got a giant," Kara blurted out. Val nodded her head with a surprisingly quiet Brianna still staring at the picture.

"Damn, B. Are you alright over there?" Adaliya noticed the same thing.

"Yeah, I'm good," Brianna shook out of her daze and searched around the room for Susie. "Fuck this. I need a drink-drink."

"We all going to need something to make this grand toast. My girl is getting better and got a fine ass dude waiting on her like the grand prize winner," Val hollered.

"I would love to toast to that," I smiled at my friend.

"What's going on over here?" An older woman walked up to the table and asked.

"Hey, Ms. Janet. How are you doing?" Adaliya spoke first.

"Ready to go. This isn't anything but a big ass party for Courtney to flaunt what she has over people. That's what happens when you spoil your child," Ms. Janet enlightened us.

"I think Courtney came out you, looking for diamonds. She is nothing like Farrah and Mitchel," Kara told her.

"We thought that would have changed with you guys being great influencers and all," she replied and rested her hand on Adaliya's shoulder. "I heard what happened to you. I talked to your mother, and she said that you were doing better. I'm so happy to see you out and about."

"Thank you, Ms. Janet. I don't think Courtney would have forgiven me if I didn't come. Especially with all the detailing, she took to make sure that I was comfortable," she threw a nod at the waitress that turned her back to us with the pitcher of water on her tray.

"Don't give her all the credit. Greyson told her to do that," Ms. Janet revealed.

"Wow," I expressed and sat back in my seat. I didn't know what these girls meant to each other or what they had been through together, but there was no need for friends like Courtney.

"Selfish," Brianna mumbled.

"That she is," Ms. Janet said and jumped when a young man and lady stepped behind her. "Why aren't you guys at the table?"

"The same reason you're not at the table. Courtney is talking about herself and the wedding. Can we go, please?" the young man responded.

"It can't be that bad Mitchel," Val smirked with her statement. He stared at her with a scowl deep enough to change his facial features.

"Don't act like you don't know how your friend is," the lady spoke.

"I'm sure that you are thrilled to be a bridesmaid, Farrah," Kara wondered.

"No. I'm not. She thinks bridesmaids are maids to the bride. Like, real-life maids. You know she asked me to come and clean her house while she shopped for lingerie."

"For the wedding night?" I questioned.

"No, for tonight," Farrah spat. It wasn't funny, but it was funny. I covered my mouth to conceal my laugh from the frustrated little sister.

"That girl is too much," Brianna said as Susie walked up with our glasses of water. "Can we please get something stronger than this?"

"What do you mean? It's an open bar," Ms. Janet implied.

"Yeah, but we are under restriction," Kara informed her.

"The hell? Susie, please get these grown-ass women some drinks. This is a celebration," Ms. Janet instructed her.

"Yes, ma'am We might have another wedding in the mix," Kara clapped and pointed to Adaliya.

Farrah forgot about Courtney and stepped forward to congratulate Adaliya. "That is great. But, how? I thought you were in the house the entire time."

"Amanzi is the guy that saved her life," Val answered. Ms. Janet and Farrah gasped and started asking questions about him. I'm not going to lie and say that we weren't loud. Our conversation was getting more attention than the guests of honor. The drinks were delivered, and it was becoming a real party. That pissed Courtney off. She stormed over to our table and pushed through her family to get to the front.

"What is going on over here?"

"We are celebrating?" Farrah announced.

"Yes! Cheers to that!" Brianne yelled.

"Cheers!" Everyone raised their drinks and clinked glasses with each other. Courtney's hands clasped together against her chest.

"Oh, guys. Thank you! You know I always knew that I was going to be the first to be married. Greyson and I came a long way," she sounded as if she prepared the speech for this moment.

"Oh, girl, please. We are celebrating Adaliya. She got a man, and we can say water without her freaking out on us. Aye!" Val raised her glass towards a blushing Adaliya.

Courtney tilted her head, confused about what was said. "Wait. Liya got a boyfriend?"

"Not a boyfriend. A man. A grown-ass six-nine man with his own business and money," Brianna teased. Before Courtney could say anything else, Brianna slid her phone over to Courtney before she opened her mouth. "I hope you don't mind, Egypt. I'm pretty sure Skye is about to be taken as well."

I loved their confidence in her. Brianna seemed like the one that spoke her mind about everything and didn't hold back. Her attitude was the complete opposite of Skye's. I didn't know what he thought about casual dating, but I was going to let him know of his admirer.

"You are so full of sh," the words paused as her mouth dropped, gawking at the picture. She couldn't believe what she was seeing either. Ms. Janet and Farrah moved in closer behind her to get a better view. I loved watching the effect that the Heart men had on women. Some natural gods took pride in themselves and their work. It showed through their tattoos and demeanor. Landon sat me down and explain every artwork of his body. The history behind it alone had me in tears. I didn't understand how much they all had been through to be who they were today. I was happy to shine a light and become a good mark on his body.

"Oh Lord," Ms. Janet whispered. As much as Courtney didn't want to show her attraction to our men in the photo, her facial expression gave her away. She didn't want to turn away from the picture. Brianna cleared her throat, sporting a smirk on her face. Courtney slammed her phone down on the table. It shook, forcing us to sit back in our chairs. Her body temperature spiked up alarmingly. No one seemed fazed about her change. They all watched as she unraveled into something that they have all witnessed before.

"This is not the time to celebrate a relationship that might not last longer than your airman career," she shot at Brianna and Adaliya.

"Damn, Courtney. Are you serious?" Adaliya grimaced. Courtney glared down at her with her nose flaring.

"Yes, I am. He doesn't look like the man that has the patience to deal with your chaotic life," she assumed. I felt the feline in me rise at her comment. She didn't know about my relationship with the men in the picture and thought that she had free range to say what she wanted. I didn't play that shit and need to interfere quickly before she said something that would have gotten her face clawed up.

"You don't know shit about my brother. He will wait forever and more for Adaliya. I think that was simple enough for you to understand," I hissed calmly and paused. "Oh, I forgot. You don't do anything simple. Let me rephrase that," I was ready to stand up and get in her face. Adaliya's hand stopped me from rising. She looked just as pissed off as I was.

"She really doesn't know shit about anything. That is why her nosey ass stays in other people's business. That fucked up fantasy world she built around herself is bland like her personality. That is why she is not settled. She wants to be remembered for something, even if it's a lie. That's why I don't pay her any mind. Misery loves company and I refuse to be an afterthought guest," she spoke with confidence before the phobia.

The girls recognized it and sat back in their seats loving the response. Ms. Janet sipped her drink and looked away. She didn't want to chastise her child then or now. To see someone else do it, was priceless.

Greyson came over and brushed his hand up Courtney's back. "Hey, is everything okay over here?"

"Yes, everything is fine. This was beautiful Greyson. Thanks for looking out for me. I appreciate it," Adaliya stood up. It was the cue that I had been waiting on since we walked in here. The other girls started grabbing their things as well, planning other places that we could go to finish off our day. Adaliya pushed her chair in and nodded for me to go ahead of her. I moved forward to lead the group out of the party. I was sure that Adaliya was safe behind me. I knew it. I didn't think that her conniving friend would take the pitcher of water and pour it over Adaliya's head.

"Ahhh! Ahhh!" she screamed and fell to the floor.

"You bitch!" Brianna yelled and tried to tackle Courtney. I grabbed Adaliya's arms and picked her up. I rushed her out of the area, moving people out of our way. She was shaking and mumbling shit under her breath for soul or something.

"No. No. No. Don't go back to that place, Liya. Come on. Stay with me. Stay with me and breathe. You got this," I coached her.

Adaliya leaned against the wall and tried to slow her violent breathing down. I rubbed my hands up and down her arms giving her all the strength I owned to overcome this episode. Her eyes were shut tightly as the water ran down her face. Val ran out with some napkins and started patting her face dry.

"She is going to pay for this, Liya. That bitch done cross the line for sure," Val promised.

"Just," she mumbled and inhaled a deep breath. "Can you please just take me home?" Adaliya requested.

"Sure, sis," I said and grabbed her hand. Val wanted to say more, but she saw how badly Adaliya needed to go.

"I will call you later," she told us and turned around. There was more yelling and cussing in the room. I wanted to go back in there and watch Brianna tear Courtney into shreds. If she didn't do it, I was going to make it my duty to do so.

We got on the elevator and went down to the car. She was admiring the letters that drew her attention when we came in the first time. She didn't look towards the water once we stepped outside. Adaliya covered her eyes with her head down as the valet went to retrieve my vehicle. I held Adaliya's hand like a child that would run wild in a candy store.

“Adaliya,” I mumbled softly.

“No, Egypt. Not right now,” she breathed out in pain. I stopped talking, seeing that she was pushed to her limit. I knew if I dropped her off home, her parents were going to need the ambulance for her again. I didn’t want that. None of us did.

My black BMW M6 pulled up to the curb. I immediately opened the door for Adaliya and placed her in the car. Brianna was being dragged out by the other girls screaming how much she was going to ruin Courtney’s life for the bullshit she pulled. Adaliya leaned forward and placed her head in her lap. She covered her ears with her hands. I pulled away from the scene, knowing that the steps she took forward didn’t mean shit. She looked as broken as she did when she woke up in Amanzi’s hut. I wanted to give him good news as I did the past couple of days. Revealing this was only going to put him in a sourer mood. Thanks to Qala for giving him their creatures to take his anger out on.

"FATHER! WATCH OUT!" CORIAN YELLED BEHIND ME. I swung my sword backward, slicing the blob's head off. I threw my hand forward toward the one that was in front of me. It paused with its mouth opened inches away from my face. I closed my hand and watched its skin fall from its body. Another one tried to shoot past me to get to my children. I grabbed the blob's tail and pulled it back. I slammed it on the ground and threw it into the blob without the head. I thrust my sword downward into their bellies sure that they were dead after that.

Femi swam up to be pissed at the creatures that started popping up everywhere. I knew that the shit wasn't that easy. But it seemed as if they were multiplying somehow. We had been making transfers since the first encounter with Qala's creature. Anything that resemble the signs that Cyann's section had, we didn't take any chances or waited for something to happen to my people. It was strange when two came upon us at one time, then three, and four. No matter what my people did, they couldn't fight or harm the creatures. There were only able to die at my hands and that made it that much harder. I had to ensure the safety of my people, but I had to protect the leaders that led them to our haven.

"Is that all of them?" Femi inclined.

"I'm not sure. We have to move fast just in case more come back," I said and scanned the area for any other imminent attack. Femi waved his hand forward, giving Corian the okay to escape his section. Corian stepped aside and allowed the Lost Village of Ontario mosogens to be filtered out into large groups around Trinity and Dafari.

"What is next?" Valin questioned. Before I could answer, felt the danger near the banks of Tampa. I growled.

"Get everyone to safety!" I told him and teleported myself to the scene. I saw Lenmon fighting off land creatures on the beach. It was the same vicious animals that we faced in Atlanta. I didn't give anything a second thought as I stepped forward and snatched the back of the creature that tried to attack Lenmon from behind. The creature turned to face me. My hand shot forward, turning into a blade that went in his mouth and through his skull. I swung my arm, throwing the creature behind me to deal with another. Lenmon had his war hammer out, slamming against the creatures' heads with a purpose. He growled menacingly at the creatures that dared to be in the vicinity of the water.

"Ahhh," a scream was heard to my left. I turned and saw a creature stalking toward the woman. Lenmon head snapped in that direction and tried to get to her. The creature he was fighting caught an opening and bit into his side.

"Dammit," he hissed. Lenmon elbow dropped on the creature's head, forcing it to let him go. Lenmon spun around with his hammer, hitting the creature and breaking his ribs. I slid across the sand and grabbed the opened mouth of the creature near the woman. I pulled the top of his mouth including his head off his frame. A creature turned on its heels to attack me. It leaped forward but got yanked back by the claws of Egypt. She hissed and ripped out the creature's throat. The ground shook as Landon stampeded his way through as a rhino. Egypt took a step away from the crowded creatures. I snatched Lenmon's collar and pulled him back. Landon ran down the rest, stomping and burying them into the sand. Lenmon was still trying to get at them.

"Stop," I hissed in his ear. Lenmon stopped struggling and calmed himself. Egypt admired Landon as he transformed back into his human form and approached us.

"You are adapting well," I complimented my sister-in-law.

"I have a good teacher," she responded and wrapped her arm around Landon's waist. "Did you get the picture?"

"Yes, I did," I smiled at the thought of Adaliya in that dress. When Landon sent it to me, I was battling one of the blobs. I handled it quickly so that I could take my time going over the mental picture. Her hair was up exposing her neck and shoulder. I have caressed her body many times before without her noticing and knew that her skin was just as soft as it looked. The small smile on her face gave me a glimpse of what I will have once all this shit was over. It wasn't like I needed a reminder. My body sometimes drifted to wherever her presence was. I saw what happened to her the first time she went into the restaurant and reacted by sending energy her way. It took everything in me to stand fast and allow my family to take care of her. Once she settled down, I released a heavy sigh. I thanked my brother and told him to continue to watch over. Skye replied she was going to be ready for me sooner than I thought. I wanted to be happy about that, but it was too much shit going on. I wanted to be free of all of this so that I could spend time with her. What she wanted, I could provide that and more. I didn't worry about her accepting what I was. She already did and was going to be ready for everything that I had to offer and more, including the answers to the unexplainable events.

"Thank you for that. It's good to see her smiling again," I added. Landon was staring at Lenmon who was foaming at the mouth.

"Are you guys, okay?" he inquired. Lenmon noticed eyes

were on him and straightened. My eyes stayed on Lenmon as I answered his question.

"Yeah, we are fine. I felt the disturbance near the water and came up. When I did, Lenmon was fighting them off by himself."

"Where did they come from?" Landon asked Lenmon instead.

"I don't know," he answered.

"What do you mean, you don't know? You were out here to check the surrounding, right?" I asked sternly.

"Not this area. I heard the woman scream and ran to see what was going on," Lenmon spoke. Egypt glanced behind us. Our attention went to the woman who was stunned by what she saw.

"What the hell was she doing out here by herself?" Egypt wanted to know.

Lenmon took a step forward to go and found out, but I stopped him. "You need to heal. Get into the water," I told him. Lenmon looked as if he wanted to disobey me. "Did you hear me?"

"Yes, Father. I just wanted to make sure that the woman was okay before I did that," he replied.

"You think her seeing you leak white shit out of your wounds is going to calm her hysterical state? No, it won't. Get into the water, now," I responded to my question. Lenmon continued to stand there as if I didn't give him a direct order. My eyes brightened at the disobedience. Egypt stepped up and tapped Lenmon on his shoulder.

"I will check on her," she spoke and went to the woman. Lenmon followed her steps not caring about the consequences of his action. Landon knew I didn't play that shit and tried to change the subject before I went off.

"Did you find your brothers?"

Lenmon returned his attention to us and sighed. He nodded his head and reached into his back pocket. "I went to the last site they were guarding and found this on the ground. That is the necklace that Trinity made Semaj before his assigned site. I watched him fight furious battles. Never was this necklace removed from his neck."

I took the necklace and shook my head. "Was there anything else lying next to the necklace that looked suspicious?"

"Yeah. There was a pile of silver dust not far from it. Another was found six feet from it," Lenmon explained.

"That was their remaining," I uncovered. "Where are the others?" Lenmon wiped his eyes and looked out into the water.

"I suspected that. That's why I told them to stay away from the shore until I found out what we were up against. I didn't want to call on you, thinking that they were trying to set you up," he retorted.

"I thought I told you to do the same thing," Landon was now getting upset.

"I know. But I had to get," Lenmon stopped himself from revealing a secret that he was obviously keeping.

"You had to what?" I encouraged. Lenmon's pale eyes scanned over mine with no answer. I was tired of this shit. I stepped into his face with a threatening glare. He was really fucking playing with. "I asked you a question," I told him in our language.

Lenmon started sweating and stuttering, which was new to me. We didn't sweat or stutter. I created them to have confidence in everything that they did. Lenmon was a leader, acting out like one of my newborn younglings. He knew he didn't have a choice but to answer my question. He never saw me speak our language in front of my brothers. I was losing my cool, and he understood that.

"I don't know how to say it," he started and got interrupted by Sipho and his two guards. They walked out of the water with their bodies in liquid form. When they got further on the beach and into the new air, their skin began to cover them, giving their bodies a defined shape. Their seaweed hair became dreads, long and untamed. The seagrass covered their bottom halves like loincloths. All three of them looked like warriors from one of those tribes with the markings of the ocean tatted on their bodies. I knew it had to be important if they addressed me out of the water. Their bodies weren't meant to stay out too long, or they would dissolve themselves. Sipho nor the other guards didn't know the language of the land and spoke freely in front of Landon.

"Father, the youngling Zuri is missing," Sipho spoke first.

"What the fuck do you mean he's missing? I thought I told you to watch over him," I spat.

"You did Father. But I had to step in to help teleport the larger groups to the haven. I instructed my two guards, Jabarrie and Gamba to look after him. As soon as I left, Zuri disappeared without a trace," Sipho explained.

I smirked.

I didn't think the shit was funny. I had to keep myself from going over and killing all the incompetent creatures that I created. If they weren't doing their job right, what the fuck were they there for? My family's theories of not creating them were getting truer by the minute. I closed my eyes and inhaled the scent of the ocean to soothe my raging spirit. I held it in for at least a minute before releasing it. I felt Landon stepping back, allowing me to handle the situation however I saw fit. It was his only option. Getting between me and my children would have been a fight between him and me.

"What is your purpose?" I said out loud.

"To build and help our people grow within my section," Sipho answered.

"To protect the shores of the water from any danger," Lenmon went behind him.

"To guard and protect the lives of our brothers and sister," the two guards spoke together.

"Then help me understand how all of you are failing your

purpose. You two aren't guarding or protecting shit if you can't keep your eyes on one youngling. Danger walked into the water from the shore of a beach that you are required to guard. If any danger got near, you were supposed to alert me or my brothers. You did neither. You oversee muthafuckas that are raising younglings that think it is okay to bully their own and have them looking for attention elsewhere. Please make this shit make sense to me," I opened my eyes and grilled them.

"Father, I didn't think that Zuri would go against your orders," Sipho spoke.

"You went against my orders! You did! I gave you the direct order to look after Zuri, Sipho and you gave that job to someone else. I didn't need you to teleport shit. You took it upon yourself to insert help that wasn't needed. You did that. Why are you so surprised at Zuri not listening when you doing your own thing? Explain that." I went off on his ass.

"He was in the room when it was revealed that he can't be detected by any of us but you. I don't know if he is testing that theory out or just being an outcast," Sipho countered. "I'm sorry that I messed up Father. I would gladly suffer any consequences for my actions later. Right now, I'm worried about Zuri and what he might get himself into," Sipho countered.

His apology sounded sincere, but there was something in his tone that wasn't quite right. I didn't have the time to dig deeper, knowing what he said to be true. If Qala got his hands on an undetected youngling, he would destroy us from the inside out.

Lenmon looked relieved that the attention was off him. I burst that bubble quickly with my next statement.

"Get yo ass in that water. After you heal, gather all the piyas for a meeting. This shit is far from over. If I have to make an example out of you to get my point across, so be it." Lenmon looked defeated. He nodded his head and walked towards the water. His body dissolved as soon his foot touched the tide of the ocean.

I stepped forward to graze the water, searching for Zuri's presence. "Fuck," I growled in land language, drawing Landon's attention. I looked around the area for any signs of Zuri's presence.

"He is not in the fucking water."

"What?" Sipho reacted angrily.

"What's going on?" Landon asked.

"One of my younglings escaped the water and is wandering around on land," I told him.

"Do you think Qala has him?" Landon's second question was.

"I don't know. But we have to find him," I said.

"Do he have the ability to walk on land without needing water?" Egypt questioned next. I turned to Sipho to get that answer.

"What did the healer say about Zuri?"

"Zuri isn't like the others," Jabarrie answered.

"We know that already," I snarled. He stepped back and allowed someone else to answer my question.

"Trudy revealed Zuri has a strong heart and willing spirit. He will excel wherever you put him. Plus," Sipho paused to take a deep breath. "She called him an aggregate."

"An aggregate." I translated for Egypt and Landon.

"He's a collection of what to be exact?" Egypt tried to get a better understanding of what was being said.

"Of everything that I created. Zuri is an ultimate," I shook my head, pissed off with myself. I never wanted one youngling to be more powerful than the other. That was that favoritism shit that I wasn't fucking with. I guessed I messed up and put too much into the seed that Zuri sprouted from. "This is not good," I whispered.

"Where could he be?" Landon was ready to help however he could. I wasn't sure where to start. Sipho and his guards stepped forward to help, but I was afraid that I would go off on them even more.

"Go back to your section. We got this," I told him and headed for the parking area of the beach. Landon and Egypt followed behind me waiting for further instructions.

"What does Zuri look like?" Egypt wondered.

"He will be in child form, no older than eight. He will be taller than the average kid, with hair down his back. He will be wearing seagrass as a loincloth. Because he wasn't assigned to any specific duty, he won't have any tattoos. We can try to look near the water banks or other beaches. I will contact the other," I stopped mid-sentence, feeling the skip of my heartbeat. I made sure that no one was in the red zones of the water to get attack by those blobs. Dafari or Femi would have made their way up here if anything else went wrong. The only other person who my heart would do that for was...

"SKYE!" I called out to my brother. The night clouds in the sky moved out of the way for the dive that he made from the balcony of Mother's house.

"What's wrong?" his dragon's eyes were wide and ready for war.

"Adaliya is unguarded. That's what's wrong," I growled and spun on my heels.

"I thought she was at home with her parents. She had a rough day and wanted to go home to get some rest," Egypt grabbed my hand and reached out to Landon, whose eyes were of his sabertooth.

"She is not home. And, she is not alone," the words rumbled out of my throat. Skye touched my shoulder as I brought us in front of St. Joseph Behavioral Health Center on N. Habana Ave.

"What the fuck?" Landon mumbled.

"Oh, no," Egypt whispered and headed to the front entrance of the hospital. She stopped once she saw Adaliya, walking toward the beach with the boy. "Liya, what are you doing here?"

Adaliya's eyes left the young boy's and reached mine. She gasped out the only air in her lungs and tried to retrieve more to do the same. I was stunned to my feet as if it was my first time seeing her. She was still in the dress that she had worn to the outing with Egypt. Seeing her in front of me, after so long, didn't lessen the effect that she had on me. I didn't know what to say to get everything started.

"Amanzi," she spoke my name as if she was dehydrated. I was willing to fulfill that need until the young boy stepped around her. His eyes were steady and sure of what he had done.

"Father," he addressed me. I took a few steps toward them, trying to behave in front of Adaliya. She took note of the young boy's word and frowned at me. Adaliya grabbed his hand to pull him closer. I didn't let that gesture stop me from addressing the youngling. He messed up in a big way and he had to be punished.

"Zuri. I thought we talked about this."

THAT BITCH!

I knew she had some issues within herself but never had I thought that she would flash out her frustration on me. I could have called her on her shit many times before we arrived at her engagement party. That whack-ass email giving us specific instructions on what we needed to wear and the back entrance to used to enter were the first of my problems. Then it was her telling me she needed to approve my guest that I wanted to invite by sending a picture of Egypt to her. Courtney thought she was the better-looking one in the group. Even after the plastic surgery to fix her nose, added hips, breasts, and ass, it still placed her last. The girls realized that and didn't bring the shit up. Brianna got on her about everything else and made her hate herself differently. We thought Bri was doing too much but after what happened, she deserved all of that and then some.

I wanted to blame myself for turning my back on her after I blasted her in front of her friends and family. The most I thought she was going to do was to tell me to leave her party. I took that away by getting up and leaving. I added insult to injury by taking her guests that wanted to celebrate my accomplishments. I could've sworn I saw Ms. Janet stopping Farrah and Mitchell to walk out behind us. There was nothing left for her to do but to use my weakness against me.

Never again!

I would never put myself in a position to be harmed that way again. Egypt was right. I made a lot of progress to moving backward and being afraid of some shit that would have me running back home. I have been spending time with Egypt, Landon, and Skye for weeks. They have helped me regain what I've lost in myself. My mother's surprising face was priceless when I asked for my cell phone. I started making calls to my job to see if there was anything that I could do minor before stepping into my position. They assured me they had something for me and were going to set up something with HR. That step alone made me feel I was fine enough to attend the party.

I was wrong.

I confused my comfort around the people that made me comfortable with the people that wanted me to be comfortable. They would have needed to spend more time with me to know what they were able to say or do around me. I haven't been around the girls for them to know how to do that and I couldn't expect Egypt to pick up the pieces every time I relapsed. I knew Egypt thought I was going to close myself off and start all over. On the ride back, I was quietly on my phone ordering an Uber. Egypt pulled up in front of my parents' home and tried to talk to me. I shook my head and got out of the car with no words. I was afraid of the idea when I heard it, but it was the only option at the moment to get better. I couldn't rely on the voice to come to me each time. I called out for him again today in front of Egypt. If she heard me, she didn't say anything about it. The entire ordeal was embarrassing. If I told Egypt what my plan was, she was going to talk me out of it. I couldn't risk that. I entered the home quietly and waited for her to pull off. When she did, I stepped outside for the car.

A black-on-black Dodge Charger pulled up with the Uber

sign sitting in front of the window. I didn't give myself time to think about my decision. I jumped in the car and gave the driver the address. He punched it in and looked back at me when the information popped up on his screen. The young man wasn't sure how he wanted to ask the question. I saved him and me the embarrassment by speaking first.

"Please, can we just... go."

He nodded his head, turned, and pulled off. I slouched down in the back seat to avoid the scenery that was calling out to me more and more as the days went on. I peeked at the water the other day and caught myself in a trance. I thought I saw someone looking at me and motioning me to move forward. I wanted to say that it was my imagination, but I have seen shit that I couldn't explain more than twice. I closed my eyes and rejoined the conversation that I was having with Egypt. I had in it my mind to revisit what I saw once I got all the way better. And better was what I wanted for myself. The young man announced that we arrived at St. Joseph Behavioral Health Center.

"Would you like to change into something else before going in there?" he asked me.

"No, I'm fine. Thank you," I said and got out of the car. The driver pulled off wishing me luck. It looked peaceful outside the peach stone wall building. I was sure that the security cameras that were posted at the door had something to do with that. I wasn't sure what to expect and kept my mind open to accept whatever help that they were going to give me. I took a deep breath and exhaled slowly.

"This will change everything," I mumbled.

"I don't think it will," a little voice spoke behind me. I turned and saw the most beautiful child I had ever seen. His auburn skin stood out underneath the moonlight. He was at least fifty-nine inches tall, which made me think he was ten years old. The boy sported violet eyes and long unkempt dreads that hung down his shirtless chest and back. He was wearing some grass shit around his waist with no shoes. I kneeled in front in front of him with a soft smile.

"Hey, dude. What are you doing out here by yourself?" I asked him.

"I am not by myself. I am with you," he answered and raised his hand to touch my hair. He twirled it around his fingers, amazed at how it felt. I saw the enjoyment in his eyes and wanted to keep it there. I tilted my head to the side and continued talking to him.

"Yeah, but I just got here," I smiled at his admiration.

"Me, too," he replied quickly.

"Oh, yeah," I said and looked around for any adults in the area. "Where from?"

"Home. I needed to see you again and make things right. I don't want you to be mad at me. I was only trying to bring you home where you belong. It's the only way I could protect you," he informed me.

"Protect me? Protect me from what?" I wondered.

"Everything," his simple answer didn't give much for me to go off on. I didn't want to disregard what he was saying and missed the opportunity of helping this young boy. But I was standing in front of a mental hospital in an evening gown with a child dressed like Tarzan. If anyone would have passed us up, they would have thought that we both belonged in that hospital. I remained open to the possibility of him needing help and continued talking to him.

"Well, I'm not in trouble. I'm doing okay now, but we need to get you home. It can get cooler at night, and I don't want you to get sick. Do your parents know you are out here dressing like that?" I tried again.

The boy shook his head with a flash of uncertainty in his eyes. "No. He can't know that I am here, or I am going to get into trouble with the person who was watching me. I wanted him to see that I didn't mean to hurt you."

That worried me. I felt what he was saying was accurate. I didn't know what asshole would cause harm to this little boy. He seemed gentle and harmless. How could he have hurt anyone? "I know, dude and it's okay. We don't have to go back to your home if you are afraid of someone there. I have a friend that works with children and help them in situations like this. We can give her a call to see what we need to do to get you some help." I brushed my fingers across his face. I yanked my hand back noticing how cold his skin was. I took his hand immediately and started blowing on it. "My God, you are freezing. Come on. We can go inside to get you warmed up," I told him and got on my feet. I headed toward the entrance of the facility.

"We don't need to go in there and you don't have to call your friend. Once everyone sees you are okay, they won't be mad at me anymore. It's near the ocean," he whispered convincingly. I thought I was going to go into a panic attack, thinking of going toward the ocean. The thought of that was drowned out by the touch of the little boy's hand. It was soothing and refreshing. It had me back-peddling away from what could have cured me.

"What is happening?" I whispered to myself.

"The change that you were expecting," the boy said and started walking away from the hospital. I didn't think of how crazy the shit sounded or looked. I was comfortable with this little boy and didn't see any detriment in what he was saying. The truth was in his bright eyes.

"Liya, what are you doing here?" I heard Egypt shout from the parking area. The little boy stopped and drifted behind me. I gazed up in Egypt's direction and caught another set of eyes that haunted yet enthralled me. The man that was the subject of many conversations was walking toward me with the power of something I couldn't explain. My heart raced and my mouth went completely dry, hoping that he could fulfill a thirst that I haven't had in months. His short hair was glossy like his creamy dark brown skin. Oh, how I wanted to feel his touch on my body and caress his into submission. I wanted to do whatever his eyes were commanding me to do. At the time, they wanted to hear his name from my lips.

"Amanzi," I easily obliged. He loved it and rewarded me with a smile that flashed off his pearly whites. If I wasn't ready for our meeting before, I was damn sure getting ready to meet my future husband that resembled the description of the man that talked to me nightly. I felt the little boy peeking around me to see the people that arrived. He stepped out on the side of me with his head held high. His light voice got deeper as he spoke.

"Father," he addressed Amanzi.

I felt that pitcher of water being dumped on my head all over again. Whatever fire that was burning for him was put out by this new revelation. I grabbed the little boy's cold hand and pulled him closer to me. Amanzi didn't care as he stalked toward us.

"Zuri. I thought we talked about this," Amanzi's demanding voice spoke.

"Talked about what?" I replied with an attitude. Amanzi stopped walking and gazed at me. My eyebrows went up, expecting an answer sooner than later.

"I don't think that this conversation is any of your concern," Amanzi spoke. I didn't know why his statement affected me so. I felt the rage of some kind building up to protect the strange kid who knocked me off my road to sanity. I felt my eyes going into a slant and a snarl released my lips.

"Clearly, he wasn't your concern either. How could you allow your son to walk out the fucking house looking like this? What the hell were you doing that was so important that you lost sight of your child's whereabouts?" I snapped. Amanzi stood his ground as I got into his face.

"I was working," he answered and raised his hand to push my hair away from my face. I batted it away, not giving a fuck about his response.

"If you were at work, who the hell was watching him? He is

afraid to go back there because he thinks that someone is going to hurt him," I revealed. Amanzi glanced down at the boy and started talking in a different language. The shit threw me off because I couldn't decipher what they were talking about. The language that they were speaking sounded like something from a different planet. I raised my hand and blocked his view. "Hell no. None of that. You don't get to talk to him. For all I know, you might be the one that he is afraid of too."

"Okay, guys. I think we need to calm down and talk about this," Egypt intervened.

"Yes, we should. Because this baby is not leaving with him," I folded my arms over my chest.

"Now, Adaliya. I don't think that's," Skye stepped up and tried to speak his peace.

"I hope you are not about to take up for your brother after seeing your nephew out here like this. Are you crazy, too? Or, is it a family thing? His ass needs to be held accountable for this shit here and if you won't fix it, I will." I said to the group. I meant every piece of the words that came out of my mouth. There was no way that these muthafuckas were standing in fly ass gear, shoes, and fucking socks on, while this kid had nothing but some lawn grass around his waist. I felt my blood boiling out of control over this scene.

"Shit," Skye mumbled, not taking his eyes off me. He backed away with his hands up, surrendering the situation back to Amanzi. Egypt and Landon stared at me with wide eyes as Amanzi sported a smirk that had me fuming even more. I didn't know what the hell was funny, but he was about to get an earful. I felt the boy's cool hand in mine, stopping my movements.

I glanced down and saw the same smile on his face. "See, Father. I didn't hurt her. She is stronger with me," he proclaimed. He was right. One-touch, had me feeling as if I could swim in the ocean and defeat a whale. I felt guilty drawing energy from him. I tried to remove my hand from his, yet his grip got tighter. "Don't," he whispered up at me.

"Zuri, I don't think that is a good idea. You can't be away from home like that until you get older," Amanzi told him.

"He isn't going back to the home that he ran from," I said with my eyes still on Zuri's. They seemed to get brighter with every second.

"Zuri," Amanzi demanded his attention. I glared up at him with something else showing in my posture.

"Don't," I repeated Zuri's words in the same demanding voice as Amanzi. I couldn't understand what he was seeing that placed the bewildered look on his face. "He is not going anywhere with you."

"You don't get to make that decision, luv," he replied, stepping forward.

"Oh-kay," Egypt moved in between us. "As I said before, we can go somewhere else and talk about this."

"What is there to talk about, Egypt? The person who you guys described as a good man is an *ain't shit father*," I told her.

"No," Zuri tugged on my hand for my attention. "Father takes care of all of his children. We are very grateful to him."

"All? You mean to tell me he has more grass-wearing, dreads having, violet-eyed children running around here," I turned and asked Amanzi.

"Not necessarily. I am the only violet-eyed, grass-wearing, dread-having child he has. The other twelve hundred and seventy-nine have blue color eyes. It would have been more, but we had to stop due to the strange activities at home. Father hasn't pulled any of his seeds out since," Zuri explained further. Egypt snorted and placed her head down. His statement came out as innocent as his little face. It was the adults around him that couldn't handle their expressions. I was one of those adults.

"Twelve hundred!" I yelled and stepped back, moving Zuri

with me. Amanzi shrugged his shoulders, confirming what Zuri said.

"No, that is not what he meant," Landon said.

"I don't need you to clarify shit. Zuri isn't going with him," I addressed Egypt with my next statement. "You have an obligation to the abused children around the world. You can't ignore this because of who is involved with the situation. It should push you more to see that your nephew gets the help that he needs."

"We will take Zuri until this matter is resolved," Landon held his hand out for Zuri. I shook my head and snatched Zuri up into my arms.

"No. I don't trust that you will keep Amanzi away from him. A report needs to be registered and CPS will begin its investigation. During the investigation, as we could see that abuse is clearly the answer, Amanzi shouldn't be able to see him without being supervised by a caseworker. If you guys don't want to do this the right way, I will call child protective service and get someone else on this case," I said. Zuri's cold arms were wrapped around my neck, enjoying the warmth of my body.

"Okay, Adaliya. We will handle this the right way. We will get an officer out here to take Zuri to a foster home until Amanzi is clear of all the charges," Egypt was taking it more serious now.

"What is a foster home?" Zuri wanted to know.

"Another place you won't be going," I said without thinking.

"That is protocol, Adaliya," Egypt informed me.

"I am not allowing my son to be held by some human shit," Amanzi hissed.

"Human shit?" I repeated.

"Amanzi, he can't go home with you," Egypt said. Amanzi didn't say anything after that which was weird to me. I have been around the family long enough to know how much loyalty was between them. Any family that would up and move to console a strange woman because their brother's infatuation was some crazy shit. I heard stories about foster homes and parents that housed young children like Zuri. Some got abused, sexually, physically, and emotionally. Brianne was in a foster home for one minute and decided that the shit wasn't for her. She used to sleep at my house and with the other girls until we graduated from high school. Brianne wasn't too forthcoming with her experiences, and we didn't bother pushing the subject. Landon, Skye, nor Egypt was going to let Zuri encounter any of that. I could've sworn Amanzi's eyes got darker when he heard foster care.

"Let's go Zuri," Egypt made the decision and reached for Zuri. My motherly instincts kicked in out of nowhere, forcing me away from the group.

"No," I growled and shook my head. Egypt dropped her arms and tilted her head. Landon stepped forward with something in his eyes that warned me to run. Amanzi floated in front of Landon, stopping whatever advances he was trying to make. Skye moved in to diffuse an escalated situation.

"Guys, come on. We don't need everyone getting upset. Adaliya, you asked Egypt to do her job the right way. She won't be able to do that if she can't deliver Zuri to the CPS caseworkers," Skye tried to explain.

"He isn't going to get dropped off anywhere. You know that. I know that. They know that. Stop playing with me," I spoke with Zuri in my arms. His body was getting warmer which was a good thing.

"No one is playing with you, Adaliya. We all want the best for Zuri. You didn't want him to go with any of us. We are the only family that he has that is close enough, to grant him shelter. Where else will he go?" Skye added.

"He will come with me," I stated and pulled my phone out of my back pocket. "I have more than enough room for him at my place until we resolve this."

"What about your parents? How will you explain Zuri's presence to them?" Egypt wanted to know.

"I won't have to explain anything to anyone. We are going to my condo, which is only thirteen minutes from here. I will call an Uber to pick us up," I added. Egypt's jaw dropped to the ground.

"Adaliya, are you sure? Your condo is on the thirteenth floor. It's nothing but eighty feet of glass, overlooking the Bayshore. I know you want to keep Zuri safe, but you have to consider your mental state. What if you have one of your episodes while Zuri is in your care? How do you think he will react to your sudden mood change?" Egypt voiced her concern.

"I would take care of her. It's my job," Zuri responded to her. He squirmed down to his feet and grabbed my hand. "I'm ready."

"The car should be here in five minutes," I said.

"You don't need a car, Adaliya. We don't mind taking you there. I will go and get the truck," Landon suggested.

"That's a good idea. I don't think that it is safe for any of you to be out here by yourselves," Amanzi stated.

"Nigga, are you serious?" I spat. He didn't react to my outburst. Amanzi motioned Zuri to follow them to the curb. As my feet moved, the decision I made began to kick in. I realized everything that Egypt was saying and didn't want to admit that her concerns were valid. I was scared, knowing damn well I didn't have any business going to that fucking condo after what happened today. I wanted to say it was the adrenaline pumping that influenced whatever confidence that was now dissolving. What had me confused was my demeanor. My steps were as strong as the others that I admire so much. The doubt that was overcoming me, wasn't showing on my face.

"Everything is going to be alright. I said that I am here to protect you. Don't you believe me?" Zuri sensed the turmoil that I was battling with.

"Yes, I believe you," I assured him.

"And you don't have to worry about today. That lady wasn't really nice to you. If there wasn't a rule against harming humans, I would have killed her right there for making you sad," Zuri added.

"Kill? Zuri, I don't think that she deserved to die for her actions," I said and peered over his head at his father. "Is this how you raise your children to handle a disagreement?"

"It wasn't a disagreement. She is a mean bitch that threw water on you after you turn your back. If I didn't have to get you out there, half-dead was how I was going to leave her," Egypt promised her.

"She threw water on you?" Amanzi uttered to me and turned back to the hospital. "That's why you were here. You were going to admit yourself to this mental hospital to get the help that I could have provided to you."

I frowned and shook my head at how wounded he sounded. "Maybe that's your problem. You are worried about saving me when your child needs to be saved. Your priorities are all fucked up." I rolled my eyes and paid his ass no mind.

"You don't know anything about my priorities," he replied and stepped off the curb.

Landon pulled up in a green 2022 Hummer. It wasn't a big enough vehicle for some of us to fit. Skye recognized that and threw a nod at us. "I will meet you guys there," he said and walked off.

"That is not necessary. You don't have to meet or follow us there. We will be fine," I directed that statement to Skye and Amanzi. Skye stopped and looked at Amanzi for further instructions, ignoring me altogether. Amanzi leaned his back on the truck and sighed before speaking.

"Why do you think we don't need to make sure you are okay?" he said with a controlled smile.

"I can understand, Egypt and Landon being there. I can also get why Skye wants to follow me because he saw what would happen if I...," I paused and took a different route. "Look. You said that you have to work. I'm letting you know you don't have to follow us anywhere because your brothers and sister will make sure things get handled. They have been doing it."

"You are upset because you think I haven't been here for you through the struggle," he countered.

"No, I'm not upset," I retorted.

"Yes, you are. I can feel it," Amanzi replied with his arms crossed over his chest.

"What you are feeling is regret. I thought you would be better than this," I gestured to Zuri. "Your son is out here in nothing, and you are worried about how upset I am that you weren't around for my recovery."

"You have been around my family long enough to know that is not how I operate. If you need more clarification on the situation, let me explain. The conversations that we have been having haven't touched the topic yet?" he replied and opened the door.

"What conversation? The last time we talk was on the beach," I reminded him.

"You and I know that's not accurate," he challenged. Before I could say anything, his son interrupted us.

"Yes. We all should talk," Zuri spoke and pulled me to the open door. Amanzi reached down and picked my dress up from dragging the ground.

"Watch your step," he warned and took my hand to help me in the car. I slid over to make room for Zuri. He sat closer to me and grabbed my hand. I began to rub it to bring him some type of warmth.

"Hey, Landon. Can you please turn on the heater?"

"Are you cold?" Amanzi asked when he got in the truck.

"No, I'm fine. Zuri is freezing," I answered.

"He will be fine. This is his normal body temperature," Amanzi clarified.

"Oh," I said and stopped rubbing. I picked up one of Zuri's dreads and twirled it around my finger. "How old are you?"

"I am thirty-two seasons old," Zuri responded. I looked at Amanzi to explain that shit further. He smiled, liking the confused look on my face.

"He is eight."

"Okay, but what is seasons old?" I wanted to know.

"Spring. Summer. Fall. Winter. We live by the seasons." Amanzi answered.

"Why? Is it something that has to do with your religion?" He shook his head and turned slightly towards me with his arm stretched out on the door.

"It doesn't have anything to do with religion. It's more of a regime. A lifestyle that I created for the safety of my children and home."

"What does that include, exactly?" I interrogate.

"The lack of clothing is one. Our language, diet, jobs, and education are all impacted by our lifestyle," he responded easily.

"If the lack of clothing is one, why is it fair for you to wear clothes and Zuri can't?"

"Do you want to see me without clothes, Adaliya?" Amanzi threw his question at me. He gave me the sexiest smirk that flirted with the possibilities that I canceled.

"Th-That's not what I meant," I said around the gulp.

"I know. What Zuri is wearing is home wear. He hasn't been introduced to any other type of clothes yet," he replied as we approached the front of the condominiums. As soon as Landon stopped, the valet opened the passenger side door. Egypt stepped out and gazed up.

"This place is so beautiful," she said. Amanzi waved off the valet and opened his door. Zuri crawled over me and stared out of the window. I was too nervous to acknowledge the site that was much better than my condo.

"I can see everything from here. Can you father?" Zuri beamed.

"Yes, I can," Amanzi's tall frame stood over the truck.

"Come on. Let's go upstairs," I said with my head down. My door opened with Amanzi blocking the view. I took advantage of that and grabbed Zuri. I jumped out of the truck and walked around to the entrance of the lobby to The Sanctuary. The desk clerk greeted us as I led the group to the elevator. I took the key out of my purse and inserted it with the access code to my floor. The doors opened, and I went to the back. Egypt came in and stood next to me. Landon and Amanzi stood in front of us. I felt crowded but safe. If I wasn't carrying Zuri, I knew she would have reached for my hand to support me.

"When was the last time that you were here?" Egypt asked me.

"A couple of months ago," I replied and concentrated on the beeps of the elevator.

"Why? Did they not tell you of the changes I made to make you comfortable?" Amanzi spoke. I glanced up at him and frowned.

"What changes?" I said before the elevator doors opened. We all got off and met Skye, who was standing near the door where the stairs were.

"I didn't have a chance to tell her," Skye commented. I entered the key and pushed the door open to the view that I wasn't looking forward to. I was completely shocked and had no words for him. Egypt told me that Amanzi was working on his end to prepare me for a normal relationship. I didn't know that he went through these extremes.

"Oh, shit," I heard Landon say and walked inside the condo.

"Oh my God. When did you have time to do this?" Egypt asked Skye after following Landon in.

"After our first outing. It didn't take that long, considering the number of windows this place has. I went grocery shopping and got some stuff that can hold you over for at least a week," Skye replied. Egypt told me how Adaliya's mother had been pushing her to get better. I didn't want Adaliya to think that she would only be safe under her parents' roof. I decided to get her windows covered with dark-out electrical blinds. That way, she could control how much she wanted to see daily. Everyone admired and spoke about the new change, but Adaliya. She walked silently towards the center of the room with her hand over her mouth. Zuri was stepping all on the couch with his dirty ass feet. As I approached Adaliya, I glared at him. Zuri fell on his ass and sat his hands on his lap. I knew we needed to talk about him fearing Sipho or any other mosogen in his section. I would have called him on his shit but, Sipho was holding something back. I wondered if his motives were to find Zuri and shut him up before he revealed the truth of his section. I didn't think about questioning any of the other mosogens about what Sipho was doing. They were going to back their leader no matter what. I hoped it didn't have anything to do with that Qala shit. I was going to wipe that entire section clean leaving no survivors.

"Liya, are you okay?" Egypt turned when she didn't hear her speak. I was standing behind her, waiting for a response as well. She hasn't been here for months, yet her scent and warmth roamed the air in her home. I had to control the urge to throw everyone out and fill the room with more of her.

"I-I do-don't know," she stuttered and sighed. "I-I," she continued saying.

"You don't like it," I needed to know. Adaliya spun around shaking her head.

"No. Nothing like that," she answered, glancing over her shoulder at the blinds. "I didn't think that I could live in this space without feeling like I was drowning. I'm okay, even with knowing what's on the other side. I was hoping that it was possible."

"For you, anything is possible," I responded. That statement drew her attention back to me and I was enjoying it. Every time she rested those pretty brown or purplish eyes on me, a sense of tranquility spread over my body. Even when she was going off on me about being a careless father, my peace wasn't disturbed. I loved the way she was protecting Zuri and the lengths she was going to do it. I felt how worried she was after saying she was going to take him home with her. My love was faking it until she made it. I couldn't help but smile at the little warrior inside of her. I brought my hand up to caress the stressful lines on her forehead. Adaliya avoided my advances by moving back.

"Why do you insist on touching me?" she asked.

"Because you are mine," I said without hesitation.

"No, Zuri is yours. I am not," Adaliya thought she made that clear. I let her think about what she wanted for now. I couldn't wait to show her the truth in my words. I pointed to the covered windows to get clarity on her feelings.

"You are good with this?"

Adaliya nodded her head, regretfully. I knew she couldn't wait to get back to herself. Her body craved the water just as I did. I could've cured her of this sickness a long time ago, but I knew she wasn't strong enough to endure me tossing her in the open water. It would have damaged her heart more than it did the first time. Somehow Zuri felt Adaliya's discomfort and moved off the couch, disregarding my stern look. He grabbed and tugged on her hand. Adaliya gazed down at him.

"We can get used to this for now," Zuri assured her she had another supporter on her team.

"For now, yes. You, on the other hand, need some clothes. I'm sure you need a bath and some rest. How long have you been out there?" She questioned.

"I have been looking for you for two sunrises. I followed you to the place you thought was going to save you from what you and everyone else here think is a sickness. I'm not understanding why we are catering to this idea of moving slow and blocking what could save you," Zuri spoke without a filter. Landon and Skye shook their head at his bluntness. Zuri was never taught how to speak to humans. I was unsure of how Zuri knew the land people's language at all. Adaliya folded her arms and glared up at me again. The sparkle in her eyes was meant to scare an average man. I welcomed the fire that had been hiding in this woman with an open heart.

"You sent your fucking child to spy on me," she spat.

"No, sweetheart. I would never do such a thing," I explained, shocking my brothers. They had never heard me speak to anyone in the manner that I was speaking to Adaliya. Landon understood only because of his feelings toward Egypt.

"I am not your fucking sweetheart, and your tone is unwanted," Adaliya spoke and tried to walk around me. I gently grabbed her arm and pulled her to me.

"*Careful*," Zuri hissed, threateningly. He was truly different. None of the other younglings wouldn't dare do such a thing. I had to talk with him when Adaliya wasn't around.

"I thought you were going to give me the time to explain," I reminded her.

"Yes, I did. You are supposed to explain Zuri's situation. Everything else isn't a factor," she countered.

"We are a factor. You may not know it now, but I will explain that along with Zuri and the rest of my children. I don't think that tonight is the right time to go into everything. Zuri is on a strict diet and needs certain nutrients to survive. I will swing by tomorrow morning with his food and clothes. The three of us can sit down and resolve this issue together," I suggested.

"We all have had a busy day. Tomorrow will be a great start," Egypt was trying to convince Adaliya to give our talk a chance. Adaliya sighed and rolled her eyes. She didn't understand that the decision was already made. I was going to be here no matter what she said.

I was ready to say that. Adaliya stopped me when she responded with a nod. "I want to know everything. Don't leave anything out or we will be making that phone call to child services," she responded menacingly. We all released a sigh of relief. We knew she meant what she said. I didn't want to deal with any more humans than I had to.

"No problem," I mumbled with my hands caressing her bare skin. Touching her outside of the water was doing something to me. I felt the temperature in my body changing to match her warmth. I knew I was making things awkward, staring at her as if she was my personal artwork. The silence and being the center of attention didn't make it any better. Adaliya noticed it as well and became uneasy. I didn't want her to feel like that in her home or around me. I dropped my tingling hands, wishing that we didn't have an audience. I smiled when she brought her hands up to hug herself as if she was already missing my touch.

"Soon," I promised and motioned Zuri to me. Egypt walked over to her and began to ask if she needed anything. Landon and Skye stepped to the side with me to talk to Zuri.

"How are you feeling?" I asked him.

"I feel fine. I overheard you talking with Lenmon the other day about the nutrients that we all need. So, I made sure that ate enough for the journey," he answered honestly.

I frowned at his reply. "When did you see me talking to Lenmon? Tonight?"

Zuri shook his head. "No. This was a couple of moons ago. I used to leave and sit by myself to understand my purpose since no one couldn't tell me what it was. That's when I saw you leaving the water. I followed you to the surface and heard your conversation about what had been going on."

"You know it is dangerous for you to leave the water without anyone knowing, right?" Skye tried to explain to him.

"I remember the exits that my father used when he wants to see our Luna. There aren't many threatening activities in those areas," he hunched his shoulders and spoke.

"Wait a minute. You been following me, Zuri?" I questioned.

"Yes. I thought you were searching for my purpose here. When I saw you with our Luna, I knew that you have found the reason for my existence," he replied.

"Who told you you were responsible for Adaliya?" Landon beat me to the question. Zuri glanced up at him and Skye, not trusting where the conversation was going. He took a step away from us and shook his head.

"I am not replying to any other question until I speak to my Luna and Father. He will let you know the answers to the questions you ask. If you don't mind, Luna needs her rest," Zuri spoke with confidence and strolled over to the front door. Skye looked at us with a smirk on his face.

"He is truly your son," he noted.

"You don't say,"' Landon added and went to say goodbye to Adaliya. Egypt embraced her with a comforting hug.

"If you need me, call me. No matter what time it is."

"I never check the time," Adaliya confessed to her. They laughed at that as if they were long-time friends, real sisters even. I was grateful for their growing relationship. It made her transition into the family uncomplicated. After they said their goodbyes, I stepped up to her and wrapped my arms around her waist to press her body to mine without permission. Her hands grabbed onto my shoulders for balance. She didn't need it. I was going to be all the balance she needed, in life and everything else that seemed off to her.

"Get you some rest. I will bring your favorite for breakfast tomorrow," I whispered to her. I couldn't help but to brush my lips against the softness of her neck. Adaliya's body shivered. As much as I wanted to stay in her arms, I had to get back into the water to check on my people. After inhaling her scent once more, I turned with a promise to return tomorrow with more answers than the questions she had.

"Don't leave her," I ordered Zuri before walking out. Zuri nodded and closed the door after us. It took seconds for us to get down the stairs and to the car. Skye leaned onto the truck, waiting for me to address the situation first.

"I don't know what's going on," I admitted to them all.

"That's a first," Landon commented. "What do you want us to do? We can keep an eye on both if you would like. But from the looks of it, lil man got things under control. He almost took your head off when you grabbed Adaliya."

"I saw that. It was a natural reaction for him, and he didn't care about suffering any of your consequences. On top of that, he shut all our questions down like Adaliya was a secret. He was ready to go toe to toe with us if he had to," Skye spoke.

"That was a totally different Zuri from the one in the water. I felt his energy spiking up every time you guys asked about her. I didn't want to say anything in front of Adaliya. He had already got her riled up by saying too much," I told them.

"Riled up ain't the word. Did you see her eyes? They turned dark when you told her that Zuri wasn't her responsibility. I thought Mother warned you guys not to give your energy away like that," Egypt said.

"I didn't give her any of my energy. Adaliya had it in her since I laid eyes on her," I made clear.

"Since when did you have eyes for a human female. I thought they were a waste of time," Landon reminded me of the words I once said.

"I think that they are a waste of time. Adaliya and Egypt are different. Besides, Adaliya's energy drew me out of the water when she was a young child. I kept my eyes on her over the years, watching her love for the water grow. I knew what she was to me, but me seeing her in Cancun solidified it. I was near, watching her as I did when she got close to the water. Her friends were walking around the beach in their skimpy ass swimsuits. Adaliya expressed how good the water looked and how much she wanted to get in it. They procrastinated until night fell and wanted to go to a party that they were having on the beach with the rest of the college students. I didn't want her to go and expressed that nonverbally. Adaliya felt that shit and looked directly into the water at me. I tried to make myself invisible to her eyes, but she saw me. She saw me and told them she was getting in alone. As she was removing her sash from her waist I went under, blending in with the water. Adaliya ignored her friends' protest of her not being able to see what was out there. She didn't care. She swam where she saw me and treaded. Her legs moved regally under water. I wanted to touch her. Shit, I needed to, but I didn't want to frighten Adaliya. I didn't know how to get what I needed at that time until she spoke to me. She said, *I always feel you. No matter where you are, I feel you deeply. Do you feel me?* She started caressing the water by easing her hands against it. I found myself drifting to her. I was still in water form when I wrapped my arms around her body. I wanted her to really feel me. I pushed her upward, so her body could lie on top of mine. To any other set of eyes, it looked like she was floating on top of the water. She knew it was more than that because her arm reached back and wrapped around my neck. We stayed like that for hours. I was tempted to pull her down and bring her home then, yet I knew what it would have cost her. She wasn't ready to meet us. Therefore, I waited," I shared.

"Damn, Manzi," Landon uttered.

"I thought it was your first time doing that on the roof in New Orleans," Skye said. Landon looked at him and turned back to me.

"Another story?" he speculated. I shook my head and stood up straighter.

"No. It's another way of telling you all that I am not letting her go."

"We not asking you to let her go, Amanzi. We want to know the next step in this process. I'm sure that if Adaliya asks Zuri anything tonight, he is going to be completely honest with her. You might have to prepare for another rejection," Skye warned.

"I'm not preparing for that shit. I saw how my absences in her recovery have left a bad taste in her mouth. If I was here, she would have recovered quickly."

"The girl saw the ocean in your eyes, Amanzi. There was no way of getting around that if her energy is pulling your element forward without any restraints. Adaliya coming here was a big step. Maybe Zuri's presence can help her heal," Egypt suggested.

"I will not put her healing process into the hands of a youngling that is not yet classified," I disagreed and made my way across the street to the ocean.

"Wait, Amanzi," Egypt called after me. I stopped and turned

slightly her way. "Why did Zuri address Adaliya as his Luna? What does that mean?"

The corners of my mouth couldn't help but go up. "Underwater, my people are guided by the sun and moon. The sun helps them rise and sets them on their paths. The moon nourishes and guides them on their journey. I am their sun, better known as their Sol. Adaliya is their moon or as Zuri called her, Luna."

"Wow," Egypt expressed with her hand on her chest.

"Yeah, I know," I said and teleported to the front gates of Port Royal. I understood how Egypt felt. Adaliya hasn't met any of my people. For her to be connected to them that way was insane.

"Father," Kamu greeted with more guards before. "There have been no activities around this part. All the mosogens from the five sections are accounted for."

"Good. Where is Amber?" I searched behind him.

"She is covering the back with other guards. Tichan and Alecey are covering the sides. We gave them all a tour of Port Royal, inside and out. That way, they will guard it better," Kamau informed me.

"Gathered the guards up and meet us in the center of the circle. We will be transporting to another place," I ordered.

"Yes, Father," Kamau replied.

I got through the gates and came upon a sight I thought I would never see in any of my sections. Port Royal was crowded with leaders, guards, warriors, teachers, and younglings that needed constant attention. This place was only able to hold so many. Packing them like this was going to weaken the electric field that I placed over the city. I knew that was going to happen and thought that I was going to balance things out once I got back. But I didn't have time to do that. I had to move them all to a bigger place that no one has ever seen. A place that Qala himself doesn't know about. There were stories and myths about the magical place that have been in storybooks or in people's imaginations. They all wrote it off when evidence of it couldn't be proven. For the first time in Mosogens' history, I will reveal this place to them.

"Father is back!" A youngling yelled from his seating area with his teacher. Everyone's eyes zoomed in on me. The once loud place became silent as they bowed down to their knees in their greeting.

"Gather your things and get with your guards from your section. We will be moving in fifteen minutes," I announced and continued gliding to the circle where the rest of the leaders were. Dafari and Femi stood by the opening with disappointing looks on their faces.

"What happened?"

"You. You are what happened?" Dafari boldly answered.

"Really," I said surprisingly.

"Yes, really," Femi continued where Dafari left off. "We know why we were created. But being here gave us a bigger purpose than the jobs you gave us. You are that bigger purpose. As one of your firstborns, I do not like it when you leave without us knowing exactly where you are going now there is a threat bigger than we can handle. You need to be guarded, Father. You are just as important to us as we are to you. We can't lose you over some self-pride of you being greater than whatever it is that we are fighting. It's not fair for you to have us worry like that. It is a feeling that I do not like experiencing."

There was no animosity in his words or demeanor. I felt his troubled heart with the others that were in the room. I sighed and rested my hands on their shoulder.

"I'm sorry sons. I didn't mean to worry you all so. Lenmon was being attacked on land by some other creatures created by Qala. He was trying to protect a human female. I arrived and took care of them with my brothers and sister," I explained to them.

"Were they other water creatures that were able to walk the land?" Trinity asked.

"No. These were the same creatures that we fought in Atlanta. I assume Qala is moving around with these things in whatever area we reside in at that time. But," I caught everyone's attention as I got in the middle of the circle, surrounded by my leaders. "Sipho and his guards made it to the surface to inform me that Zuri has left his section."

"What?" Femi stepped ahead of everyone.

"Yes. I found him and he is safe with..." I took a deep breath before letting them know something else I kept private. "Your Luna."

Everyone gasped with their eyes wide, filled with love that I recognized in myself so long ago. The love of a mother was the world's greatest gift. To them, Adaliya didn't disappoint them or led them to stray as my mother did. They, like me, were waiting patiently for her to realize our existence.

"How did he find her? Lenmon and the others had been on the surface for years and didn't detect her anywhere," Dafari inquired.

"I didn't send them on the land to look for her," I replied.

"Luna's energy can't be ignored. There is no way that they shouldn't have sensed her," Valin's confusion was evident.

"When I found out Qala's motives for my mother and brothers, I blocked out her energy to protect her from him. I didn't want Lenmon or any of the others to swarm and scare her. I wanted her to be in peace until everything was safe," I explained. Trinity's eyes were trained on me the entire time. I knew she was going to figure out what was going on with the right amount of answers that were given. She sadly shook her head before speaking out loud for everyone to hear.

"She was the woman that Zuri attacked in the water," she said huntedly. The leaders didn't want to believe the shit. They all looked up at me for confirmation before reacting. I gave them a sharp nod.

"Wait, Father. What does that mean, then? Does she not

want to meet us now that she thinks we are monsters?" Coral questions encourage everyone to ask theirs. I stood quietly, giving them the time to vent their concerns. Some started crying, thinking that the outcome of things was worse than they thought.

"She hates us!"

"We will never meet our Luna!"

"Zuri messed it up for us!"

"He needs to be punished!"

I held my hand to keep them from saying anything else that they couldn't take back. Of course, what Zuri did was unthinkable. But if he was guided properly, none of this shit would have happened. When everyone was silent, I continued talking to the group.

"First off, she doesn't know that Zuri was the creature that pulled her under. We will sit and talk to her about that together when I go back up there. Second, she doesn't hate. Adaliya is pure of love that blesses your lives every time she touches the water. You've felt it numerous times when you were once lost. It was your Luna that helped you with those decisions," I made clear. They all smiled with that hope that they have had since before the blobs' arrival.

"If Zuri found her that easily, what if Qala send someone after her like they did Landon's mate? We need to be up there, guarding her against them," Valin expressed.

"That's why you all are moving again. I am going up there to be with her," I said and motioned everyone to go outside near the Mosogens and younglings that were standing and waiting for further instructions. The leaders stood next to their group and instructed them to hold hands.

"Where are we headed?" Trinity quizzed. I inhaled the water into my lungs and closed my eyes. Once everyone got close together, I answered Trinity's question with one destination in mind.

"Home."

"I LOVE IT WHEN YOU PURR LIKE THAT BABY. CAN YOU DO IT again for me?" I was nice about it that time. She loved it when I played polite. It gave her a reason to disobey. Egypt's sleek back was dipped down with her chest pressed to the bed. I was deep inside of her addictive warmth, loving the way she molded around my dick. Egypt's walls tightened, making sure I didn't pull all the way out. She rotated her ass on me then jerked up. That ass clapped and eased back slowly to my pelvis. That forced my eyes closed and a moan so loud that probably woke the neighbors.

"Nothing is for free Landon. You gotta pull it out of me baby," she spoke over her shoulder. Her eyes were glossy and filled with a hunger that weaken me. I could have pulled that purr out of her in many ways, but there was one that I thoroughly enjoyed. I backed up and ignored her protests of feeling empty. I kneeled and placed my tongue on the top of her clit, licking her from the front to back. Egypt sat up on her knees and released a purr with a soft roar. She never could handle this position. Egypt tried to roll over to place me between her legs. I stopped that by wrapping my arms around her back, bending her forward for easier access to my treat for this evening. She groaned her surrender and took the pleasant assault.

I didn't understand how niggas got this wrong. Pleasing Egypt this way was the easiest. The way her body trembled while my tongue looped and sucked her shit was what I thrived on. She rocked her body toward my face, feeding me that good shit that couldn't be produced by no other. I tried to withdraw every fluid from her body like I had been on dry land, deprived of water.

I made matters worse when I placed two fingers in her tunnel. Egypt bucked, almost getting away from me. I held her down with one arm, begging for her release. Egypt's legs trembled. Her groans became a scream that unleashed her juices into my mouth like a sprinkler.

"That was not the purr that I was looking for," I informed after a hefty swallow.

"What did you expect?" she moaned out of breath. I released my hold and pushed her down to lay flat on her stomach. I crawled over her body and straddled her legs. My heavy-veined friend lay on her ass. I parted her cheeks and slid inside her. The snake in me hissed.

I moved in and out of her sleekness while Egypt moved against my body. She looked back at me and licked those thick lips. I leaned forward and captured them in a scorching kiss. My thrusts became wilder. Egypt latched on my lips with sharp teeth, keeping me where she wanted me. I rested my full weight on her as my release got closer. I felt my sabertooth's teeth growing out of my mouth. Egypt let go of my lip in time for me to jerk her neck to the side and bite into her shoulder. We both orgasm with the sounds of the jungle in our bedroom. I unlatched my teeth from her shoulder and licked her wounds closed.

"I think someone is going to call animal control on us," Egypt joked. I laughed and kissed her on the cheek before rolling onto the bed. I tried to bring her with me, but she declined like she did the last couple of nights.

"Come on Egypt. You can't be mad at me still after what we just shared," I said. Egypt climbed out of the bed and covered her body with my t-shirt.

"I'm not mad at you, Landon. I want to know why you think it is a bad idea for me to meet my father. Saying because you said so, isn't sitting well with me. If you want to lay next to me again, I suggest you come up with a better answer than that," she retorted.

"You know why. He is a threat," I answered.

"How?" she countered with one simple word. She had been asking me this shit for over a week now. I knew she was going to press for more answers. After telling her how the nigga was camped out at Adaliya's place, I thought she was going to drop the shit. She asked me why he was there, and I couldn't answer that because I didn't know myself. She wanted to confront him herself about it and I told her that wasn't going to happen, demandingly. Egypt was a princess in her own right. She didn't like being told what to do without probable cause. I have been dodging the shit until I addressed him myself. I didn't have the time for creatures popping up and terrorizing humans. I knew that this was some part of Qala's plan to distract me from whatever Nesbate was trying to do.

"So, you are going to sit there and stare at me as if I didn't ask you a question," Egypt spoke with an attitude when I didn't answer her.

"It's complicated," I told her the truth. She felt that and shook her head.

"That's not enough. The next time I ask you this Landon, I want answers. If you don't give them to me, I will go somewhere else to get them," she threatened. I was on my feet and in her face in seconds.

"I don't take threats kindly," I assured her.

"And I don't issue out false ones. I have accepted this new life of mine with open arms and no regrets. I heard one side of the story that seems to be inaccurate due to all the shit that has been going on here. My father is stalking Adaliya, and no one wants to find out why. What would he be gaining by doing such a thing? I thought about it and came up with one conclusion," she said and stepped closer to me. "You and your mother are on good terms. Why ruin that by finding out something else about her that may cripple your relationship again? It's her truth that you are not motivated to seek out because it may also reveal the true purpose of your existence. If that's what it is, then that is fine for you. I need to know my history. I need to know that my purpose is much more than being your mate."

Egypt got on her toes and kissed me on my lips. "Goodnight, Landon," she said and walked out of the bedroom. I stood there thinking if that was the real reason. Mother and I have been working together with Skye on getting my land back secured again. She never commented on anything I did negatively or remarks that could be taken as such. Mother accepted Egypt as family. I didn't want to fuck that up.

"She needs answers, though," I mumbled to myself. It was my job to please my mate at any cause. I went to my closet to get some clothes. I threw them on and went to visit Mother. She was sitting at the piano smiling knowingly.

"I do not have any secrets that will cause any doubts in your relationship, son," she started. I walked over and hugged her. I sat on the bench to watch her play.

"Then you won't have a problem with telling me what Nesbate will say that would have Egypt thinking twice about being a part of this family."

Mother reached for the wine glass that sat on top of her piano. She took a small sip and hunched her shoulders. "Nesbate is angry because I didn't want to birth any of his children and share my wealth of the world with him. He may label me as a conceited woman. A selfish one that only cares about my creations. He is entitled to his own opinion of me. Do I think what he has to say will deter or put a wedge in my and Egypt's relationship? Not at all. That was why I insisted on their meeting. She will tell the difference between the truth and lies," Mother responded.

"I know that. I just don't want him to do her anything when she decides to stand up for you or me. You know that is in her nature, to protect what's right," I added.

"It is," she smiled. "Loving you is also in her nature. Trust her son. This one isn't going anywhere," Mother revealed. I exhaled a sigh of relief.

"That's refreshing," I said. Mother continued with her soft melody. It was enjoyable and peaceful. I was wondering why things couldn't be like this all the time.

"The greed of people is a major cause of the chaotic events in the world. Some of them greedy for love, money, attention, power, and truths that are more deadly than good," Mother answered my thoughts.

She already told me I didn't have to worry about Egypt finding out something that could look at any of us differently. The only other person who was searching for some truth was Adaliya. "Are you saying Adaliya will reject Amanzi?"

"That is not what I'm saying. That girl has loved Amanzi since the first time she laid eyes on him. She isn't going anywhere," she blurted. I was surprised at the straightforward answers. Mother was on a fucking roll. I decided to push a little more.

"What about Qala, Mother? What is it you are not telling us about him?"

"That is complicated, son," Mother said the same words I told Egypt.

"A lot of this is complicated. We are getting through it day by day, but it would help if we knew the entire story," I pointed out. The music continued when Mother removed her fingers from the keys to her piano. She stood up and held her hand out for me to take. I complied and followed her to the white couch in her family room. I waited for her to sit before taking my own.

"I think that you have gone through certain ordeals to understand the *complication,*" Mother said before telling me the story of Qalaneive.

"Do you want me to think that your only intentions were for me to find out that my daughter had mated with Landon? If so, you are just as stupid as these things you created," Nesbate stated while cutting into his steak. Dr. Uganja told me that Nesbate arrived in Florida days ago and witnessed Skye guarding his brother's mate. I didn't know what the conversation was about. What I did know was that Nesbate didn't like what was said. He asked for me to meet him out in Tampa to discuss what I wanted. We were at a restaurant called Fleming's Prime Steakhouse on Boy Scout Blvd. I was sitting in front of him while keeping my eyes on my surrounding. I had been careful with staying out of public. I didn't want to be seen by any of Amanzi's piyas. Those muthafuckers were strong and a nuisance. They had his strength and didn't give up until they or the enemy were lying dead.

"You of all people know what I want," I replied to his statement. Nesbate placed a piece of steak in his mouth and savored the flavor of the raw meat. He was being dramatic as fuck. Nesbate picked up the napkin to wipe his dry ass mouth.

"I know what you want. I told you over and over again that it cannot be done," he responded.

"Don't you worry about that. What I want from you is to keep the group occupied on the land. I can't do much with Skye flying around looking for any trace of me, but I have a plan that will slow him down. Landon has been showing your daughter the ropes by killing my creatures. I thought with a bigger opponent, they would need to use more than the puny strength that they have displayed the past weeks," I told him half of my plan.

"Hmm," he grunted and cut another piece of his steak. "I thought she had three. What about the other one?"

"I have that one under control as well," I noted.

"I don't think so. I saw Amanzi on land fucking up shit with his people. I was going to intervene for the hell of it, but my daughter came to his aid. She is beautiful. Nothing like her whore of a mother. It was amazing to see her shift into an animal that isn't of my bloodline. I wasn't ready for that. I guessed she had to give Egypt a piece of her to do that. When all she had to do was to be with me. Those bastards didn't need to be created," Nesbate sat and reminisce the many rejections he encountered with Mother Nature. He was relentless with his attempts. He tried everything to get and keep her attention. Mother Nature was bored with the power and his arrogance. He didn't know how to shut that off and that made him a nonfactor. It was nothing like a god with a wounded pride. They held grudges forever.

"Revenge will be sweet then," I announced. Nesbate dropped his fork and shook his head.

"I'm not looking for revenge, Qala. I can give two fucks about her rejecting me. I always had a bigger plan in mind when it came to Mother Nature. I guess that is why you are still struggling with trying to defeat her. You are derailed by hate and it is destroying you. Your plans are elementary along with those impractical creations," he insulted me. I leaned forward on the table with my arms folded on top of each other. I wasn't going to cause a scene, but I knew I had to make my point very clear.

"My creations are as strong as the children you abandoned. Is that why you allow them to die because your sperm wasn't hitting on shit? The only reason Egypt is stronger than the pathetic bitches you call sons is that I injected her with my blood. Mother Nature made the transformation tolerable with one touch. She is what she is because of us. Not you nigga. But," I said and sat back in my seat. "You can be the dad that was absent her entire life and comes around because of the wealth she gained. It's typical around the parts where Egypt is from, so you don't have to worry about being the first to do that."

Nesbate's eyes were brightly blinding. He smirked and rested his hand on the table. His fingers started rubbing against the white tablecloth. What I said was hitting on some true shit and he knew it. It was written all over his face. I picked up my glass of water and dropped it. The glass was scorching hot. The customers next to us were fanning themselves with the menu. I noticed beads of sweat on the waiter's forehead when he rushed over to clean the mess up.

"Oh, wow. I guess the AC went out over here. Would you guys like another table?" he asked, wiping his arm against his forehead.

"No need. We are done here," Nesbate spoke while staring at me. The waiter ran off holding Nesbate's plate with his apron.

"It's crazy that you would say something like that. You know, the part about Adaliya being what she is because of "us". Do you need to be reminded of who you used to be, Qalaneive? Because a god you are not. You played one long enough to understand the reality of our powers. My shit is pure. You are just another creation," he reminded me. I didn't give him a reaction like he did. I sat back in my seat and jump back on topic.

"Are you going to go after them or not?"

Nesbate stood up and readjusted his jacket. "If I am going after my daughter, I guess I will have to go after them."

He looked across the restaurant at a woman sitting at the bar. She was with two other women discussing a guest list for her wedding. "I guess I should start with her," he mumbled and made his way to the small group. I thought he was up to his old tricks until I heard the woman introduce herself as Olivia. I got up and walked out of the restaurant. He was playing a dangerous game. Skye was the calm one out of the group. Fucking with his mate was going to cause funnels and shit out of the sky.

Before I went back to Atlanta, I had to make another stop. I was surprised that Ali didn't tell me about the mess between Amanzi and my land creatures. I didn't understand why he was out here fighting them when the Golks were wrecking his homes up underwater. That type of mess usually kept Landon busy. I guessed with the help of his new mate, shit been easier for him. Skye burned half of my creatures with his dragon fire. I was going to take care of him in another way. Now that Nesbate was working on his plan, I could focus on what I needed to do to bring my love back. It took a few years for me to figure shit out, yet I was getting closer to the finish line. Dr. Uganji and Dr. Feeble made a test concoction for me to try on someone. I didn't want to do it on a human. I knew they were weak and couldn't tolerate the toxins that were used to create them. I came up with the idea of using the potion on Nelor. I had no idea that Landon was going to leave her as he did. When they made it to their mother, I stepped out of the shadows and claimed my test subject. Dr. Uganji thought it worked well on her because she wasn't dead longer than ten minutes. That pissed me off, thinking of how long it took me to find Cherish, my true mate. She was as beautiful as the sunrise. The first time we met, I knew she was the one. My heartbeat was different, the way I talked was new, and my view of the world had changed. It needed to be for both of them. I didn't hear the news from her lips. Cherish left a card on our bed sealed with a sonogram picture. I couldn't wait for her to come back from the store to celebrate. My life was going too well for comfort, and I knew she was going to make me pay for it. I felt the tremble starting before a massive earthquake took place in

Atlanta, Georgia. I immediately teleported out of the apartment and into the middle of the street. Houses and cars were falling through the biggest crack in the street. People were running around in a state of panic, as shit was falling out of buildings, crashing and killing others. I didn't know if she was testing me or not. But I wasn't saving anyone until I found Cherish. I zipped past bystanders, looking for the only one that mattered. I got to the grocery store that wasn't far from our apartment. I rushed over to the hectic scene and felt no signs of her.

"CHERISH!" I yelled her name in my thunderous voice. I frantically searched for her, picking up cars and tossing them bitches aside with people in them. Some woman gasped, surprised at how strong I was. I pushed her ass out of the way and stormed into the grocery store. Customers were holding on to stuff that wasn't sturdy enough to keep them from falling on their asses.

"CHERISH!"

The grocery store's roof was collapsing as I walked through the aisle calling out for my love.

"Help us! Please!" Lui, the manager screamed. I turned to see that he was trying to hold a shelf of cans over a woman and child. The child looked to be two years of age. He was bleeding from the head and sobbing. I moved towards them and tossed the shelf over the others. Before they could move, the roof came down onto my shoulders. Lui jumped up and tried to help with the weight.

"No! Get out of here! Go!" I ordered. Lui took the woman by the shoulders and drag her ass out of there. I flew upwards with the roof in my hands still. I flung it and continued my search.

"Where can you be, baby?" I whispered. It took minutes almost to an hour for me to find her. She was wedged between a car and surprisingly the roof I threw from the grocery store.

"Excuse me. Are you okay sir?" an elderly woman interrupted one of my painful memories. I was in the middle of the sidewalk. Pedestrians were walking around me, familiar with ignoring their surroundings. I couldn't stand this new generation. They were too in tune with whatever was going on with their phone. If any of them would have accidentally bumped into me, they would have needed a stretcher quickly. I disregarded the older woman and walked around her. My problems would have given her a heart attack.

"I think that holding burdens around makes people bitter. Whatever you are going through is written all over your face. It will be alright," she said to my back.

"You don't know shit, lady," I responded without looking back.

"I know if you pray, forgiveness will be given," the elderly spoke again.

"Your God isn't real," I informed loudly.

"Then pray to yours," her remark had me turning around. The old woman with pale grey eyes smiled at me and turned in her walker. She took small steps on the crowded sidewalk. Three young men were walking, not paying attention to where they were going. I tapped my feet on the ground, causing them to fall and roll out of her way. I thought she was going to stop and check on them. The elderly woman took the clear path that was given to her. Once she got to the corner, she gave me one final look and wink her eye. The pale grey was now gold and filled with power. I sneered, knowing that this bitch was playing with me for real. I made a step to go in her direction, but she was gone in a blink of an eye.

That woman was full of shit. She used to tell me how much she disliked walking around and mingling with humanity. It made her feel weak.

"Lying bitch," I said and cut through two buildings after reaching West Columbus.

I stood over the sewer and called out his name, "Ali.".

Water started leaking from the sewer, forcing the top to

bubble up. Ali's body formed from the dirty water into the man I sprouted him out to be.

"Yes, Father," he spoke.

"Why is Amanzi making land calls? Are you not keeping him busy enough?" I went in.

"He was trying to protect one of his children that were fighting off the creatures that were near the water. I didn't know that they were going to be in the area," he responded.

"They weren't supposed to be. They gravitate to God-like energy. Not even his piyas would have that type of effect on them," I countered and stuffed my hands in my pants.

"It doesn't matter. It will be his last visit for a while. The Golks have been multiplying. Soon we will take over the rest of the sections he created for his Mosogens. We are winning Father. Finally, we are on top with everything going for us."

"You never celebrate too early, Ali. The brothers always have some shit up their sleeves. The new power that my creatures were chasing is connected to them somehow. We will have to find out who this person is because we don't need to have any other surprises," I implied.

"I can do that," Ali suggested.

"No. I need you to continue with what you have planned. If Amanzi does leave the water, I don't want him to have anything else to go back to. Crush all that shit," I gave him what he had been asking for. Ali showed his gratitude with a sinister grin.

"As you wish," he melted back into the sewer to start his new reign of terror. On the other hand, I couldn't return to Atlanta until I find out about our newcomer. I didn't need anyone else interfering with a situation that was going to get them killed.

WHY DID HIS WORDS HAVE A MAJOR IMPACT ON ME?

When I went to bed last night, I couldn't get his words, his face, or his touch out of my head. I was hoping not to say that he was a part of me sleeping past twelve. I couldn't help but to replay his voice over and over. It was like the sound of the sea I didn't remember the last time I slept so well without the nightmares. I guessed having someone that relied on me to stay sane was helping me more than I thought. If it wasn't for his presence, the stuff that he said was intriguing enough to have me interested in our conversation with his father. The knowledge that this kid possessed about the water was astonishing. I thought I was a freak about the primary element of life.

After everyone left, I closed my eyes and released a deep breath.

"Maybe you need a cup of water," Zuri suggested.

My eyes popped open at that. I shook my head and gave him a shaky smile. "I'm fine. They were right. It has been a long day and rest is what we both need. Come on, I could show you to your room."

Zuri grasped my hand and squeezed it. The upcoming anxiety cleared right away. I was filled with energy that had me ready to run miles around the beach. *The beach?* There was a time when I couldn't think of that word without freaking out. I wanted to fill my feet in the sand and smell the saltwater in the ocean. The need for it was truly overwhelming.

"I told you I can make it better. All you have to do is ask," Zuri's entrancing eyes pulled me in. They were the same as his father which made it difficult for me to do anything else.

"What can you do? You are just a child," I said, curious about how he was going to answer.

"I am not the child you think I am. I know I can do much more than talk the talk. I am my father's son," Zuri shrugged his shoulders.

"Well, I am looking forward to the talk that could prepare me for the walk," I countered walking towards the second floor.

"It's nothing to prepare for really," he insisted. "It will be quite easy. You have already had the many sunsets to adapt to him. We are a product of him and everything that he protects. You will blend well. I promise," he insisted.

"Okay, baby," I answered. I wasn't sure of what he was talking about, but the who was very clear. As frightened as it was at first to look into his eyes, I was delighted with the opportunity to see what I have been missing for these past few months. Shit... I could hear the ocean waves clashing when he held me in his arms. I thought I was going to faint and embarrass myself in front of him again.

"I'm not a baby," Zuri stopped and told me. "I am a youngling from Sipho's section."

"Sipho? Who is that? Is that person your father left you with?" I suspected.

"Sipho is not a person. He is the chosen leader of the Pavlopetri section," he explained. I stopped on the stairs and grunted.

"Pavlopetri? Isn't that the oldest submerge city in the world?" I asked.

"Yes. It sits between Elafonisos and the beach Punta in Southern Laconia. We have been there for many sunrises," Zuri answered.

"Wait, Zuri. Time-out. The city that you are referring to is in Greece and underwater. How did you get here, from Greece?" I was too confused at that point.

"It wasn't that hard. The currents that my father created can get us anywhere in the world faster than the boats that humans use. It helps us get to each section when there is trouble faster. Father and my older brothers and sister have been using the currents a lot since the attack on Cyann's section. That was why he didn't know where I was. He was too busy fighting off the enemy with Femi and Dafari," Zuri went on. I paused hearing those names. Femi and Dafari weren't common names in any area. I decided to voice out the other names that were spoken in my conversation with Sol.

"Is Trinity and Valin with him as well?"

"Yes! Trinity is one of our first and most respected healers. She is usually stationed at Port Royal. Valin is the leader of Point Fermin," he recited everything that I already knew. It was like experiencing déjà vu all over again. I turned and asked him about what Sol, and I didn't talk about it.

"Who is the enemy?"

"Qala. We don't know much about him, but Father had to help Landon fight him when we were in Atlanta because he tried to take Egypt. Qala and his creatures were at a great disadvantage. Landon's main beast mated with Egypt. No one can defeat Landon's sabertooth," Zuri continued.

"Oh-kay," I said while nodding my head. "Landon has a sabertooth tiger as a pet?"

"No, Luna. Landon is the sabertooth. He is the king of all the land creatures. Just like, Skye is the king of the sky, and my father is the king of the water. All animals obey them," Zuri enlightened me.

"Who assigned them to be these, Kings?" I asked only to see what his answer was going to be. His story becomes more of a fantasy. I have never heard of someone changing into some animal, unless it was in those books I used to read while I was in college. We were standing outside of the bedroom where he was going to be sleeping in. All the rooms were well furnished with beds, desks, a walk-in closet, and a connected bathroom. I opened the door and motioned for Zuri to walk in. He did and answered my question at the same time.

"Mother Nature created Father and his brothers to protect the land, sky, and water. Father didn't trust the creatures that she created before him, so he made us."

"Us, as in your twelve-hundred siblings," I added.

"Twelve-hundred and seventy-nine," he corrected and stood near the block window.

That was another reason I adored this place so much. The natural lighting made it possible for me to keep my lights off. The house was pitch black when we walked in. It felt like I was cut off from the world somehow. As much as I appreciated the thought and effort of keeping me safe, it didn't feel like home.

"This is not your home," Zuri was now standing in front of me with a stern look on his face. I wiped the worrying off mine and placed my hands on my hips.

"How do you know what I am thinking?"

"Because I know you," his bright eyes conveyed those same words. In them, I saw he believed in everything that was said tonight. Zuri didn't stumble over his words as he spoke about his family and father. Like any other child his age, he wasn't animated, nor did he smile while jumping up and down on my sofa. I didn't like it and had every intention of changing that.

"Hey. How about this? I will run some water in the tub for you to get nice and clean. After that, we can check the fridge for some ice cream," I tried to brighten his stern face.

His brows deepened more at my suggestion. "What is ice cream?"

"What is ice cream? Are you serious right now? You never had ice cream before?" I almost yelled. Zuri shook his head.

"I don't eat anything that isn't plant base," he explained.

What type of shit was this? The kid had to be involved with a cult or something. Denying a kid with such a sweet treat had to be abused somewhere in the world. They were treating this kid like he was some type of... fish. I wasn't going to stand for this shit. His father could be mad at me all he wanted. There was no way that I was feeding this baby plant shit.

"We are going to eat ice cream tonight," I said and walked to the bathroom door. "I can't believe your father didn't at least give you a chance to experience other things before deciding this shit for you. I don't fucking get it. Wait 'til he brings his ass over here in the morning. I am going to curse his ass out. For now, take your bath. I am going to get you one of my shirts and a pair of shorts to wear. They are going to be big, but you can roll the shorts up to keep them from falling," I instructed and pulled the towel from the cabinet above the sink. I sat it on the counter and checked the temperature of the water. It was lukewarm which was right for his cool temperature. "I will be waiting for you downstairs," I stated and kissed him on his forehead before leaving him in the bathroom. There was a storage closet next to his room where I kept all the clothes that I couldn't fit or didn't like. I placed them near the bathroom door and knocked. "I left it on the floor," I announced.

"Thank you," he responded. I brushed my hand down the door and went to change into something more comfortable in my bedroom downstairs. Just like Zuri's room, mine was in complete darkness. I hit the switch to turn on the light and moved around the room as if I had been staying there. I gathered my nightshirt from my drawer and went into the bathroom. I grabbed a face towel and placed it under the running water. I lathered it with my Ocean soap from Bath and Body Works. I started cleaning myself off in deep thought about what was happening.

I wanted to ask him more about his lifestyle with Amanzi. I couldn't care less if anyone thought I was being nosey. I was around Egypt and Skye almost every day. Egypt and I had plenty of conversations about her life. She never went into detail on how she and Landon met. I didn't ask which probably gave her the impression that I didn't want to know. "Hmm," I grunted throwing my nightshirt over my head. I turned the water off and went into the kitchen to get our treat together.

"Damn, no ice cream," I mumbled looking into the freezer. I closed it up and went to the kitchen cabinets. "They had to be something sweet to eat around here." I found a pack of Oreo cookies and had an idea. I pulled two cups from the top shelf and grabbed the gallon of milk from the fridge. We were going to go old school, something that my dad used to do with me when I was younger. Dad would talk and listen to all my stories, fiction or real and eat an entire pack of cookies with me. It was another one of my favorite times we shared. I always knew that I would do this with my children when I had some. The security and comfort I felt during that time were what I wanted Zuri to feel. I needed him to know that he had someone that cared enough to help him in his time of need.

I heard little footsteps descending the stairs and perked up. Zuri came in with the clothes and the towel that I gave him. His little grass skirt was wet as if he jumped in the tub with that thing on.

"Why didn't you put on the clothes I gave you?" I wondered.

Zuri shrugged his shoulders. "I don't know how," he voiced. My face remained passive. I walked over to him with my hand out for the clothes.

"Let me help you," I mumbled. I took the towel and dried him off, I grabbed the shorts and asked him to step in. Once I was close to his hips, I tried to detach that grass shit from around his waist. Zuri grabbed my hand and shook his head.

"I feel more comfortable with this on," he said. I nodded and proceeded to put on his shirt that fell below his knees. Zuri took a glance at his new wardrobe, touching the shirt that covered his body. He then looked up to me for approval.

"You look awesome," I smiled. He accepted that and went to the kitchen counter. "You will have to be awesome and practically a genius to perform the task I have plan for us. So, we don't have ice cream, but we have the next best thing," I started. I picked up the cookies and pointed at the milk while introducing them to Zuri.

"We are going to take this Oreo and dunk it in the cup of milk. Once it gets nice and soft, we are going to eat it," I explained further.

"It doesn't take a genius to do that," he replied. I leaned forward and poked my lip out.

"Well, when I was younger, it took me four times to get it right. I kept leaving the cookie in the milk too long and it crumbled. My father and I stood up all night until I got this right," I demonstrated. I pulled the cookie out of the glass and held it up for him to see. "See! You try," I encouraged.

Zuri took the cookie and dunk his entire hand into the glass. I laughed out loud and took his wrist to pull his hand out.

"Nope mister, it doesn't take a genius to do that," I said. I took the napkins and wiped the table of the milk that spilled. I poured him some more milk and guided his hand into the cup. "cradle it and don't crush it. Then..." I helped him bring it to his mouth and got a glimpse of his teeth. They were sharp and shaped like shark teeth. I wanted to get a closer look, but Zuri closed his mouth quickly and chewed.

"This is great. I never tasted something like this before," he said excitedly and snatched another cookie out of the pack.

"I'm happy you like it," I whispered with my head tilted

downward. Zuri didn't give me another chance to see his teeth. I sat and watched him enjoy himself while talking about his family. I wasn't sure of what type of bedtime stories they told him, but he was running with this shit for sure. He told me about the different *sections* that his siblings resided in, which fucked me up because they were all sunken cities that were destroyed by earthquakes and fires. I didn't bother to enlighten him on that fact since I was enjoying the tales myself. We went to bed long after that on the couch. Zuri didn't feel comfortable with me in the room by myself and decided to stay in the living room. I wasn't too happy about his decision and remained out there with him. Zuri cuddled up next to me with his eyes on the door. I didn't know how long he was awake because I fell asleep. I woke up to a very energized Zuri. The volume of the television was high. I took the remote and lower it down. I placed it on the table and went to the bathroom. When I got out Zuri was standing in front of the television with the remote in his hand changing the channel. He stopped when he came across Aquaman.

"Can we have more of those cookies?"

I walked into the kitchen to gather items we need for the breakfast that our guest promised us. I placed dishes and glasses on my white marble table located in my dining room area. The crystal chandelier that hung over the table didn't give off the light that I needed to brighten the room.

"What the hell?" I mumbled and picked up the remote for the blinds. I pressed opened and walked back into the kitchen. "No cookies in the morning. Your father is bringing some breakfast over. On top of that, I don't think that your father is going to be so happy with me giving you cookies," I stated.

"Father won't get mad at you. It is physically impossible for him to get upset with you about anything. You are his better half," Zuri replied.

I frowned at him saying that. "If your father told you that, I am sorry to inform you he was lying to you. I am no one's better half. I am just Adaliya," I countered from the kitchen.

"You are not just Adaliya. You are our Luna. The mother of the water. You have no choice but to be his half," he claimed.

I shook my head at the nonsense. There was no way that I was going to fall for the bullshit that came out of his mouth. Water was something that I found myself not wanting to be near. If his family stayed near the water, I knew it was going to be bad all the way around. Not to mention, the infatuation I had with the *thing* that approached me when I was younger. Every time I saw a body of water, I felt him watching me. That gave me the notion to enter the water without fear or thought. Once I did, I felt him caressing and holding me instantly. I didn't understand why he wasn't there for me when I needed him the most. It wasn't something that I want to think or talk about. Amanzi was close to what I thought I wanted and to see that he was an *ain't shit ass nigga,* messed me up. I slammed the dishrag in the sink and leaned on the counter.

"Courtney was right," I mumbled to myself and sighed. I felt my head pounding, frustrated with the situation.

"I don't think she knows shit about what you and I have," a deep mesmerizing voice was heard from the other room. I frowned and walked out of the kitchen. My eyes rested on a very sexy Amanzi standing near the couch with bags full of stuff. He was dressed in some navy draw-string waist beach shorts and the same color shirt that was supposed to be loose to fit. The shirt was pressed against his muscled chest and fell below his hips. I couldn't do anything but sigh. That man was too fine to be so fucked up. I inhaled and caught the whiff of cinnamon French toast with double bacon and my favorite French vanilla-flavored syrup. At that moment, my stomach sounded off with a loud growl. Amanzi smiled and proceeded to the table with the goods.

"Zuri, I have clothes and food for you. I will help you change as soon as I get Adaliya squared away," Amanzi told him.

"I don't need help Father. Luna showed me how to put clothes on last night. See," Zuri replied and showed off the clothes he slept in.

"That's good son, but I have clothes that will fit you. Here you go," he held out the clothes for him to take. Zuri came over and took the items from Amanzi's hand.

"After we eat this, we can get some more cookies and milk," Zuri yelled behind him. Amanzi eyes went to mine.

"Cookies and milk?"

"Yes," I answered while taking the food out of the bag. "I'm not understanding why that child was deprived of anything as simple as cookies and milk. You ought to be ashamed of yourself."

"I have my reasons," he mumbled.

I stood up and placed my hand on my hip. "And I can't wait to hear it."

"You will. After we eat," Amanzi ordered. He pulled out some grass shit in a container and set it in front of an empty chair. He pulled out a bigger one to place it near the seat that I was going to sit in.

"Is that all you two going to eat?" I wondered.

"This is all we need to eat. We don't have big appetites," he concluded.

"I understand that, but you don't want any bacon or chicken for that salad?" I asked.

"No, thank you, sweetheart. I promise you that this is enough. Please sit," he pulled my chair out. I sat down and allowed him to serve me my food. He drizzled the French Vanilla syrup all over my French Toast and bacon.

"How did you know that this was my favorite?"

"I know everything about you," was his answer. I found it a little strange and scary until I thought of the times I went out with Skye and Egypt. This was something that I always ordered when I was out with them.

"Oh. Egypt must've told you what I like," I said.

"No. I told Egypt your likes and dislikes. If you recall the times, you guys were out, you never had to order anything. They did the ordering for you," he replied.

I did sit back and thought about what he was saying. Skye always removed my menu out of my hand and ordered for me. "How?"

"Like I had been telling you. I know everything about Adaliya. Why do you think that my feelings for you are so deep? It doesn't have anything to do with the small encounter that we had when I rescued you from drowning. We have met before, actually, we have met many times before your accident," he explained.

"I would have remembered bumping into someone like you," I replied.

"You may not remember, but your body does. That's why it shivers every time I speak to you. That's why it drifts toward me. It wants to be close to me because I am where you belong. Always have, always will be," he went on to clarify. I noticed my body leaning more into him as he spoke. I shook off the feeling and pushed my food to the other side of the table.

"I guess all of this is in your explanation as well," I walked around the table and replied. Amanzi glanced at my movements and smirked.

"Pretty much," he sat and grabbed his fork from the napkin that was on the table. Zuri made his appearance with some beach shorts and a pretty grey shirt that brought out the color in his eyes. He came around the table to sit next to me. I reached over and opened his container before pushing it to him.

"There you go," I muttered. Zuri dug his hand into the container and grabbed a fist full of food. "Aye, boy. Use a fork."

Zuri looked at the utensils on his side and turned back to me. "We didn't use these with the cookies and milk."

"We didn't have to. Here," I picked up the fork and showed him how to use it. He opened his mouth and crunched on the grass. I squeezed my eyes shut at the disgusting sight of their food.

"What is that?" I finally asked.

"This is a Sesame-Ginger Vegetable Quinoa Salad with cranberries and walnuts," Amanzi responded after stuffing his mouth.

"I like the different flavors," Zuri added.

"This is your first time trying this out?" I wanted to know.

"Yes. When we are fed in the section, it is usually not in this entrapment or with the stuff that Father explained. The ocean gives off its own flavor, which we have grown accustomed to," Zuri answered. That had me turning to Amanzi.

"Can you please explain this to me?"

"Yes, I will. After you eat," he noted.

"It doesn't take much to eat and listen," I picked up my fork and began to eat.

"It doesn't. I want your undivided attention. That way, I will see if I need to go with Plan B."

"Which is?" I snapped. Amanzi smiled and shook his head.

"Eat, please."

I rolled my eyes and did what he asked. Zuri had his eyes on the television, finishing up the last bit of his food. Amanzi had finished and kept his searing eyes on me. It was uncomfortable in a way that made me want to cover myself up. His eyes dropped with the sudden thought, which made me drop my fork.

"Why did you do that?"

Amanzi avoided eye contact as he answered. "Because I don't want you to feel uncomfortable."

"How do you know I was feeling that way? I didn't say anything out loud. I thought it. You and Zuri have that shit bad. Whatever I thought, he answered my questions right away. You did that the moment we met. Is there something I'm missing?" I probed.

"Are you finished eating?" he voiced. I pushed the plate to

the center of the table and folded my arms. Amanzi took that as a yes and began to tell me what I wanted to hear.

"You said that we have never met before. That is untrue. The first time we met was when your father brought you fishing. You were at least four years old. Your father had his fishing rod stationed at the front of the boat. You both were reading up on the different types of fish that were in the water when the string began to tug. Your father hopped up to retrieve the rod and started winding the handle. I heard him telling you you needed to hold on. The boat was rocking with the strength of the angry Warsaw Grouper along with the wind that was forcing the waves to hit the boat. I heard your whimpers and cries for your father to help you. He was too caught up with making the big catch. He jerked with all his might, pulling the Warsaw out of the water. It frantically wiggled and flopped into the boat, jumping up and hitting you in the face. The impact of the hit caused you to fall overboard and into the water. At first, you struggled. Your arms were flapping around, trying to reach the top of the water. Your father jumped in to get you, but the water didn't want to let you go. Your essences shifted the flow of water. It took me by surprise that someone that young had those capabilities without any help from, me or my mother. The water wanted to keep you and pushed your father away from rescuing you. I ignored the same feeling and intervened in water form to carry you back to the surface. While in my arms, you didn't cry. You kept your eyes on me as if you knew who and what I was. Your eyes shined as the brightest, yet darkest color jewel of the ocean. I was stuck and wanted to know more about you. From that day forward I knew what you were meant to be," he finished. My hands were completely sweaty. I brought them down to my shirt to wipe them dry. I took in what he was saying and didn't remember that event. But I knew out of all people, that not remembering something didn't have anything to do with it not happening. Yet still, it was unbelievable.

"I think that you have mistaken me for someone else. I never had an accident like that with my father," I denied still.

"You have. That memory is suppressed with all the others that you have about me. The only one that you remember is the one I left for your eyes only," Amanzi revealed more. I gasped shaking my head. There was no way for him to know the words of my admirer. I thought he pulled it from my thoughts, but I wasn't thinking of him at that time. For him to know that, made me feel betrayed.

"You are not supposed to know that," I frowned and was ready to stand up.

"But I do. I know that this is where you do not belong. I know you are more comfortable in the water. I know you missed the way I touch and caress your body," he said with his eyes more than the words that came out of his mouth.

"This is a very inappropriate conversation that shouldn't be had with a child at the table," I interrupted. I snatched my plate and brought it to the kitchen.

"You said that you wanted to talk," Amanzi said right behind me.

I spun around and faced him. "Yeah, I did. I wanted to talk about why your eight-year-old son is walking around this bitch with a hula skirt on, talking about living underwater with a muthafucka that wants to hurt him. That was supposed to be the center of the conversation. Not this shit," I waved my hand between us.

"Zuri's reasons for being here have everything to do with you. He feels your energy even after I disguised it. You are calmer and more aware of your true nature when you are around him," Amanzi revealed.

"My true nature? I don't even know what that means," the frustration in my tone was evident. Amanzi moved forward and cupped my face in his big hands. He gazed down at me with those swirling eyes. I got lost for the minutes that we were standing there. Amanzi's cool breath brushed my lips, encouraging my eyes to close.

"No need to be confused about who you are. Open your heart, babe. Let me show you," he requested. I was speechless. As much as I wanted to submit to his demand, there were a couple of things that were bothering me. What I was feeling was hard to put into words.

"I think," I started and stopped. What the hell could I have said to make the shit sound right.

"Tell me this Luna," Amanzi tried to help. "How did you sleep last night?"

"It was uhm... it was okay, I guess," I opened my eyes and stammered over my words. The way he was looking at me made it hard for me to speak correctly.

"Just okay," he questioned with his eyebrows up. Afraid to speak, I nodded my head. "It had to be better than good. You ran Zuri's bath and checked the temperature by placing your hand in the running water without fainting. You gave yourself a wash-off. You woke up and opened the blinds when you noticed there wasn't enough light. Okay is an understatement because you are more than okay. Your true nature is showing without your permission."

"What? What are you talking about? I didn't do any of those things," at that point I was confused.

"Yes, you did Luna," Zuri stepped out of the dining room area and replied. I shook my head and began to back up. Amanzi release me noticing that something was wrong.

"Adaliya, are you okay baby?"

"Bruh, stop with the baby shit. I am fine. I didn't do these things," I countered and turned away from him. I paused at the brightness of the window. I knew they were closed when we woke up and didn't remember how they opened. I thought I was going to turn away, yet I moved forward to get closer. The waves were moving all in the same direction which was odd. I had never seen anything more in sync. They got bigger with every attention I gave them. I raised my hand and slid it up the window. A deafening whistle came from the water forcing the glass in my home to shake.

"What's happening?" I whispered.

"It misses you. The water wants their Luna home. Don't you feel it?" Amanzi answered for me. My blood ran cold like the water that almost took me out. I inhaled deeply, choking off the air that became foreign to my lungs. My mouth was dry. Everything was too dry.

"This is not possible," I whispered roughly. Amanzi came behind me and pressed his front to my back. He wrapped his arms around my stomach and clenched the nightshirt that I was wearing.

"All is possible, when it comes to you, Adaliya." The water got rougher, pushing up on the beach as if it was trying to get to me. Big waves were knocking over boats and the people that were in them. I closed my eyes as my anxiety began to pick up. His words. Those were the same words that he used to tell me when I was unsure about anything.

"No," I pushed off the window and out of Amanzi's arms. "This can't be real," I said out of breath.

"It is very much real, Adaliya. You belong in the water with me," he replied before his eyes changed colors.

"Oh shit," I gasped and back into the wall.

"It's okay," Zuri comforted me. He grabbed my hand, and I snatched it out of his grasp. None of this shit was real. If I was dreaming, I needed to wake up and try this day all over. My head started throbbing, and the room was getting blurry. Amanzi was standing across the room and got in front of me in seconds, causing me to get dizzier.

"It's a lot to take in, I know. But this is not a dream. I am the one that you have been searching for. I am Sol. The one that will give you everything you wish for. I will show you and then I will bring you home," he promised.

"I don't want to go. I can't go into the water," I cried.

"You will," Zuri told me out flat.

"Sleep," Amanzi commanded. With nothing else to say, I obliged and entered another calm dream.

"Are we going home now?" Zuri voiced after I scooped Adaliya up and rested her on the couch. The cries from the water were still loud, begging for me to bring her to it. It seemed as if the water was remorseful to her as well. We all missed her in our lives and needed her to get better to come home.

"No. I will allow her to rest. That was a lot for her to take in," I said as Egypt and Landon walked into the condo. They both were in similar beach wear as Zuri. Egypt was sporting a one-shoulder forest green bathing suit. It wasn't meant to look as alluring as it did, but my sister's goddess made everything look that way. Landon had on multi-green swimming trunks with the matching color tank top men's vest shirt with a hood. The shirt was thin enough for anyone to see the outline of his abs and pecs. I was sure that they were going to explore the beach a little more after dropping Zuri off.

"Where am I going?" Zuri read the situation more than he did my mind.

"You are going to visit Lenmon. I need him to teach you how to work with the land people. Your vernacular towards Adaliya shows you need training in that area. I don't need you talking about our way of the world to the humans so freely," I explained.

"I thought you ruled the leader of the piyas incompetent. If he is that, why would I want to learn from him.? I know more than he can teach me. I wouldn't say the things I say to her to anyone else. I am supposed to tell her the truth," Zuri responded.

"Lenmon's actions will be dealt with. I need you to do what I say. I know you are supposed to tell her the truth, but in portions and on my time.," I ordered.

Zuri sighed like the child he was and continued going back and forth with me. "You were taking too long. She should have been known about her people and where she belonged." He wasn't disrespectful nor was he being impolite. He was as blunt as I was.

"Regardless of how you felt, it still wasn't your place. Before you open your mouth to speak on anything know that your tongue will perish along with your duty as her guard. Do you understand that?" The words were spoken with a different type of stealth.

"Yes, sir," he replied too quickly.

"How did everything go?" Egypt strolled over to a sleeping Adaliya. "We saw the ocean outside and thought that we needed to make it up here sooner so that you can check on whatever is going on down there. I have never seen the water so..."

"Boisterous," Landon finished.

"It wasn't me. The water was trying to get to her," I told them.

"Wow," Egypt expressed and glanced down at my heart.

"That is some power brother," Landon added and brushed his hand over Adaliya's forehead.

"We know. That is why she belongs in the water. As long as she is on the land, it will get worse," Zuri spoke.

"I won't let that happen," I concluded and motioned for them to leave. Egypt reached her hand out for Zuri to take. Zuri walked over to take her hand and saw Adaliya twitch. His eyes zoomed on her and made a detour towards us. Zuri kneeled and pressed his forehead to hers and whispered in our language, *"You will always be my mother."* He kissed her on the cheek and stood back on his feet. Egypt's hand was still awaiting his. Zuri looked at it and shook his head.

"Ready," he announced and walked out the front door. They both were waiting for an explanation from me.

"He is very attached to her," was my answer.

"You think," Landon replied and took Egypt's hand to go after Zuri. I turned my attention back to my Luna who was in a peaceful slumber. To see, touch, and breathe her in, felt like a dream come true. I didn't consider myself a pervert, caressing her body as she slept. Shit... she was mine. All mines. She was lucky I didn't wake her up with my head between her legs. The slight memory of what she tasted like had me licking my lips. My brothers always clowned me for my celibacy. I never had the urge to be with any woman but Adaliya when she reached a mature age. I had been patiently waiting for her to notice me for who I was. I caught myself many times talking out loud to her. I would hear her responses like she was sitting or lounging right next to me. Her words embraced me as the water did her. I yearned more for her voice and a sense of acknowledgment. I wanted her to see me and not doubt what I felt. If I had to show her the magnitude of love that I carried for her, I would do that for the rest of my existence. I rearranged myself and picked her head up to rest on my lap. I sat and waited unwearyingly for her to wake up to me.

THE MOVEMENT in my lap forced my eyes to open. I didn't realize I closed them. Watching Adaliya sleep brought me so much pleasure and assurance that I was that comfortable to stay in her peace. I took a deep breath and released it with a sigh, quickly peeked out the window. Judging from the way the sun sat in the sky, it was past noon. I assumed things were going well with Lenmon since I didn't hear a word from Landon about

Zuri's progress. I knew he was going to be a handful and have Lenmon ready to toss his ass back in the water. His arrogance and demeanor were of no other youngling, which was going to test Lenmon's patience. If Lenmon knew what was best for him, he had better complete the task I gave him without the complaints. Zuri questioning my motives for sending him to Lenmon pissed me off even more. He also knew that shit wasn't right amongst our people. Thinking about that shit had me getting upset all over again.

"Don't," her permissive voice declared. I glanced down and gasped at the sight of her. The color of her skin was shimmery with a gilded hue to it. Her hair was wavy and hung from my lap to the floor. The frightening woman that passed out early was no longer present at that moment. For the first time, I was seeing my true Luna in person. Her pretty vantablack, blue-rimmed eyes stared up into my violet ones with all the answers. I smiled down at her and brushed my hand over her cheek. The feel of my touch affected her the way I knew it would. She turned her face into my hand and brushed her lips on it.

"Hmm," a small groan fell from my mouth. Her pillow-soft lips smirked and revealed something else that I wasn't ready to see. She pulled me closer in with her eyes, swallowing me into an abyss that was deeper than my reality. I gave in, prepared to see a blissful future starring us and our children.

That wasn't the case. I saw Atlantis in its darkest hour.

I appeared above the waterfall, standing on the edge of it. The thick silver cloud filled the once clear ocean water that held the sparkling glow around our home. I inhaled the scent and residue of death. I peered over my home for the reason of the foul odor. Near the bridge that led to the gates of Atlantis, my mosogens were on their knees with tears streaming down their faces. I was in the center of them all, standing in my rarest form. I felt the anger and disappointment rolling off me into my creatures in the water and on the land. For some reason, I needed them to feel the pain that I would have once covered them from. The Water King flashed a glare at the others, thinking of eliminating everyone at that time. He rose his hand to do so... but in a far distance, I heard my name being called. I looked beyond him and saw someone floating towards him, trying to save the lives that he no longer wanted around. Ignoring her, his hand moved in a forward motion. The mosogens shrieks were sirens in the ocean causing death to all water creatures that were in the vicinity. The Water King then turned to his new arrivals to do the same thing. I shook my head and leaped off the edge, merging into the waterfall. As I shout from it, the water followed me like a shooting star to attack my supreme self. I couldn't allow it to hurt her. I wouldn't accept failing her again. The floating interrupter held the same fear that she held in her eyes when she was dying in her element. The added fuel to the already incinerating fire, caused the blow to the back of the Water King to be heavy and strong. He stumbled and swung blindly behind him. I dodged it and stepped back into the silver dust of my family. I whirled my arms around, bringing their remaining together to form a huge ax in their honor. I didn't understand what would cause me to act out so mercilessly, but it wasn't going to end with her life. The Water King turned to face her again and went to strike.

"Amanzi... Amanzi..." she shook with fear and tried to get through to me.

"Nooo," I shouted as her eyes zoomed in on me. Adaliya opened her mouth to call me again.

"Amanzi," her voice was louder. I blinked and found myself back in the condo with Adaliya, staring at me with concern. "Are you okay? I have been calling your name. Look at me," she requested.

"I am looking at you, Luna," I told her. She shook her head and wiped my face.

"You are not. You were looking through me and weeping. Are you okay?" she asked again. I didn't know what I was. Seeing what my Luna wanted me to see, fucked me up. I lost complete control over myself, to the point I didn't recognize her. If my Luna was to ever lose her life at my hands, I would never forgive myself. Her death would cause more sunken cities than the world has ever witnessed. That pure thought had me tearing up again. I didn't want to alert her to what was going on. I nodded my head and tried to get on my feet to put space between us. Adaliya shifted herself to sit on my lap and palmed my face.

"No, Amanzi. You need to sit down. You look pale and drained. Just... sit for a minute until you regain your color at least. Do you need some water?" she inquired. At the sound of that, my throat and body went dry even more.

"Yes," I answered. Adaliya climbed off me and went to the kitchen to retrieve the water. I placed both elbows on my knees and placed my head in my hands. My thoughts were everywhere. I needed to calm down before the water reacted to my emotions.

"Here you go," Adaliya brought my attention to the water bottle in her hand. I took it and mumbled thanks, before opening and downing it within seconds.

"Can I have another, please?" I asked her.

"Umm... sure," she ran to get more. I allowed the water that I consumed to heal the dryness of my dreadful thoughts. Adaliya arrived in front of me with three extra bottles. Pleased with her thoughtfulness, I finished off all three bottles and sat back on her couch.

"Wow. I'm happy that water doesn't have that effect on people's skin like yours. If that was the case, it would be over two-hundred dollars for a case," she joked.

"Not only that but the beaches would also be filled every day including the wintertime," I went along with her. She gave a nervous giggle before responding.

"That would be hard on the Piyas, right? I know they aren't allowed to show who they are in front of the *humans*. You don't want your secret getting out."

I couldn't have been happier with her bringing the subject of our conversation up on her own. I thought about giving her more time to adapt to what was said by taking her for a walk, bringing her to one of her favorite places on land, or refreshing her thoughts with Cookies and Cream Boba Tea. She thought we needed to do a due over and I prepared to do so once she woke up.

"Do you want to go out for a minute and get some fresh air?" I inquired. Adaliya's arms went around her body instantly with a shudder.

"I'm fine here," she pretended.

I regain enough of my strength to stand on my feet. Adaliya moved back to give my wide frame room to create my personal space. As demanding as I wanted to be, I knew shit wasn't going to go my way if I carried her ass out of there. I licked my lips and continued with the patient route that has gotten me this far. At the same time, I needed to let her know what being fine has done to her.

"You were fine staying in your childhood home with limitations. You were fine when you went to your so-called friend's event, and she threw water on you. You were *fine* when we were talking this morning and you passed out. Fine is only good for the time being. I want you to be always at your best," I informed her.

Adaliya sadly smiled at that and dropped her head. "I don't know what that is anymore."

"We can find that out together," I insisted, reaching my hand out. Adaliya thought on it for minutes before backing away from me. "Adaliya, this can be the way for you to get better. You have me here in the flesh now. I'm not going to let you falter, baby."

Adaliya smiled and waved her hand for me to stop. "I'm just changing clothes, Amanzi. Is that okay with you?"

I took a glance at her nightshirt and thick socks. I saw her in less many times over. It didn't matter what she had on. I adored her in whatever she had on as long as her legs were out. Those long semi-thick legs glistened without water or her body oil. They were smooth, soft, and athletic, meaning her leg lock would be on point. *Fuck.*

"Amanzi," my name out of her mouth caressed my soul.

"Yes, sweetheart," I breathed that out.

Her blushing cheeks revealed how much she loved when I called her that, despite her rejection before. Adaliya's lips parted for the air to escape gracefully.

"I will only be a minute," she assured me.

I regained my seat on the couch and sat back. "Take your time. I'm not going anywhere." She nodded and disappeared into her bedroom.

I PULLED MY PERIWINKLE SUNDRESS OUT OF MY CLOSET AND laid it across my bed. If he was who he said he was, I knew we were going near the water regardless of my condition. He repeated this to me and made me promise I would give in to him when it was time. I didn't know if this was that time or not, but I wasn't going to renege on my word. It was close to the summer out here, so the weather was going to be hot. I loved dresses I could go bare underneath. Feeling the light fabric on my skin made me feel as if I was in the water. I realized I didn't need a reminder of it when he was around.

He was here with me. The man that told me many stories about life underwater was sitting in my living room waiting to explore options with me. My heart swelled knowing that. I had so many questions to ask and needed them to answer before we went any further. My mother was right. I would have gone after the thing that tried to take my life. But it was only because of the confidence he bestowed on me. I needed to recover from this ordeal by any means necessary.

I slipped into my dress immediately. I wasn't about to put on all that fucking lotion, sweating and embarrassing myself. I moved into the bathroom to brush my teeth again before walking out to retrieve my sandals that were in the closet near the front door.

Amanzi stood to his feet and assess my attire, praising my body with his demeanor. I paused a bit before walking towards the door. "Let me grab my shoes and we can go."

"You don't need them. We are going on to the beach," he said and took my hand.

"Well... the beach is not right outside the door. I have to cross a major highway and walk some miles. The concrete is hot, and I don't want to risk stepping on glass, rocks, or other shit. I need shoes on my feet," I replied.

"There is nothing that your feet can't withstand. We will be fine," he assured me and walked out the door and in front of the elevator.

"Your country ass feet may withstand lava rocks, but I don't think mine will. I just got a pedicure two days ago and know how sensitive they are afterward. It won't take long. I can grab my sandals and be back before the elevator reach our floor."

The beeping of the elevator sounded off, killing that plan.

"If you feel that way, I will step on the hot concrete, rocks, and glass for the both of us. How about that?" He told me. I frowned while walking onto the elevator, looking around as if I saw germs on the well-cleaned rug.

"This is so country. My mother will kick both of our asses if she sees us out here without shoes on," I implied.

"This is not country. This is us enjoying nature that was created to explore."

The elevator stopped to allow some other tenants on with their dogs. I scooted behind him when the dogs came sniffing at my feet. Amanzi thought that exploring nature was walking around barefoot. He was more than welcome to explore the dogs licking on him.

"Another reason I and others wear shoes," I whispered. The dogs were hairy and almost bigger than their owner. She was a petite little creature with nothing grounding her to earth. I swore if she didn't have those dogs, the wind would have carried her ass away. The stranger's puny arm jerked on the leash she held around those dogs to keep them from getting to us.

"I'm sorry. They are not bad dogs," the woman cited what was clearly her opinion. The dogs were growling and shit which made me very uncomfortable.

"That is unacceptable," Amanzi stated loudly.

The woman's eyes were down and focused on pulling them away. Amanzi glanced at me and flashed a smile that revealed his pointy teeth. I gulped, thinking that he was about to make a scene. I peeked over his shoulder and watched Amanzi sneer. The dogs ran back to the owner, tangling her with the leash.

"Oh. Oh. Bruno. Bentley. Stop it right now! Stop!" the owner yelled. Once the elevator door opened Amanzi guided me out of the elevator, leaving the mess behind.

"Why risk exposing yourself like that? That woman could've looked up and saw you," I told him.

"Risking exposure isn't something that we too much fear. There are a lot of unexplainable things that are going around in the world that people list as either urban legends or paranormal activities. She could have said I did whatever to her and people would have looked at it as her being a racist toward a black couple. Someone would have run with it and the truth would never be told accurately. Besides that, people in the world need to feel relevant again by discovering such events. They are only okay with something being superior to them if they had a hand in them being superior. That is a fact," he schooled.

"I don't think that's the case," I defended.

"In your case, it may not be. But others dream to be a part of something big no matter the consequences. It could cause someone's reputation, relationship, and sanity. That is why I despise humans. They aren't grateful for what is given to them," he countered. Amanzi got to the curb and was about to step off. I grabbed his hand and tried to pull his stern body back from getting hit by a car that zoomed past us. Amanzi didn't blink or showed any interest in the car. His eyes were on our adjoining hands. My small one clutching his massive one seemed like an awkward fit but matched perfectly in a way. His hands were almost softer than mine with clean nails that appeared to be sporting JINsoon clear polish. Just... perfect.

"You need anything Adaliya?" Amanzi drew my attention back to his face.

"Uhh..no. I mean, you have to look both ways to cross the street. That car almost hit you," I informed. Amanzi face frowned and looked down the street at the car that was two blocks down already.

"Hit me?" he rebuffed with a teasing smile. "I don't get hit, Adaliya."

"If you go out into the street without looking to see if it is okay to cross it, you will get hit, several times. It may not cause you any bodily harm, but the drivers and their vehicles are going to suffer. So, can we do this as humanly possible, by waiting for the right time to cross," he allowed me to pull him back on top of the curb.

"As you wish," Amanzi commented. I didn't think how difficult it would be to stay on such a major highway. The traffic wasn't bad unless people use this as a detour route. As soon as the last car passed, Amanzi gazed at me to get the okay to cross. I nodded my head and led him across the street.

"That wasn't so bad, was it?" I teased him after we stepped on the curb. There was an iron railing where pedestrians leaned over to look into the water. Amanzi stepped in front of me. He dropped my hand and placed his arm around my shoulders.

"It wasn't. It's something that I have to get used to if I will be escorting you around," he replied and started our walk with him blocking my view. I kept my head down and continued with our conversation.

"If this is something that you have to get used to, who trained the piyas to live on the land?" I countered.

"I taught Lenmon, Gazo, and Prada to live on the land with my brother's help," he answered easily.

"Who taught you?" I followed up with.

"No one. I live many years to adapt and know the bare minimum of cohabiting with humans. I taught that to them, while they lived and learned the rest from experiences," he stated.

"Were there times you had to help them through those tough experiences? Heartbreak is one of them. I needed my father for my first one and I," I couldn't finish with Amanzi interrupting me.

"What heartbreak?"

"Trust me, it was nothing that you have to worry about," I informed him.

"But, I do," he said.

"Can you focus please?"

"My mosogens aren't made to fall in love with their opposite. They have a certain purpose, and nothing can deter them from that," he finally answered.

"But, why? How is it you want them to live and blend in with humans if they can't enjoy living it? I don't find that fair," I commented.

"It's not about being fair. They were created for that purpose."

"Is that what you were created for?" I had to know. His motives didn't seem to be anything like I assumed them to be. Sol talked about his people with passion and love. The shit that was coming out of Amanzi's mouth was mechanic.

"I have many purposes," he revealed. We walked silently on the sidewalk with him on my right. I didn't want to look his way and catch the view of the water. I tried to shut my peripheral vision off, but it wanted to see the beautiful sight. I hoped that walking around with him will lessen my anxiety. With his hand still in mine, it did. I inhaled the water scent and felt as if I was near my true home with him. My eyes started at his extremely large feet, to his calves and muscled legs. His shorts pressed to his thighs with each step he took. I got bold and positioned my hand flat against his nicely shaped abs. I brushed my hand up and down them as my eyes kept moving upward to his covered chest that hid the rest of the tattoos that crept out the top of his shirt. They wrapped around his throat to the back of his neck then down his back. Amanzi was walking around like an art museum by himself. I would love to explore more of him...

"You can if we can get to the beach. I'm trying to be human-like and not remove my shirt. We don't want people to suspect anything, do we?" he read my mind again.

I laughed and shook my head. "You might create a traffic jam."

"You think so," he looked around himself and disagreed. "There are more eyes on you than they are on me. Check it out," he requested.

"Yeah right," I doubted and pulled my eyes away from him to look where he instructed. Men and women were slowing down in their cars to stare at me. One man across the street from us gaped at me openly while walking with his girlfriend. She rolled her eyes and slapped his face.

"Oh shit," I hissed. "What is going on?"

"The same thing that happened when you all were on the plane and people moved when Landon requested it. We are natural gods that gather attention wherever we are," he answered.

"I'm not a god," I declined.

"No, you are not. You are a goddess," he corrected.

"I don't feel like it. I feel helpless and troubled. I can't stand on my own two feet without others' strength and guidance. That's a weak goddess," I admitted. Amanzi stopped walking and turned me to him.

"Needing strength and guidance doesn't make you weak,

Adaliya. That in itself makes you stronger than you will ever know. Seeking counsel from your elders or more experience individuals help you to understand another part of you that is trying to evolve with your big heart. I admire and adore the woman that you are growing into and the queen that you will be. Weak will never be a word that will fit your description," he preached that to me with the water behind him, nodding and agreeing with what he said. Dolphins were flipping in the air and splashing into the water. I couldn't ignore the show that it was putting on for me. I smiled and walked around Amanzi to get a better look near the railing. My hands shook when I reached for the only thing that was stopping me from falling over. Amanzi grabbed my waist and tugged me back to his body. My eyes closed and my head relaxed on his chest while he walked us the rest of the way.

"Look, Luna," he directed. I took a deep breath before opening my eyes to the dolphins circling each other making symbols I made out easily.

"Oh my God! This is so beautiful," I commented. Amanzi's hands drifted down my legs in a smooth motion. His lips brushed against my neck as his face lowered into my neck

"You have to understand that your presences do something to the water and the creatures below it. Having you here in my arms is more than a dream come true. It's the beginning of a fantasy that plays like a rerun each time I close my eyes. You are on your search for this guidance but all I want is to fulfill a purpose that was created when you fell over the boat. Acceptance. I need you to accept and want me the way you always had and not be afraid to show or give into it. I need that more than I need the water, Adaliya," he confessed with an open heart.

I turned in his arms and prepared to tell him that until I saw what he meant in his eyes. The ocean that I loved the most was a mirage in them. It caught me off guard. I blinked twice before steadying my attention into the whistling waves. I reached up and palmed Amanzi's stern face.

"I am working on it but if you are by my side, I know it will be sooner than later," I told him honestly.

Amanzi's forehead dropped on mine gently. "Thank you," he whispered in an echo. Those sexy ass lips caressed and took me under. Amanzi opened his mouth and slid his tongue inside mine. My arms went around his neck to pull him in deeper. He fisted my dress, wanting to rip it off my body. The wind picked me up and wrapped itself around our bodies bringing them closer together. It was the most natural feeling I have felt in a while. Our soft moans were more than tunes to the audience of the ocean. It was a sweet melody that our hearts created before this moment. My tongue skid across his lips, teasingly and begged for him to take it further on its own accord. Amanzi obliged by sliding his right hand up my back and grabbing the back of my neck. His left hand squeezed my ass roughly, forcing me to squeal. I didn't want them peeping toms to get a show out of us. If we kept going, I knew my legs were about to be wrapped around his body. I broke the kiss and backed away. I could tell by the pressure of his grip. He didn't want to let me go.

"We have to stop..." I opened my eyes and paused. We were no longer on Bayshore Blvd. We appeared to be on the Ben T. Davis beach which would have taken us over thirty minutes to get to if we were still walking. I depended on that time to prepare myself for the white sand and the sunny shore of my favorite beach. It was the best place to soak up the sunlight for that natural tanning. Others sat under the palm trees, enjoying the freshwater breeze. The sparkling water from afar looked like crystals sitting on top of it. I did a one-eighty, stopping at the children playing in the small tides that brushed up the sand. I began to feel some sort of resentment when the mist of the ocean kissed my skin the same way Amanzi did. I felt the welcome back greeting as if the water itself cloaked around me. A small laugh and a tear fell from my eye. I knew he was what he told me he was, but never have I witnessed his true capabilities. I turned to face him and asked. "How?"

"I'm trying to get you to that sooner part," he dropped his arms and grab my hand. "We don't have to go into the water. We can walk the beach and enjoy each other," he told me. I didn't answer. I went along with his plan of action and listened as he talked more about himself. He revealed he had the ability to teleport wherever his mind took him. That was one of the reasons why crossing the street or wearing shoes weren't things he needed to have or do. He told me stories that I recalled as private moments with my secret admirer. I was embarrassed and satisfied with the fact that we experienced each other before. It may have not been a physical penetration thing going on, but the way he stimulated me emotionally and mentally sparked something fierce in me. I knew if Amanzi would have said the right shit to me, my pussy would start leaking and throbbing with the anticipation of him. If it wasn't his words, his body was the next best thing. Amanzi obliged my first thought and removed his shirt. The tattoos were as amazing as the waves in the water. I didn't think that the colors would show on his darker skin. I saw the blues, reds, and greys with no problem. The one that stuck out the most was the bright orange upside-down triangle that was outlined with white, green, and blue circles. Amanzi got approached by three groups about his tattoo artist. Amanzi smiled and told them that his artist wasn't available any longer. That was when Amanzi revealed to me I was the only one to see his tattoos in color.

"For your eyes only," he uttered. I kissed him on his bare arm and rested my head on it as he entertained the men. I felt like a proud wife or spouse of a man that spoke with such power and his stance backed it up. Mother Nature knew the right ingredients to create this masterpiece. I couldn't wait to meet and tell her how grateful I was for her creation. But there were also questions about his passion and his sexual behavior. If everything was self-taught to him, who was he learning this shit from. I remembered the sleek way he moved against my body in water form. If Amanzi showed me more than that, I was going to be in trouble. Touching his bare skin was a tease within itself. I wanted to stroke his body and that dic...

"How about I fill you up?" his voice interrupted my last thought.

My cheeks were on fire from the humiliation of him being in my head. "Amanzi," I said his name breathlessly. "Can you not read my thoughts?"

"Your thoughts were yours, that time. I would like to fill you up, as in getting you food. We have been walking for hours now that the sun is setting. I thought you were hungry,' he gave me a teasing smile that reached his eyes. We were standing in front of a Whiskey's Joe Bar and Grill. I didn't know that we walked down this far. I hoped they weren't anyone around when it was time for us to get home. Amanzi was going to have to teleport us back or call an Uber driver. Amanzi cleared his throat to get my attention. "But I wish that I wasn't pretending to be human. I would love to know what you were thinking about."

"Something that you have thought about many times and acted out in water form. I don't know if I should feel assaulted or not," I spoke.

"I acted only when you desired me the most. If there were any signs of restraint, I would have stopped. But if you feel that way now, I'm sorry," he quickly apologized.

"I don't want you to be sorry, Amanzi. I would have liked it if I could participate more. That's all," my boldness response caused a flash in his eyes. I knew I was thinking something of a sort, but never would I have thought of saying it out loud. This man did that to me and it low-keyed scared the shit out of me.

"How about we get you something to eat and fulfill these obligations of yours in a place of your choosing," he insisted. An unknown chill crept up my spine at his declaration. I never heard anyone speak about what my obligations were. I knew they weren't anything ordinary. The man himself wasn't ordinary, nor was he inexperience. Amanzi had to have fucked some mermaids or traveled to many lands to be with different types of women. "No, I haven't. You will be my first as I will be yours." I was ready to comment on that when the hostess approached us.

"Good evening, will it be just you two?" she greeted while flipping her bleached blonde hair over her shoulder to show off a large amount of cleavage. They looked fake, like her lips, hips, and ass. She was standing in front of us looking like a real-life plastic doll.

"Yes, ma'am," Amanzi spoke loud and clear with a hint of an accent. The pretty young hostess was caught off guard. She stopped and gawked at him.

"I'm. I... I'm not that old for you to call me ma'am," she told him while staring at his chest. Amanzi smirked and removed the shirt off his shoulder to place it on. I didn't find her stuttering amusing or cute.

"You don't have to be an older woman to be called ma'am," I snapped.

"Yeah. Yeah. Yeah. You are right. This way please," she turned and walked faster to our table. She placed the menus on the table and left us without another word. Amanzi smiled and pulled out my chair.

"I don't think that she meant anything by that," he stated.

"That may be true. I thought I needed to inform her that all women, young, middle-aged, or old can be addressed as ma'am. I don't know what the big deal was," I sat and picked up the menu.

"It was your tone, sweetheart. She didn't want to battle with the goddess that pops in and out with her appearance. Do you not feel her when she comes through?" Amanzi pulled his chair out and sat across from me.

"I don't know of this goddess that you are talking about," I replied.

"You do. She has been present the majority of the times when you and I have been together," he admitted.

I gazed at him over the menu and thought about the times Amanzi spoke of. Nothing alerting came to mind, which made me think she was an illusion that he made up for me to believe that I was really meant for him. "I don't remember someone taking over me at any of those times."

"Tell me this. How did it feel when you were in the water, willingly?" he was specific.

I hunched my shoulders, wanting that feeling to remain a secret. At the same time, I couldn't put in words what I felt then. The world seemed more realistic underwater than it did on land. I would swim, close my eyes, and get lost in a world that I created in my head. I would be swimming with the sea animals or joining them in an underwater adventure. Sometimes I would lie in the soft seagrass and watch the water move with the motion of my hand. It felt so real. And, then he comes along and lies next to me. He places his arm and leg across my body while resting his head on my shoulder. I provided the comfort that he needed to lead as he offered the consistency of love and desire. He implanted the education that I needed to nourish our offspring to be the best warrior, guard, piyas, leader... shit. My eyes got wide as a revelation of my fantasy was real. Amanzi didn't say a word. He allowed me to think and recover all things that I didn't know about myself in those seconds. Was I her? Was I this goddess that he proclaimed I was? Because in that form, I felt free. Free to do whatever I pleased and not give a fuck about who didn't like it. But....

"Why didn't she appear when I needed her the most? Why weren't you there?"

"I was on the outskirts of Earth talking to my family about some other activities that happened before your incident. We have been dealing with an enemy that was somehow created to destroy what Mother Nature gave birth to. We were born to protect this from him," he waved his hand all around, towards the land, water, and sky.

"Okay, but I thought you can feel me whenever I need you. Shouldn't you have felt that before that thing grabbed me? By the way, what was that? I have never seen or learned anything about what I saw," I wondered.

"Oh, that. I thought we could discuss other matters before revealing your attacker. It's an explanation that has a story behind it. I want to get the facts and everything to it before I address that matter," Amanzi replied.

"So, you know what it is," I sat back in my seat and sighed. "That is weird. For me to be the goddess of the water, why would anything from the water want to kill me? Does it have anything to do with the enemy that you guys are fighting?"

"No. It was nothing like that. He wasn't trying to kill you. He wanted to bring you home," Amanzi revealed.

"Home? Which is what exactly?" I questioned.

"You will find out soon. As far as your goddess showing up when you needed her, you have to be at peace with where you are. You were in a state of panic and thought of death while you were supposed to be in the safest place in the world," he responded.

"How do you be comfortable while dying and knowing that you don't want to die?" I countered.

Amanzi rejected my statement. "I don't want you to ever be comfortable with dying. I want you to be complacent. You were looking for me but the entire time all you had to do was to trust yourself."

"Sooo.... you are saying that all I had to do was to trust myself to breathe underwater and it would have happened?" Amanzi heard how unconvinced I was.

"Yes. You did it before," he responded and took the menu out of our hand as the waiter approached.

"Good evening. I am Dan and I will be your waiter today.

Can I start you, beautiful couple off with some drinks? We have a special on our margaritas and mojitos," Dan greeted us with a million-dollar smile. He was the type of guy that enjoyed his job. I didn't know what the uniform policy was, but he was dressed like he was going straight into the water after he got off.

"She would like the loaded island fries with a sweet tea and lemon. That will be all," he ordered and passed the menus to the Dan.

"Okay. Do you want to keep the menu just in case you want something else?"

"No, we are sure," Amanzi spoke.

"How do you know I am sure? I might want dessert afterward," I jumped in.

"You don't. When you used to come here, you would order the loaded island fries with a sweet tea and sit out near the water. You never finish it all because it gets cold while you stared at the water and spun the ring on your finger. You will ask for a to-go plate so that you can warm it up in the microwave once you get home and eat it over a movie," Amanzi told me.

Dan pursed his pink lips and wrote my order on his notepad.

"Wait. What if I want something different today? What if I want to try something new or order from the dessert menu? Is it too much for you to ask me that before making that decision for me?" I ran off with the questions.

"You are not the type of person to try something new to eat when you are particular about what you eat. If dessert is what you want, we can stop on the way back to get you some ice cream or your other favorite... cookies and milk," he finished and directed his last statement to Dan. "That will be all."

Dan walked off smiling at the display of a man that knows his woman. If he knew that this was our first date, he would have thought that Amanzi was a stalker.

"You are my obsession Adaliya," he corrected my thoughts with a searing look. I exhaled and blushed at his statement.

"You aren't eating anything?"

"Our appetites aren't that big. Salads, seeds, fruits, nuts, and whole-grain meals will be enough for us. Liquids are the most essential part of our diets. That's because we swim all day. We hate feeling heavy in the water," Amanzi explained.

"My mother would always tell me don't eat before swimming. I thought she was telling me that to keep me from going into the water. She used to hate doing my hair afterward," I joked.

"No, she is right. You can catch massive cramps in your stomach that will enable your ability to swim," he countered.

"Liquor has the same effect. I couldn't concentrate or think clearly when I fell overboard. To this day, I don't know what we hit," I thought on it.

"It was a boulder that was created by the adversary," Amanzi shared.

"Qala, right. He is the one that is after you guys," I started. Amanzi sat back stunned that I knew that information. "Zuri told me about this before our conversation this morning. I guess he prepared me for this moment. You did, too," I continued.

"Right. I needed you to know some of these things so that explaining the major parts of our lives could be understood." Amanzi nodded his head and exhaled. The coolness of his breath reached my lips. I licked them wet, drawing attention to what he loved about me. He was ready to lean forward and capture them in a kiss I knew was going to make me forget what we were talking about. I sat back and kept on track.

"Okay, Qala. He targeted the cruise ship because of me?" I whispered.

"I believe so. That was another reason Landon, Skye, and Egypt stayed close to you. They didn't want him to notice his failed attempt and try to come back to finish the job."

"But, why? I haven't done anything to anyone. Why would he want to kill me?" I felt I needed to know.

"Because you are my everything. And, without my everything, I am nothing," Amanzi said in a faint voice. I could tell that he didn't want to admit that out loud, not knowing who was listening. I looked around the restaurant and got pissed. I hated I was a weakness that couldn't protect myself. I had never been the type to allow others to fight my battles while I sat in the corner all helpless. There were all types of shit going on in the water that needed Amanzi's attention, and he was here trying to convince me I was stronger than I was acting. I was a disappointment. I saw that shit in my parents' eyes, my friends, and Egypt before she dropped me off at home. I hoped to not see it on Amanzi's face. I didn't want to be this pathetic-ass person or an easy target. I wanted muthafuckas to think twice before they came after me to get to him.

To get to him.

They wanted Amanzi.

They wanted to hurt him. Kill him and destroy what was ours.

Ire emotions rose inside of me. My hands began to twitch with my breathing. The wind kicked up and began to turn some tables over.

"Woah! The meteorologist needs to find another job. There was no way they didn't see this shit starting in the Gulf." Dan walked up to us, holding my plate. "There has to be bad weather coming. That's the second time that has happened since I been at work today."

"What?" I looked up at him and asked. His eyes, along with most of the patrons were standing and looking out towards the beach. I turned my head and saw a wave coming towards the shore. It wasn't any regular wave. It dove under and came up bigger each time. I stood and felt it tugging for me to get closer. I closed my eyes wanting to be near and touch what was mine.

"Your emotions are controlling this. Allow me to calm you down," Amanzi stated behind me. His arms went around my waist so gently as he pulled me to his front tightly. His hands were flat against my stomach, holding me still to place his lips near my ear. I thought he was going to kiss and nibble on it, knowing that it was my spot. He released a soft whistle that sounded like the music from the seashell. The raging storm inside of me settled as he said it would. My body swayed side to side. I found the strength that I was looking for in that small act. I could tell by the noise of the crowd that the waves had died down as well.

"That's magic," Dan commented and sat my food on the table.

"Box it up," Amanzi stated, not wanting to let me go. I smiled, thankful that he said something because I wasn't moving or hungry anymore. Amanzi was feeding me all the nutrients I needed.

"I could hold you like this forever," he mumbled.

"I would like that," I sang. My body relaxed as he spun me around to face him. Amanzi continued rocking my body into submission. My heart was settled along with my soul. Zuri was right. There was no type of medicine that the hospital could have given me to make me feel how I did. I wasn't floating. Looking into his enchanting eyes, I was swimming in the purest water. The temperature was the same as Zuri's body, cool and refreshing. I was willing to do whatever he asked me to do, go wherever he wanted me to go, and believe whatever he wanted me to believe. I knew he wouldn't tell me any lies or hurt me intentionally. His reasoning for not being there for me then didn't matter. In reality, he has been there for me through this entire process, keeping my mind and sanity intact. His unconditional love and undying faith in us had not wavered. I was content with those findings. Others may have thought that the situation was crazy and odd, but I thrived on it. I knew I was different, obsessing over the water like I did or being a girl from the poor part of Tampa, majoring in Marine Biology. My goals were unrealistic to those that didn't understand my passion, and here I was standing in front of a man that was a part of what I wanted to know. He was my fascination. My love. He was my everything...

"And without my everything, I am nothing," I voiced loudly. Amanzi's sparkling smile understood. He leaned forward and planted a sensational kiss on my lips. I drank that shit in and begged for more with a groan. He pulled back and was ready to ask what I was willing to say.

"I'm ready, baby. Take me home."

Without any other word, Amanzi squatted and picked me up. I wrapped my legs around his waist with my back to the water. I heard it calling out for me and couldn't wait to join it again. Amanzi got near the shore and froze. He backed up and placed me on my feet.

"Not now," he said serenely, but I knew differently.

"What's wrong?" I demanded.

"I have to take care of something first," he answered and nodded behind me. I turned and saw Egypt approaching us. "Egypt will get you back to the condo safely," he wanted to explain further. I forbade it and kissed him quickly.

"Go. I will be fine," I rushed to him. I took a step back, on the side of Egypt. Amanzi gave me one last look before diving into the water.

"Is it really that bad?" I directed to Egypt.

"I come to realize anything that is dealing with Qala is bad," she responded and looped her arm in with mine. "But I am happy that he told you who we were. It was getting harder keeping this secret from you."

"I knew that something was going on with you. You used to purr for no reason," I laughed.

"You are a very friendly person to be around. My purring comes natural around you," Egypt noted and looked ahead of us. "You guys walked from the condo."

"No. He teleported us here," I answered.

Egypt looked surprised and beamed. "Oh, my brother isn't playing with you. He tries to get you home-home."

"Yeah. He and Zuri made that perfectly clear," I told her and thought of the little violet eye kid. "How is he? When I woke up, he was gone."

"Amanzi wanted him to train with the Piyas since he vowed he was your protector and guard. I don't think that Amanzi knows that for a fact because he wasn't the one that gave him that purpose. Overall, all the mosogens are your protector," Egypt supported.

"I can't wait to meet the rest of them."

"They are quite the bunch, but you will love them just as much as they already love you. You can tell by the way they speak of you," Egypt commented and glanced around the area. It was getting dark out. A few people were packing up their things and getting ready to leave. "Do you want to take the shortcut to the condo?"

I wanted to wait for him near the shore with open arms. I knew he was going to need it after dealing with the mess underwater.

"He needs you safe, remember," Egypt reminded me.

"Right! Shortcut it is," I said and closed my eyes. The air escaped my lungs and rushed back in. I coughed hard feeling the difference in the atmosphere.

"You will get used to it. There will even be a time when you will do it on your own," Egypt announced.

"Amanzi told me that there will be a lot of things that I will do once I connect with the goddess in me," I said.

"He wasn't lying. Ever since I mated with Landon, I feel connected with the land and its animals. They look up to me like, I'm their creator. I will have to get used to it, yet I am up for the challenge. With Landon by my side, I could conquer all."

"And, when he is not by your side, you are just a cat shifter that took on a burden that has placed you in the path of their nemesis," a man's voice spoke. He walked out of my bedroom, carrying one of my shirts. The strange man lifted the shirt to his nose and inhaled. Egypt hissed and yanked my arm to place me behind her.

"What are you doing here, Qala?" Egypt addressed. My eyes zoomed in on the man that we were talking about. I guessed we spoke his ass into existence. The audacity of his stupid ass to be standing in my home sniffing my shit. Qala was on some bold stuff. His glare didn't invoke the fear he hope it did.

"I am here... for her," he dragged out and tossed my shirt to the floor.

"You will never get her," Egypt promised. Qala flashed her a smile that made its own statement. Egypt's long claws grew from her fingers and yelled. More people started popping up and stepping in front, placing me near the front door.

"They won't be enough," Qala grew his talons and stood up straighter.

"They won't, but I will," Egypt stated before hell broke loose.

SHE WAS FUCKING READY!

My baby was ready to come home and be with our family. I wasn't going to ask her any questions or make sure that I was where she wanted to be. I scooped her ass up and carried her to the entry of our life. When the water touched my foot, I felt the negative activities surrounding the homes that I made for my people. They weren't in one area. They were in many at one time. I had to make sure that they didn't take over my territory. I called out for Egypt to take Adaliya back to the condo. I wanted to tell her I was sorry for the delay. She planted an understanding kiss on my cheek and demanded me go save our family.

I dove and blended in the water. The first place I came upon was Port Royal. The sight was unbearable. Blobs covered my city like an umbrella. The bigger ones stuck to the breezeway of the bridge, while the others sucked the seeds of my younglings out of the ground. I frowned at the barbaric action and wanted them all dead. They were sitting at the entrance waiting for my mosogens arrival. I held out my hand and released waves of knives toward them. One of the blobs head went up at the sound of my attack. It was too late for it to move. The wave went through its mouth and sliced three others behind it. They alerted the others, and they all came in my direction at once. I jerked my arm, which formed a multiple arrow shooter. Like a machine gun, arrows went flying through the bodies of the blobs connected with the only main organ that mattered to me. Chunks of them fell to the seafloor in a pile. When I finished the last of them, I focused on my destroyed section. The mosogens didn't have a reason to return to this part of the section, not even for memories. I raised my hands gesturing for the city to rise from the seabed. I clapped my hands and watched the city fold itself, destroying all the history of the once-lost city. It wasn't something that I was proud of, yet it had to be done. I needed to eliminate any area that they were hiding in. Judging from their past destinations, they were all in places where my mosogens resided. Meaning, that I had to destroy every section to keep them in the open.

"Father, we thought..." Trinity spoke behind me and stopped. She was staring at the destruction of their birthplace. Dafari floated forward with his hands on his head while Femi's emotions triggered Valin's. I should have known that they were going to meet me here. I didn't want them to feel that type of loss.

"I'm sorry, children," I mumbled.

"It's fine father. I would rather see it demolish than to have these things covering it," Dafari turned and stated. "We all were sitting around trying to find out what we can do to help you kill these things. I know you may not like it, but Trinity came up with an idea that can assist you."

"Yeah," she whispered. She backed up to where we were standing. "When I was healing Monco, I had to disperse more of my energy to bring him back to full health. It confused me at first because Monco didn't have any physical injuries. And, then it hit me. Those things aren't hungry for our flesh. They need the energy that you have given to them to survive. That was why the force fields were weakened around the other cities where we found them."

I nodded my head agreeing with what she was saying. "That

is a great observation, Trinity. When I arrived here, the vitality was completely drained."

"If that is the case, maybe we don't need to be in one spot. We thought we can lure them out and let you kill them. You can use us as bait," Valin continued with their thoughts.

"I don't need you guys to lure them out. I know where they are coming from," I said and turned to go in that direction. "When we first arrived at Cyan's section, I noticed that there was a lot of energy coming from the no-go zone. I think they took some mosogens down there to feed some of the other blobs to help them grow or make more of them. I will go down there to see what I can find."

"Father, we can be of some type of assistance," Valin argued.

"No. None of you can. I need you guys to go back home. I will have to take care of this by myself," I ordered and teleported over Cyan's section, appending an attack. To my surprise, Cyan's section wasn't covered in blobs. They were none in sight. I found that strange, since the energy from below changed the density of the water.

"What the hell is going on down there?" A familiar voice said behind me. I looked over my shoulder and saw Skye swimming awkwardly. I would have expected Landon to greet me with his presence. Skye was always doing shit by the book. He had to have been under the radar to be underwater without Mother snatching his ass back to the sky. "You could have told us we were able to come down here with you."

"You can't be down here, Skye. Go home," I told them instead.

"We are all able to be in each other's element. I swim around in the Pacific all the time. It is Landon that is afraid of the water," Skye responded.

"The last time I stepped out of my territory, it gave Qala the opportunity to step in my shit. I don't want that to happen to you,

Skye. Landon has his stuff under control and more help than he did before," I stated.

"First off you don't have to deal with this on your own. You think you can, by demanding your children to vacate the premises shows you are either stupid or selfish. I would like to vote for the stupid option. Because you know Qala isn't that bold to be in the sky that is closes to Mother. And, unlike you, I use the resources that were given to me to my advantage. I have eyes everywhere," Skye spoke.

"But Skye," I tried to convince him to go back to the surface.

"Stop it, Manzi. You know that there is no way for you to handle this by yourself. Your mosogens-your children are worried about you and decided to reach out to their uncle because you were being stubborn. You can do all that flashing of the eyes at them to get them to comply with your demands. The shit doesn't work on me. You are my little brother, and we are going to do this together," Skye made perfectly clear before looking down into the no-go area. "Now tell me what the plan is."

Talking to him was obsolete. I knew they were able to sustain my element as I did theirs. I wasn't comfortable with them being here. Their unwanted opinions on my way of life were the topic of many of our conversations during our family gatherings. Seeing how my mosogens lived was more ammunition I was giving them. It was too late to cover the mess that was made by the blobs. I opened more and allowed him to see what was going on in the submerged city that had been buried in the lagoon of the Qiandao Lake.

"Whoa! Singapura. This was really the Atlantis of China. I hated they submerged this place for Xin'an hydroelectric and river dam," Skye indicated.

I shook his head and moved closer. "They could have, but at the time that was the best decision that was ever made. Their inadequate ability to reserve fossil fuels or preserve energy beyond the electricity that they received through hydropower. I know Landon miss this city though. I kept the place up well underwater. I love the way the detailing on the animal carvings," I brought his attention to the walls of the entry to the city.

"I remember Landon telling me he felt the spirits of them every time we visited," Skye added.

"They are still here. It is a way for me to have a piece of you guys here with me," I made known.

"This is amazing, Amanzi. Landon would love to hear about this," he admired. I didn't want him to get caught up in sightseeing.

"Thank you. But I know you didn't travel down there to see the Lion City. The first attack was held here and some of my children were dragged down below," I implied.

"What is this?" Skye held his hand out and spread his fingers. Slim stretched from them, causing his fingers to be sticky.

"That is what the blobs are made of," I answered and moved to the edge of the cliff, where it got thicker. "I will clear the way for you," I replied and stepped off into the darkness. I left a clear path for Skye to get through easily. The further we went down the thicker the water got. I looked to my left and right, seeing chunks of those things' flesh floating around like jellyfishes. The shit was disrespectful. I felt the toxins polluting this entire area. That was why most of the people in Cyan's section were getting sick. They were right above all this mess, inhaling it all in without knowing. A cleansing was going to be needed after I destroy whatever he released in my water.

As we approach the end, the cliff that my city rested on began to break off, creating a space in another area below it. I held my hand to stop my brother from moving forward once I landed on the rough surface. Ahead of me, was a rocky pathway that led to an underwater cave.

"That bitch in there," Skye whispered to me. I looked at him and frowned.

"Didn't I tell you to stay yo ass back?" I replied.

"Yeah, but I decided not to listen. Did you know that this was down here?" he ignored my attitude and asked.

"Yes," I answered.

"Then why you didn't come down here when everything started happening," Skye added. I released a frustrated sigh before responding to him.

"Because... I had to get my people to safety and fight the things that were terrorizing them."

"But, after that though," he continued.

"You can go back to the surface with all this shit," I mumbled and moved forward. We maneuvered around the hard large rocks, careful to not make any noise. I paused as something fell, landing in front of me. I gazed up and was surprised at what I was seeing.

"Go," Skye instructed after I stood still for seconds. I pointed upward to draw his attention to what stopped me. Blobs were coating the roof with their bodies moving in and out. Bubbles formed around them from all the sucking that they were doing. "What are they doing?"

"They are absorbing the vitality that I placed in this area so that my garden of younglings will grow and the force field that keeps the divers away," I retorted. It was sickening watching them get to fill up on my energy to kill my people.

"Let's kill them muthafuckas, then," Skye's dragon claws began to grow.

"No need for you to break a sweat brother," I growled. My glowing eyes flickered at the water that was behind us. The seabed began to shake, producing a tsunami underwater. Skye and Landon pressed their bodies to the stone wall and watched the water transforming itself into ice. It went through the blobs, slicing them all in halves. The top part of their bodies dropped to the surface, while the other part of them remained stuck at that top. Skye marveled at the pile that was stacked in front of the entrance.

"Yeah, I see what you mean. That shit was too easy," Skye remarked.

"They were a distraction. The real focus should have been on him," I nodded towards the cave. The aura that was coming from it was as toxic as the shit that was coming out of those blobs. Whatever he was, he was watching and waiting for the time to introduce himself. He didn't come out to see what the commotion was all about. He was patient and okay with me killing those fucking things. If he felt that way, he must've been one of Qala's greatest creations, by far. I took a couple of steps forward before he or it decided to appear at the opening of the cave. Even with us being underwater, I could see how smarmy his body and hair were. His creamy pale skin looked to be wrinkled because of his long stay underwater. He was tall like me and had white eyes.

"It is nice to finally meet you Amanzi. Welcome to my home," it hissed. Skye stared at the intruder as if he had lost his mind. This asshole greeted us like we were visitors in his shit. I grunted, feeling insulted at his existence.

"This is not your house. And, we are not your guest. I'm pretty sure your maker that put you here, knew that already," I spat.

"My maker," he sarcastically said. "He is my father who places me in a position to rule a territory that will be opening shortly. As you can see, my children are getting comfortable and making visits to yours. It's a shame how provincial they are. A trait that they picked up from their father no less. But they are not as tough as I thought though. As powerful as you are, I thought that the will of royalty would seep into their genes, which had me worried at first. After visiting your "sections" I was truly disappointed. The king of the water runs, and hide were the only choices you had to protect your family. I was preparing for a fight and now I'm playing hide and seek. Pathetic."

I frowned and looked around the area where he sat up camp. "Hiding? You are the one that stays below sea level nigga and I'm hiding?" I questioned. I released a sinister laugh that chilled the water around us. My brother and I noticed the prodigy of Qala quivered.

"Don't ignore it. That chill that is running up your thin-ass spine is a warning. It's telling you you have fucked up. You have bit off more than you can chew and swallow this shit is going to be difficult for you. That is something that your father should have taught you. The same thing I trained mine to do. When it's a battle that they can't fight, as their father it's my job to step up and take the situation into my own hands. Unlike yours, he sent you here to die when he instructed you to come after my family. That's a punk-ass move because I was a problem that he couldn't handle. Just like your blobs, you are here to distract me from whatever plan he has in motion. We are going to cancel that shit, just like I am going to do to you."

My promising words didn't do anything for him. He grunted like the disobedient shit that he was and stood his ground. "You can't touch me."

I sneered and teleported in front of him. I snatched him up by his scrawny neck and lifted him off his feet. "Another lie he told you," I scolded. I took my brother's advice and finished him quickly. My arm jerked into a pendulum blade that swiped through his midsection. Like his stupid blobs, the bottom half fell to the seafloor while his upper body stayed in my hand wiggling. I tossed him aside and waited for him to disintegrate as his children did. Instead, his body evaporated into the ocean floor. Through the cracks of the ground, he reemerged newly regenerated. His head was up with his eyes closed. The creature exhaled and dropped his gaze at me.

"Like, I said. You can't touch me," he bragged. I felt myself changing into something that would touch him until Skye called my attention to what was going on behind me. I turned and saw the blobs that I killed were multiplying. The ones on the ridged roof grew their other halves and continued to suck the remaining energy out of my city. I was shocked at this new revelation. They couldn't be killed by me or my mosogens.

"Well, thank you for increasing my army. But this put you at a disadvantage. Go get your mother, Amanzi. Because this is a battle that is too big for you," he commented. He pursed his lips together and whistled. The blobs lifted from the ground and started swimming towards us.

"I can try to kill them," Skye released his metal wings underwater.

"No," I told him and looked back at my intruder. I didn't want to risk them multiplying again. I looked back at the intruder who had a smug on his face.

"Run, King. That is what you do best," he taunted. I moved to him and stopped at the sound of her voice.

"Come to me."

My body straightened up right away. She was calling out to me. That could only mean one thing. "Uhhhh!" I growled and teleported to where her energy led me. Adaliya's condo was filled with my wounded piyas and Egypt.

"What happened? Where is Adaliya?" They tried to bow down in my presence. I shook my head and moved to Jernia, who was falling over. Her hand was covering the hole in her stomach. "Why aren't you in the water?"

"We needed to make sure that our Luna was okay," she mumbled weakly. I gestured for the other injured ones to move forward. Skye went to the bedroom door that was blocked by Oklan and Brun. I nodded for them to allow him to go in.

"I am here now. Go and heal," I ordered.

"Father," I heard Zuri call. My piyas were standing still on the wall with their attention on the bedroom. I entered and saw that Egypt was standing near the bed with Skye approaching her. Zuri was in the bed that was placed in the center of the room with Adaliya. She looked like she was resting from an exhausting day. I got to her in seconds and placed my hand on her head.

Adaliya's temperature was normal, along with her vitals. Baby girl was still in perfect health. Knowing that I turned my eyes to Lenmon who also was sporting some war wounds.

"What happened?" I asked calmly.

"We heard Egypt's call for help. We appeared at Luna's home where Qala was waiting. He wanted to take her and do whatever. We fought. He didn't try to kill us, which was strange. He stabbed, burned, and clawed some of us, but all of our injuries were superficial. We all could heal from this by stepping in the water. When we were down, Egypt stepped in and started fighting him. He raised his claws to hurt her, and Luna yelled. Her scream made him stop. We all did. I looked up, and she was... she wa..." he got choked up.

"She turned into something that low-keyed scared Qala into a shock. That allowed me to strike him in his chest. He pushed me away and tried to teleport out of here. We found out that Adaliya's scream was a call to the water. It broke through the glass and snatched Qala. I don't know where he went or if he got loose. Adaliya wanted to follow him. Lenmon and Zuri convinced her to wait on you. Hearing your name, she came to and passed out. Again," Egypt finished.

"You had that part right. He was trying to distract you to get to Adaliya. This fool is a weak one for that," Skye stated.

"But why, though? Don't he know that coming after Adaliya will cost him his life," Egypt thought.

"He nor his son don't think that. I will have to come up with a way to kill them both," I snarled.

"We will come up with a way to kill them. You are not alone in this, man," Skye reminded me.

"Yes, father. We are here to help you as well," Lenmon concluded.

"The only help I need from you right now is to clear everyone away from this room. Make sure everyone is healed and get some rest. There are many things that we have to talk about," I glanced up at him to make sure he got the point that I was making. Lenmon nodded his head and did as I ordered. The only ones that didn't leave the room were Zuri, Egypt, and Skye.

"Now can we take her home?" Zuri's impatient ass said.

"Not yet," I said while caressing her face. "As her guard, you should know that." I glared at him.

"I know that. That is why she should be in the water right now," he went on. I knew it wasn't the right time but his attitude over Adaliya's was bothering me.

"My brother asked before who assigned you to be Adaliya's guard. You said you felt it. I would like to know how that came about."

"I can't explain it. It felt like my purpose. I thought you knew when you came to visit our section after meeting with her," Zuri replied.

"Why would you have thought that?" I questioned.

"Because you saw her without clothes on. I thought you saw our unique mark," he told me. I took my hand from her face and intertwined it with the other.

"You weren't born with a mark, Zuri," I responded.

Zuri got out of the bed to walk to me and pulled his ear down, revealing something new to me. The triangle was right-side-up with waves crashing the inside of it. I leaned in closer knowing that I had seen this symbol before. I pulled back and turned towards Adaliya. My hand went easily to the mark on the inside of Adaliya's thigh. It was the same as the one that Zuri had, but the colors were different. Zuri's triangle was shaded in with the different blues of the ocean. Adaliya's mark was the same color as her skin tone.

"She has to be my purpose. No other human or mosogen has this mark on them," Zuri noted. I couldn't argue with him on that. I haven't seen this mark on anyone else and I have lived centuries.

"How do you feel when you are around her?" I queried.

Zuri inhaled a deep breath and released it with a soft sigh. "I feel like... like I'm home. I am right where I belong. If she was to be in the water with me, I won't have to worry about fitting in or following rules that are against everything that I value. With her, I am all," he expressed. Zuri's eyes glowed with these acquainted feelings. My children's expressions toward her are different from what Zuri described. I sat back and addressed everything that he said.

"That was another thing that I wanted to talk to you about. Adaliya is under the impression that someone in the water will hurt you if you return. I haven't punished any of you for the bad behaviors that had been displayed for a couple of sunrises now. Even when you scared Adaliya to death, I still didn't react the way my nature insisted me to. But now, you are afraid of punishment so severe that you would drag Adaliya in the water in the condition that she's in, to prove a point that we have already established was a mistake," I spoke with a steady voice. He had to understand that this was a major problem, yet I didn't fault him at all. I blamed the older mosogens that were supposed to lead by example. What Zuri was explaining was something different entirely. Our values were always about the water and my people. The water had been disturbed, but it never went against us. The only other thing that I could think about was my people being the problem. If so, my punishment was going to be felt around the fucking world. "Is there something I'm missing Zuri?"

The glowing in Zuri's eyes became dull. He gazed down at his feet with shame, which wasn't a trait that I instilled in my people. I sat and waited patiently until he got himself together to talk.

"Sipho hasn't been a good leader, Father. Whenever any of us do something wrong, he would punish us," Zuri briefly explained.

"By doing what? Did he make you guys do double shifts or stop feeding you? What?" I queried further. Zuri maintained eye contact when he revealed some unsettling news.

"He killed them."

"What?" Skye frowned. Egypt placed her hand over her mouth, stunned by the news.

The chill in his words stopped my blood flow for a second. I knew if I would have looked outside, the water itself would have sat stilled. Zuri's feelings about what was going on in Sipho's section were shown in his eyes. He had seen the shit happen before.

"How the fuck did I not know this? I haven't been giving anyone my energy like that, to be distracted by what was going on in my home," I spoke harshly.

"He did it every time you left home. Whenever I came back from visiting my Luna, I would always notice someone missing from the group. I didn't say anything. No one will. We are afraid of ending up like the others," Zuri kept going. I waved my hand for him to shut the fuck up. What was building inside of me would have taken the entire building down. I didn't want to wake Adaliya up with the roar that was ready to release from my mouth. My heart was throbbing faster than normal. I hated not understanding why shit was happening to me. There was something seriously wrong with me not feeling my people being hurt underwater.

"There is a reason for that," Zuri commented and sat on the other side of Adaliya. He picked her hand up and placed it on her stomach. "When you travel on land or sky too often, it weakens your bond with the water."

"That is not true. My bond with the water can never be withered, no matter where I am," I told him.

"So is mine. My connection with everything in the sky remains strong," Skye confirmed.

"It may seem that way after you return to the sky from being away from it. It's a welcoming feeling that you receive that makes the bond stronger. Overall, you are weaker on land, just like the others would be weaker in your territory. That's how everything works. It's the balance of everything. That is why you all were created for different elements. It's also why Luna sleeps and passes out so much. She has been thriving off the energy of the water for most of her life. She has been going without her natural supplement for some sunrises now. It will be difficult for her to breathe each minute she stays on land. Her body needs to rejuvenate like the piyas. It needs to be submerged into the water," Zuri continued with this theory. I knew he wouldn't have gotten this information based on a couple of visits on land with Adaliya. I raised my guard and stood up straighter. Zuri had his head down with his attention on *his Luna*. His protectiveness over her was uncanny. When I told the other children about her, they wanted to come up here and protect her themselves. I told them no, and they didn't have any other objections to that. Zuri didn't take no for an answer. He wasn't going anywhere without knowing that their Luna was going home into the water where the creatures were. I felt his energy before and assumed that he was mine.

He had to be mine.

I remember the moment that Kiaz brought him to me when he was only a season old. I had a few younglings born with blue eyes, but Zuri's were my color. I didn't think anything of it until now.

"Zuri," I called for his attention. He reluctantly gave it to me. "Who are you, son?"

"I'm Zuri, Father," he answered quickly.

"And," I encouraged him to keep going.

"The protector and guard of Luna," he responded.

"Who told you that?" the question was simple yet demanding. He knew I was getting upset with this back-and-forth shit. He moved to stand in front of me. Zuri's eyes told me what I felt from the beginning.

I snarled something furious before launching off into the sky. I knew she had something to do with this shit. She sat her conveying ass right there and lied to me in my face. Mother was always ready to blame shit on Qala or us. It was cowardly and sickening.

I landed in the middle of her living area, interrupting her and Landon's conversation. The shit looked deep, but I didn't care. Judging from the sword that was now in my hand, they both knew that something was about to go down.

"Amanzi," Landon said my name in a warning. My eyes stayed on the pale gold ones of the woman that I tried my hardest to understand. The woman that I loved unconditionally, played me like I wasn't that nigga that would fuck her shit up. The sharp edge of my sword tapped her marble floor, cracking it.

"This doesn't have anything to do with you, big brother," I told him.

"It's not what you think, Amanzi. Please sit down so that we can talk about this," he replied. I shook my head and pulled the sword up to examine it.

"No. I'm tired of talking? Aren't you?" I inquired Mother. She moved to the other side of Landon.

"You are not big on what I have to say, Amanzi. So, do what you came up here to do," she replied. I grunted and smirked at her.

"No, Amanzi! Wait!" Landon screamed. I swung my sword towards him. It dissolved going through him and returned solid when it reached Mother. She raised her wrist, blocking the attack with her bracelet. Landon dipped his shoulder and tackled me. He tried to run me into the wall, but my body became my element, forcing him to crash through it. I appeared in front of Mother with hands wrapped around my body. Skye pulled Mother back and got between us to calm me down. Egypt appeared next to Landon.

"Move back, Egypt," Landon growled. "Whatever it is we can handle this a different way?"

"Nah, fuck that! She told me she didn't have anything to do with Adaliya drowning. Come to find out, she was the one that created Zuri. She put his ass in the water to spy on me on my people," I told them.

Landon's hold loosened up a little. Skye turned to Mother for her reaction to what I was saying. The conceited look on her face had my feet moving. Skye held his hand up for me to give her some time to explain.

"Mother?" Landon spoke behind me. She walked over to the couch and gestured for us to have a seat with her.

"I am not sitting down with you, Mother. I knew you had something to do with this shit. Your answer was too fucking clean. Tell me now, why you have Zuri in my fucking water?" I demanded an answer.

"Zuri isn't there to harm Adaliya. I guess he has your trait of being impatient," she replied casually.

"What. The. Fuck. Is. He. Doing. Down. There," every word was pronounced with more venom than the next. I felt my sharp teeth coming out, pending an attack.

"He is there to protect his Luna," she repeated the same thing that he said.

"If that is the case, why did he try dragging her down into the water? Come on Mother. You have to start making some sense," Landon requested.

"He wanted to bring her home. There are a lot of activities that are happening in your water. You have leaders killing your younglings because he feels like he knows what is best for the water. Just like the creature that Qala created. Everyone thinks they know what is best for your kingdom, because the king that was created for it, is never there. You are always where you are not supposed to be," she threw in my face.

"Who is killing your younglings?" it was Landon's turn to ask.

"Being there for my brothers is where I'm always going to be needed. These fucking games you are playing are going to have you left alone with all this shit to protect," I hissed instead of responding to him.

"Your brothers didn't need your help. Landon was always capable of getting back to himself without your help. Egypt was going to bring him back to life, just as Adaliya should have made you realize that the water is where you need to be. Zuri knew it. He saw what was going on and needed to bring back the balance to your civilization by bringing the Queen home," she responded.

"Bring back the balance? It would have never been off if you didn't send Zuri. You wanted me to see things your way and reasons I should rely on the creatures you created. Zuri brought out the worse in my people. He encouraged Sipho's behavior, just like he encouraged and touch my piyas. They have all been acting out due to their unknown interaction with Zuri. He fucks up everything he encounters," I noted.

"That is not his purpose. You are his father," Mother tried to remind me

"I am not his father!" I roared.

"Yes, you are, Amanzi. He was created in your image. He is you in a kid-like form," Mother added.

"What the fuck does that mean?" Landon's aggravation was coming through.

"He brings out the worse and the best in people. It depends on how they receive him. That is why Adaliya's fear of water slightly diminishes when she is around him. She will receive you better with Zuri," Mother commented and directed her eyes at me. "You felt his calm energy. You know he would never cause any pain to any of his people or Adaliya. That is the reason you left him alone with her."

"You don't think that this was something that we needed to know beforehand," Skye wondered.

"It didn't have anything to do with you Skye, nor Landon," Mother replied.

"But it had everything to do with me. When I came up here the first time, you should have told me. What was the reason for you keeping this from me?" I questioned.

“Everything had to play out,” she insisted. I shook my head, baffled by this entire situation.

“I never thought that you will go through these extremes to have some type of control over what I do,” I spoke.

“Amanzi, I don’t want to control you. I just want you to understand where your priority lies. Doing what you were created to do is being there for your brothers,” she implied.

“Okay, and what are we created to do Mother? What! It’s the same question we have been asking for centuries and still don’t have a definite answer to. You expect me to behave in a way that would make your sitting on this throne up here more relaxing. We are in a battle for what?”

“You are in the battle more with yourself than anything else. You may think that you know who and what Amanzi is, but you have no idea of the major gifts that were bestowed upon you. You have found yourself more confused about who you are in the last couple of days. That’s because you want to be a better creator than me. In a sense, you are just like me Amanzi. Zuri didn’t have anything to do with the behaviors of your defiant piyas or Sipho. Your piyas are hiding a secret from you they think you can’t handle. The same secret you thought of keeping from me because you thought I was going to ruin what you love. Why else would anyone go out of their way to help a human woman, whom their father so calls despise? Sipho’s arrogance is what you displayed many times over by doing the very opposite of what I asked you to do. They are all showing you who and what you are. You give them warnings and don’t want to punish them because you think that there is a better way to resolve this. I made a lot of critical decisions that I don’t regret. I had to better the world and my children by making examples of people many times over. I will do it again and again until it is done right. You may not agree with my methods, but they are valid. Just as your next decision,” she implied.

“You don’t know what my next decision will be,” I told her.

She giggled and reached for her small crystal ball on the table. "I know your next decision, Amanzi. It's going to hurt you more than it will hurt them, but it needs to be done," her eyes glowed as the water rose in the ball. It began to clash, causing the ball to tremble in her hands. "Like me, you are a creator. The King of the water. It's about time that you claim what has been given to you and rule with an iron fist. That way, the enemy will surface and will be easy to kill without my help," she advised me. The water in the ball became ice, breaking the crystal. Landon and Skye stood next to me, waiting for another outburst. I never understood why she did the things she did and told myself that I wouldn't be like her towards my children. Her punishments seemed severe at the time. I thought of how Landon was before with Nelor and then Egypt. The pain and suffering he went through prepared him for his true mate. I had been suffering from losses and dealing with them accordingly. I wasn't sure if I could get through this pain alone. My fist was curled up in a tight fist as the tear slowly ran down my face.

"Amanzi," Landon grabbed my shoulder and pulled me into a hug. "Let me go with you."

"Me too," Skye said behind me with his hand resting on my back. I cleared my throat and stepped out of Landon's embrace.

"No," I wiped my face and spoke. "You guys stay in your territories. I got this."

Without talking or a last glance at my mother, I appeared in the water amongst my people that were settling into our new home. Each section leader had an area for their group to build their homes, near the bridge that led up to our castle.

"It's wonderful here Father. The energy is powerful and peaceful," Trinity ran and told me. I nodded my head and walked around her. "Father."

I ignored her call and continued down the path. Trinity motioned for the others to flank me. They knew that something wasn't right about me. This place was our sanctuary. We had no other choice but to be happy here. The smiles on the younglings were priceless and something I haven't seen in days. The light in Cyan's eyes were back and filled with life. It should have been a rejoicing moment. Sipho was talking to his general, unaware of the trouble that his section was in. As I approached, the guards smiled and nodded my way. Sipho turned and greeted me with a smile.

"Father! This place is wonderful. We have set up near the bridge so that we can be near you and the Luna," he spoke loud enough to alert the others to greet me properly. They all kneeled with their heads bowed down. Sipho bowed his head and reached for my hands. He placed his forehead on it and glanced back up at me. His group tried to get on their feet, but I didn't allow it. Sipho heard them struggling and looked back at them. They were straining against my hold Sipho reached for Jabarre's arm to lift him. Jabarre screeched from the tugging. Sipho dropped his arm and turned to me for answers. "What's wrong?"

"A lot is wrong with this picture, Sipho," I said and walked around him. I began to count the mosogens and the younglings in his group as I spoke. "I was unaware of the activities that you had for your section-unaware of the other set of rules you had set out for my children."

"The only rules that we have Father are the ones you have for us," Sipho argued. The ticking in my head got louder.

"What about the additional ones that had Zuri running away from your section to look for Luna?" I wanted him to admit the shit that he was doing.

"I told you, Father. Zuri ran off because he was being disobedient," he stuck with that stupid answer.

"Disobedient?" I stepped forward and questioned. Sipho nodded his head and watched me as I passed him up. I walked in between the mosogens that served this prick without stopping the bullshit that would have been easily frowned upon at the other sections. Their eyes were moving from side to side. I was truly disappointed in them all. I snarled with disgust and continued with this long-overdue dialect.

"Do you know what a leader is, Sipho? A leader recognizes his faults and accepts counsel from the ones around him. I, myself have learned that trait. I thought that my mother or brothers didn't know me well enough to tell me what I needed to do with my children. I shut their thoughts out and did what I thought was best for you all. Mother always told me it took a village to raise a child. I didn't think that her statement was directed at me since I am the King here. But I was wrong. I was wrong for ignoring her and the signs that you all have been showing me lately. I have been wrapped up in my family's business that I neglected the fact that a monster was being created within my own family. The rules that you set out for my people Sipho, wouldn't be anything close to what I would have done for their "*petty crimes.*" I may scream, which would have been all that it took for any of you to snap back into reality. But that's not the case here. You all need to see me in action. You all need to see me angry. You need me to make an example out of one of you, to get the fucking point. You all need to see me act like her!" I roared. The typhoon that was brewing started rising at my foot. The knees of the others shook, threatening to fall with their brothers and sisters. Sipho backed away from the upcoming storm. My eyes got hollow with his movement.

"Why are you backing up, Sipho? Are you afraid that I will punish you the same way as you did the younglings that trusted you?" I questioned with fury behind me.

"I haven't punished anyone, Father," he replied. Sipho sat there and lied to me with a straight face. I didn't know what part of me this nigga brewed from, but I had to reevaluate myself quickly before making more children. Dafari stepped forward with a strong grimace on his face.

"What did you do, Sipho?"

"I didn't do anything!" Sipho yelled at the group. He was

trying to convince the other leaders that began to circle around us. They all knew that he was hiding something from them.

"What did you do?" Femi repeated Dafari's question with his two-bladed sword out. Sipho glanced down at the glowing weapon, knowing that things were about to get serious. He wanted to look innocent by holding his hands up to further justify his actions.

"I didn't do anything that any of you wouldn't do. We have to have an order. Everyone needs to understand that we are absolute. We are law. We are not only sprouted from the seeds of our father. We are the souls that the water has harvested over the many years of slavery. It was because of the ignorance we bared that made it easy for those animals to take us from our homes. The lack of knowledge of who we truly were, crippled us in believing that someone else can make us a better person. We were already kings and queens until it was stripped from us. Making us start all over again, to worship some God we have never seen was ludicrous. Now our true God stands here and is angry at the actions I made to keep my sections stronger. They all had to go. We couldn't be weak. It was what those things felt the most. They preyed on the weak and attacked at full force. I couldn't allow that to happen to my people," he spoke to the group.

"You couldn't allow that to happen to your people?" I countered. The temperature dropped in the water. Sipho remained calm but stayed on guard while the others stared at him.

"If you cared about your people, punishing them with death wouldn't have been your only solution," I spat. "And the ones that follow you would have told you better. But they didn't. Evidently, they all feel the same way. What you all didn't know, was that your leader Sipho wasn't as strong as he is now. I allowed him to follow around with Dafari and Femi to become what he wanted the most. I didn't turn him away or punished him when he asked for the chance to become something more than what I assigned him to do. I encouraged and motivated him to pursue what he wanted. Everyone rooted for Sipho to become the section leader that his brothers and sisters were. He did it with help. So, tell me how, the so-called weaker ones couldn't get help from their leaders. Why didn't any of you help them the way he was helped?" I pointed at Sipho.

Regret and guilt were now the expressions on their faces. The comfortability that they had with this was an eye-opener. I didn't know what they thought was going to happen once I found out. I was beyond screaming or threatening them. It was time for action. Sipho dumb ass stared at me with no remorse. I nodded my head and felt the blade taking over my arm. The heavy weapon dropped in the sand before I picked it up and swung it at the mosogens in the first three rows, destroying them. The dust formed and became a fog in the water instantly.

"Noooo!" Trinity screamed out. Dafari held her in his arms as the massacre continued. I swung and killed every last one of them, while Sipho stood his dumb ass right there crying. I didn't know if the tears were for them or the fact that he was losing everything that he worked for. When the last of his section was gone, I strolled in front of him with a menacing look.

"Your ignorance is the reason for your behavior, Sipho. You think you are a reincarnated king of the lost souls of my waters. They would never come back to this fucked up world that we live in. They would never be okay with the shit that you are doing. You would know that if you knew my people. MY PEOPLE, SIPHO! You have no authority over what I want for the mosogens and youngling in any section that was created. Because of that, I sentence you to the same punishment you gave those younglings. DEATH!" The word pushed out as I pull the water from his lungs, leaving him in a hollow state. I opened the connection of Sipho's pain to the others. When Sipho dropped and started wheezing, everyone was on their knees feeling the same shit. I normally wouldn't do this, but I had to make them see. They had to see that there were consequences behind their actions. With no compassion or consideration, I reached back and swung forward, ending the life of one of my leaders. The screeching sound of mosogens and younglings sounded off, shaking the seabed. I felt the tears rolling down my face and the ache in my heart. It was a lesson that I also had to learn. I couldn't show any leniency to any of those that disobeyed me. Their consequences may not be death, but they were going to wish that it was.

"AHHHHHHHH AHHHHHHH!"

I jumped out of my slumber and onto my feet. The noise that was coming from the bathroom had me on guard and ready for anyone that was hurting him. I ran to the screeching sound and stopped in my tracks. Zuri's pale body was under the shower, shivering. He was scratching at his peeling skin as if it was offending him. I jumped in the cold water and wrapped my arms around his slimy body.

"Zuri. Calm down, baby. Come on," I tried to console him. Zuri jumped and slammed us into the wall. The impact forced me to let him go. Zuri leaped out of the tub and ran out or flew out of the room. My vision was too blurry to tell the difference. I called out his name, but it was in form of a whisper. I shook the pain in my back off and went after him in my drench clothes. Zuri was in the living room, screaming out the broken window. His screams were getting louder and more violent. I seriously had to rub my eyes after seeing the window shake under his tiny little fist.

"Zuri," I mumbled. He turned around and the bright violet that was his normal eye color was dull and lifeless. He opened his mouth flashing his sharp teeth and screeched at me. Zuri leaped from the window and lifted my sofa with one hand. He tossed it across the room, along with everything else that was in his way. The strength that he was displaying should have scared the hell out of me. But I didn't know what he was going through.

"Stop this, Zuri! Let me help you," I pleaded. Zuri ripped out one of his dreads and threw it toward me. I didn't think to dodge it because it was his hair. When it fell to the ground, it began to turn green. I frowned and looked back at him. His body was now marked with scratches and bruises. I couldn't let him hurt himself anymore and didn't think about the danger that I was putting myself in when I got in front of him while he was holding my television up above his head. Zuri's glossy glare reached out to my soul. I told him through my eyes that I wanted to help and soothe the pain that he was in. He recognized what I was offering and was ready to accept it until the pain struck him again. He winced and tossed the television over my head. Zuri growled and leaped over me to get to the front door. He snatched that locked door from the hinges and threw it at the elevator. With heavy breathing, Zuri broke through the door that led to the stairs and flew down them. I ran after him as fast as I could. The door opened with other tenants that were waiting for the now broken elevator. Zuri ran completely over them and crashed into the glass door.

"Oh my God What was that?" a lady hollered on the ground.

"That's my son," I said naturally and trailed behind him. Zuri ran across the street with no regard for the oncoming traffic. "Zuri!" I yelled and jumped in front of a 2021 black Tesla. I slammed my hands on the trunk of the car. I hissed something causing Zuri to turn on the vehicle. Even in his state of pain, his protectiveness over me kicked in. He jumped on the top of the car and started beating on it. The white male jumped out, ready to confront me and Zuri about his damaged car.

"Hey! What the fuck are you doing?" he hollered at the wild boy.

"Don't fucking talk to him like that!" I responded instead. He turned his attention to me and took a huge step back. Zuri's head snapped back in the direction of the water and started breathing again. He flipped off the car, flashing off and on towards the beach. Before he got into the water, I snatched his arm and wrapped him in mine. My legs went around his small waist, clamping him down in the sand. I rocked him back and forth, whispering comforting words in his ear.

"I'm here, son. I'm here. It's okay. Whatever it is, I will make it okay. I promise," I told him. The growling and vibration of his body became a silent hum. He rocked with me as his eyes stayed shut. I looked to the water and saw the brewing storm that was happening somewhere in it. The water wanted to be calm, but the waves were rough, crashing into each other violently. I didn't like seeing it that way. I sat my chin on top of Zuri's head and wished I could be the peace it needed.

"It's okay," I whispered more to the water.

"I don't think that your concern is in its right place at the moment. Maybe thinking of how you are going to get out of this situation should be your main priority," a male spoke behind me. I looked over my shoulder at the tall man that was looking out into the water. His tone and look were God-like. Almost as if he could be related to Amanzi. His golden glow was natural. The hair that these girls buy to make their wigs were pushed back by a thin headband. His linen clothing didn't move as the breeze kicked up some of the sand. I knew something was off and decided to address him, anyway.

"Excuse me."

"The water, it has so many rulers that it is hard for it to remain in control for one. I don't understand how she thought Amanzi was going to have a handle on it all. It is as if she was setting him up for failure. That's what parents do when they despise one of their children. They give them an unthinkable task to fulfill to watch them fail for pure amusement. I thought he would be the smarter one and leave her high and dry. I guess I was wrong," he spoke and glanced down at me. "What I wasn't wrong about is the beauty those boys attract. I had a chance to get personal with one of them. My. My. My. Skye is going to have a thrill with that one. But you... you will be something different for Amanzi. This connection that you two built through your small interactions will spark something deep in him. Something that will allow him to be the ruler that his mother tried to make him out to be. It will make a pleasing sight to watch. I would love to see how he will grip the mass of hair on your head when he gets deep inside of you," the stranger reached out to touch my hair. I dodged it and got to my feet with Zuri. I grabbed his hand and pulled him tightly to my side.

"I don't know you and your comments are disrespectful. I and my son will be leaving now," I responded and tugged Zuri.

"I'm sorry, but I can't allow you to leave and be with him," the man said. I was ready to curse him out until a crowd of whatever crawled up behind them. "You are his strength. You are the other half of his power. I can't allow you to mate with Amanzi, King of the water. You will die right here," he finished and took a step back. A snarl was released from a man that had a snout long enough to touch me where it stood. I jumped back, knowing that I didn't have a chance to get out of this. Zuri stepped forward and flashed his pointy teeth at the creature.

"Zuri, no," I said. The thing accepted his challenge and launched at him. Zuri caught the creature and rolled on top of him. With new claws that I haven't seen before, he dug into the thing's stomach and pulled out some shit to toss at the others. One of the creatures caught the organs and ate them. I held my hand over my mouth and gaged.

"Luna!" Zuri yelled my name. Something slammed into my body, forcing me to the ground. I rolled over and saw a slobbering mouth ass thing standing over me. Zuri dipped his shoulder and tackled it away. He pulled me up and placed me behind him. Once I was out of the way, Zuri went on full attack mode in the crowd filled with those things. He picked one of them up by the arm and slung him into the crowd, breaking its arms and using it as a weapon to fight off the others. I was too scared to marvel at the strength that he was displaying. I looked around for something to fight with. A broken log was hidden in the beach grass. I ran over to pick it up and trussed it in my hand. The thing had its claws up to tear through Zuri's back. Without thinking, I swung with all my might, breaking the log over the back of our enemy. The thing flinched a little and swung around to face me. I didn't give it time to register who was attacking him. I kept swinging with what was left of the log to the creature's face. Even when the chips of the bark started cutting in my hand, I continued my attack until I was snatched up by the back of my neck.

"Ahh!" I yelled.

"It's a shame that he won't be able to taste how sweet you are," the stranger whispered in my ear before his grip got deadly tight.

"No! Let her go!" Zuri stood in front of me and demanded. The stranger chuckled at the threat that was in a childlike voice.

"I will not let her go and there is nothing you can do about it boy. Go back to the water and get your father to deal with me," the stranger ordered.

"I said. Let. Her. Go," the growl released from his mouth with every word.

"I applaud your efforts. That is the fierceness she instilled in you. But you have enough common sense to know that this is a fight that you can't win," he replied. Zuri didn't have any words left after I hissed in pain. He had his arm out and curled his hand up. It began to mold itself into an anchor hook. Zuri's arm dropped into a chain with the hooks in the sand. He stared the stranger in the eyes while letting out a war screech, slinging the chain and hook towards the stranger. He caught the hook before it connected with his face and examined it.

"Interesting. Which one of them gave you this unique

power?" Stranger said. Zuri didn't answer with words. His other arm transformed into a blade that was straight and curved like his hooks. Zuri thrust it towards the stranger's stomach. The stranger moved my body in front of the blade. Zuri pulled it back quickly while stepping to the left and right into the hook that pierced his neck.

"No. Noooooo!" I yelled.

The man dropped Zuri and spat at him like he was nothing. That didn't sit well with my soul. The same energy that built inside me when I saw Qala, was coming up with a vengeance. I place my hand on his chest and watched him fly back, letting me go in the process. I didn't worry about what happened. I crawled over to Zuri and rolled him over. He was gurgling some blue shit out his wound.

"Zuri," I cried and touched the hook. Zuri squealed and wheezed for me to stop. "Okay. Okay. Okay. Tell me what I need to do. Please, baby. What do I need to do?"

Zuri 's arms were in weapon form. He couldn't move his neck or talk much. I had to follow his eyes that were directing me to the water. "You want to go into the water?" I asked and didn't wait on an answer. I scooped my baby up, careful not to hurt him. The snarls of the other monsters were getting closer. I turned around and back peddled to the water. The man was recovering from my attack. It had to have done something more than I thought it did. He had a hole in his shirt that revealed his skin that was tortured. He looked down at it, surprised that he had been touched like that. If I knew how to conjure this Goddess on will, I would have hit his ass with something harder. He must've known that the power I demonstrated wasn't shit compared to what I could do.

"He is going to be mad at me for doing this, but I just can't help myself. You will be perfect," he mumbled and waved his hand to the side. The creatures that were about to attack us, bodies bent backward and fell out of his way. He walked toward me, which made me take a step back. My body froze at touching the water conscience.

"Luna..." my baby used all his energy to say that. I gaze down at him and saw his life slipping. Zuri was willing to go up against a mob full of creatures and a man that wanted to kill me, to save me. It was my turn to ignore this fear and save him. I closed my eyes and resumed my steps deeper into the water. I felt the water reaching my waist and released a small cry.

"You don't have to go. I can eliminate that fear for you. Come here. Let me show you," the man offered. I opened my eyes to see that he was still on the beach, afraid to touch the water. His eyes were glowing yellow like the sun. The mesmerizing light in them tried to pull me in. There was something wrong with that picture. A few minutes ago, he wanted to kill me. Now he was begging me to come to him differently. I wasn't falling for his luminosity. I made that clear by stepping back and stumbling over a rock.

"Oh," I sobbed as the water covered most of my body with my chin hitting the top of it. I got back to my feet, but Zuri's body slipped out of my arms and into the water. "Zuri! Zuri!" I called out looking for him. I squatted patting the ground with my head up to the sky. "Zuri! Please answer me! Please..." I started panicking. I didn't want to look down into the water, unprepared for what I was going to see. My heart was throbbing out of my chest with every second he didn't answer. I took my chances and stood to my feet to glance down into the darkness. I didn't see anything.

"Zuri," I whispered. I didn't plan on going back to shore, where the man was still waiting for me. He was smiling, thinking that it was my only option. It was a familiar touch that made that a true thought. I didn't have to wait for anything to register. I turned and ran back to shore. Sleek arms wrapped around my waist and pulled me back. I reached forward, needing something to hold on to. There was no use. I was dragged under and immediately started fighting.

"Luna," Zuri's voice was a soft melody to my ears. I stopped fighting and peeked over my shoulder. The arms were still in place, while my capturer moved to get in front of me. Zuri's face was of the little boy that rescued me from the mental institution and the danger of the beach. But his skin began to shed and change into the creature that invoked the fear of water in me. I remember the hesitation that Amanzi had when I asked him about my attacker. Revealing that it was Zuri would have made me call him a liar. I stared at the childlike boy with wide eyes and mouth. The water rushed, forcing me to blow it out along with the air I encased in it. I kicked my legs to reach the surface. Zuri held me still. I pointed to my mouth letting him know I needed air. Zuri shook his head and pressed his hand to my cheek.

"You have all the air you need, Luna. Relax and trust your element," Zuri instructed the same thing that Amanzi told me. I didn't know how to trust or allow the water to be my air. I felt myself choking and losing the battle once again. My body started jerking, after releasing the air I had left.

"Don't give in to the panic. Believe that the water is all that you need. Believe in it as it believes in you," I heard Zuri's voice in a distance. Even in the water, the tears rolled down my face. I surrendered to it more times than I could remember because of what I felt. I felt I was home and not some intruder that snuck in the back door. After the traumatic event, water continued to be my first love due to the influence of a man that held me in his heart. I hung onto that in the safety of my parents' home and the condo, yet we were still in a foreign place. The cool water brushed against my face as we glided through the ocean currents exploring life as I have always dreamed with the man that I dreamt of. What excited me the most was the way his lips moved against mine. They collided against each other like waves and then blended in with the rest of the ocean.

With the rest of the ocean, I thought. And that brought me way back to another vision that I kept a secret, even to myself. I was lying in bed after spending time with Egypt one evening. I took a quick wipe-off to get to meet up with him in my imagination. When I closed my eyes, he was on the other side waiting for me at the top of the waterfall in Guyana. I glanced down at my clothes that mimicked the grass skirt that he was wearing. My breasts were covered in a strapless seaweed top that was crusted in diamonds and a rare Tahitian pearl. Sol lifted his hand out and smiled at me.

"Let's go home," he asked me. I rushed over to him, stepping on the soft rocks that the water flowed through. I got to him and slipped my hand into his. He nodded his head towards the waterfall that hid the secrets to too many escapades. I gazed down the heavily misted stream that blocked the ending of it. I knew I was only bold enough to do this while he was standing next to me. Sol pulled me into his arms to kiss me and turned his body away from the waterfall.

"Do you trust me?" he only asked what he already knew.

"Yes Sol," I responded.

"Good," Sol said and took a step back with me clingy to him. The wind lifted my hair from my back, blending it with the water that encased us both. I leaned my head back and felt the water hitting my face. Sol's head dipped to my neck. He placed his tongue on my throat, swiping upward to my chin. He grabbed it with his teeth and pulled it down, forcing me to make eye contact with him. Sol's eyes were bright enough to show the reflection of my eyes that mimicked the Vantablack pearls I was wearing.

"You are so fucking beautiful," he whispered over the loud rush of water. I gave him that girly blush that awarded me a clear glimpse of this God's perfection. Sol had no flaw in his appearance. He was absolutely gorgeous. I was in my own heaven. I brushed my hands down his face enjoying the natural feel of him. The natural feel of the water going in and out of my nose and mouth. The natural way that the water clothed me in its element without any reservation. That was the time that I completely gave into the water.

"*Not death,*" Amanzi's words came bursting through. I

relaxed my body, not giving into the death, but to the water itself. I closed my eyes and inhaled the liquid as normal as if it was air, releasing it out of my nose. I did it once more before opening my eyes to a smiling Zuri.

"You did it! I knew you would," he said clutching me. I hugged him back, satisfied with making him proud of me.

"Thank you," I shocked myself and spoke. "I can talk underwater?"

Zuri pulled back and nodded his head. "Of course, you can. How else would you communicate with us?"

"Right," I replied and looked up to the surface. "How long do you think we will have to stay down here?"

Zuri frowned not understanding why I asked him that. "Forever."

That snatched my attention away from the top to him. "What do you mean?" Zuri was ready to explain before he cringed up in pain. "Zuri, what is wrong?"

"It is father," he winced in agony. The last time I saw Amanzi, he jumped into the water to address the trouble that he had sensed. I felt it too.

"Which way?" I asked him.

"His home, Luna. He is at home," he answered. I knew exactly where they was and closed my eyes to think of the place where my love took me. The water pushed out of my lungs for a split second and came back in. My eyes popped open to the cries of the water. I saw the mosogens and younglings on their knees. Amanzi grew in size, glowing in gold. His features were crumpled up in pain and anger. Silver dust drifted into a large cloud toward me. I reached my hand out and snatched it back feeling a pinch of what had Zuri hollering for help. Amanzi swung around to face his other children that were begging for mercy with their eyes.

"Amanzi!" I yelled and started swimming forward as fast as I could. The children saw me coming and breathed a sigh of allay.

Amanzi's visage didn't falter. The muscles in his back were bulky and tight. The tension that rolled off him made Zuri clutch my arm. He was in no condition to protect me and tried to do it, anyway. I unwrapped Zuri from my arm and motioned for him to stay put. Zuri shook his head, never seeing his father in this form of action before. I rubbed his arms up and down to soothe him. "It's okay," I whispered. Zuri indicated he understood what I needed to do and fell to the seabed on his knees.

I turned and approached Amanzi slow, still. His heavy breathing meant that he was on the verge of doing something that he was going to regret. Once I got close, I slid my hands up and down his back.

"You don't want to do this," I started.

"You don't know what I want to do," he countered in Sol's voice. It caught me by surprise and had me stammering a bit. I got back on track and leaned my head on his back.

"I know you wanted us to be a family. I know we can fix this," I replied.

"There is nothing to fix. They have disobeyed me time and time again. It is time for me to show them who I am," he raised his hand toward his children.

"You are not their ending. You are their father, their guide, and their Sol," I reminded him.

"I am their creator, and this doesn't concern you," he grilled. My head automatically lifted from his back. The gentleness of my hands fell from his body, leaving him to tense up again. The last time he told me that shit I was ready to slap the fuck out of him. How dare he offer me everything to tell me it didn't concern me? Who the fuck did he think he was? Who the fuck did he think he was talking to?

I took in a deep breath and settled my violent emotions that were ready to burst free. I simmered it down but had to let him know I was a bit different. I wasn't shivering at the sound of the water... fuck I was the water and he had me fucked up. I floated backward and rotated my neck with my eyes closed. My aura shifted the entire mood. Amanzi peeked over his shoulder before making another move and that was the smartest thing he did.

"You are wrong, Amanzi. Everything that is in this water or has a connection with it, is my concern. You were under the impression that you were the only one that decided the faith of my children. I have been gone for a minute and we all know that it wasn't by choice. What I have endured affected my children's behavior. But destroying them will be destroying you and you don't want that to happen. So put your hand down Sol, their Luna is here and ready to heal their broken hearts," I divulged. My voice rang through the water. Zuri came and stood by my side. The one that had the mark of a healer saw Zuri's mobility and tried to stand to her feet. Her legs were a bit shaky before she stood to her entire height. She stared at me over her father's shoulders. I opened my arms up to let her know it was okay for her to move forward. She stumbled on her journey to me and fell into my arms with a fresh pair of tears running down her face.

"It's okay, sweetheart. It's okay. Your Luna is here," I told her and looked at the others that were still on their knees. "Come, children."

They all started rising against their father's will. They crowded me and inhaled the glow that returned their light to them.

"Luna..." they all called out my name for attention and talked all at once. I stood there and enjoyed their voices. Amanzi finally dropped his arm. He started walking away from the group with his feelings of failing us somehow on display.

"Amanzi," I called out his name. He stopped and turned to me. I patted the back of the healer. I nodded my head at her and the other children before making my way to him. The brightness of his tattoos was gleaming underwater. I placed my palm in the middle of the triangle and heard him sigh. He covered my hand with his, pressing it harder on his chest.

"You are so," was all I could get out. Amanzi sealed my lips shut with a kiss. I felt the passion, love, and all the other emotions that he had been feeling. The one that stuck out the most was sorrow. He hated it had to get to this point to get me to come home. My welcoming back should have been a joyous occasion. But growing up with my family, sometimes, it takes tragedies to bring families back together. It may have not been convivial that he had plotted, but it reminded me to never leave them astray again. And on everything I loved, I wasn't going to tolerate anyone taking me from them again. Because at this point, anyone could get it behind mine.

"THAT BITCH! THAT FUCKING BITCH! SHE KNEW WHAT SHE was doing. She had this shit planned the entire time," I yelled and tossed the table around, barely missing Dr. Uganji's recovering body. After leaving the alley with Ali, I was on my mission looking for the energy that attracted my creatures. I followed the tracks that led me to someone that looked as fragile as glass during an earthquake. I didn't ignore her, though. There had to be something about this woman, and it was. The light... the energy that I was searching this earth for was placed into this one being. On top of all that shit, she made her the mate of her son. That spoil bitch.

"Redecorating, I see," Nesbate walked his dumb ass in and stated. I alerted Dr. Uganji to move everything to The Perfecto Garcia Brothers Cigar company that was abandoned in Tampa off N. 16. The rustic brick building was standing strong and was the best spot to set up my permanent location. The multiple windows of the building were covered up by the shutters. The first floor was an open space. The basement was bigger with walls that set up everything we had to do in sections. In the last room of the hall lies a fridge coffin. I normally didn't move it, but I knew I was going to want her closer once I got my hand on Adaliya. Dr.

Uganj must have known that I found something because he didn't ask any questions and proceeded to transport all the rest of the creatures and the equipment there. That was how Nesbate ended up with the creatures to go after Adaliya.

"Now is not the fucking time. Tell me you got her," I demanded. I was surprised at the power she showed me. I didn't warn Nesbate about it. I told him that Amanzi's mate was up for taking. Him being who he was, jumped at the opportunity to get back at Mother Nature.

"No, I didn't. She is a feisty little thing," he stated and shook his head. "But you knew that already."

"I just found this shit out. She wrapped me in fucking water and threw me out of the window," I revealed.

"Yeah, well she hit me with a blast that I knew if she was at her full potential would have damaged me. I haven't encountered anyone like that before. I mean, I am God and look at myself as being superior to any. To think that someone could hurt me or kill me isn't sitting well with me. That had me thinking... of your plan of action. You wanted to get rid of me?" he asked.

"I thought you were strong enough to grab her. That was the only reason I sent you after her, God," I sighed and gestured to the workers to clean up the mess I made. "Where is she?"

"She has gone home," Nesbate answered. He was too busy looking at my equipment to recognize my facial expression.

"What do you mean she has gone home? She went back to her condo?" I conjecture.

"No," he said slowly and picked up one of my test tubes that held some of my elixir that created my creatures. "She and that little runt went into the water. I waited for her to return but she didn't."

"Fuck!" I groaned. "She is going to destroy him," I mumbled.

"She can be a destroyer of this entire world. Just imagined what would happen if she channeled all that power in the center of the world," he spoke nonchalantly.

"That is why she shouldn't be in the water with him," I growled.

"You didn't tell me that. You only told me she was up for taking. I would have been better prepared for an encounter with the Goddess of water, another adversary that you will have to beat to get to her. And I'm sorry to tell you that these kitchen-made creatures won't be enough to help you with that goal," Nesbate commented and tossed my shit to the side. He walked to the entry of the room and stopped at the door. "Good luck," he stated and walked out. Nesbate didn't mean that shit. I knew he had something else under his sleeve and was going to wait for me to fail to step in and try whatever was going on in his head.

"Set up quickly. We will have to be ready whenever everything comes to a head. I will alert Ali on what I need him to do," I instructed Dr. Ugnaji as I made my way down the hall. To be so close but so far away from getting what I wanted was becoming an agitation that was going to lead to many deaths. The sad part about all this was she knew and didn't give a fuck when I told her it was my mate that she killed. The bitch laughed at me. She laughed, knowing that I was going to destroy the world and dared me to do so. I went into the room and strolled to the silver and glass fridge casket. Her beauty was still intact, lying there in a white baby doll dress with a scoop neck. The body that I loved the most was covered in ice. Many times, I thought her lips shivered to be touched by mine. I knew that missing her this much was making me see shit. I didn't care. Believing what I was seeing versus believing that it will never come true was my best option. I rested my hand on the glass frame and sighed.

"Sooner than later my love. I promise," I promised her. It was a promise that I planned on keeping.

I WANTED HER SO FUCKING BAD RIGHT NOW. THE WAY SHE introduced herself and stood up for the children had me loving on her even more. I was impressed by her demeanor and the way she allowed them to talk to her. She sat in the middle of the circle and listened to everything that everyone had to say. She congratulated them all for their markings and their jobs. They all soaked that shit in, craving the love of their Luna. Some emotions were being displayed in my mosogens that I have never seen before. I guessed that was what Mother was trying to tell me. In a sense, I became like her trying not to be her. I should've known what the look in Lenmon's eyes meant. I saw and have been through those emotions ten times over. I hated they had to hide that from me, thinking that I was going to destroy what they loved. Somewhere down the line, I fucked up. I didn't have the time to tell them the difference between Mother and me. I was going to show them all that I was understanding of any other self-made purpose that they accumulated while being born. It was a mission that I was going to accomplish more with Luna by my side. She truly brought out the best and settled the worst in me. I appreciated her more than she would ever know.

"Look at her," I mumbled to myself. She wasn't in her natural state, but she was using her energy to breathe and speak underwater. Her hair flowed behind her like a silk wrap that blows in the wind. Some of the younglins played in it, laughing and enjoying themselves. She rubbed her temple and looked out into the water for something. I moved to ask if there was anything that she needed, but her attention got snatched by another healer.

My protective diamond gravitated toward her making sure that she didn't get overwhelmed with the attention that she was giving. Deanon of Cyann's section reached out aggressively to hug her. Femi stepped up and held his hand out for Deanon to come correct. Adaliya waved Femi off and beaconed Deanon to come as he was. Deanon heeded the warning of his brother. He approached her with tears in his eyes ready to break. Adaliya, ever so gently, granted him to do that by whispering to him. None of them didn't understand the English language that she was speaking. It didn't matter to them. They were happy with her being in their presence.

"Luna, I have this for you," Zuri glided through the circle. He held one of the women's loincloths in his hand. "I thought you would be more comfortable in this. If you want, I could show you how to put it on."

Adaliya smiled and stood to her feet. The others did the same to get her reaction to their gift to her. Adaliya reached out and touched the jewels that her seaweed loincloth was dipped in gold and encrusted in jewels of various colors of blues and blacks.

"I think you will need help putting this on, but we can help her Zuri. Thank you so much for bringing it to her," Trinity told him.

"But I can help. I'm always supposed to help," Zuri complained.

"It's okay Zuri. You can help me with something else," Adaliya assured him. Zuri nodded his head and passed her clothing to Trinity. Trinity motioned for Luna to follow her to the

Port Royal section. The other females trailed behind the two hoping that they also can lend a helping hand.

"I'm going to hunt for food. Do you think she is capable of eating our food? Do you think we should ask Lenmon to send her something?" Valin spoke.

I moved to the group and shook my head. "I don't think that she would enjoy the food that we have just yet," I responded and sighed. "I didn't know how much you guys needed her. And for that, I apologize."

Dafari placed his hand over his chest, accepting my apology. "Thank you for her Father. She is the best thing that we could have asked for."

"She truly is. I'm happy that she showed up when she did," Femi added with his eyes on me.

"I hope you aren't looking for an apology for my behavior," I countered his statement.

Femi looked over at Dafari who peeked at Valin. Valin brought his attention to me to address what they all were thinking. "We know it seem as if it was the only option because we were warned many times about what was going on. We were all prepared for it. Yet, laying eyes on Luna changed that. We didn't want to die. We wanted to live out the purposes that were beyond the ones that you gave us. We wanted to know what it was like to live in this world with her."

"It's amazing Father. Her energy brings out the best in us," Dafari concluded. I knew they were going to be affected by her presence. She did that for the people that were around her. They all tried to make sense of it, but their opinions were wrong. They were all wrong about who she was, and it was going to shock them when the reintroductions will be made.

"I am happy that she does that for all of you. She does the same thing for me," I admitted.

"Wow! You are so beautiful," one of the younglings

expressed. My head swiveled in that direction to the now crowded area.

"Oh, my Father," Dafari's shaky voice proclaimed as he stumbled forward. Valin didn't say anything. His emotions were worn on his face. Femi rested his hand on my shoulder before moving to the crowd. We have seen so much shit these past sunsets. There were deaths and toxic toxins that were being released by the blobs in this water. All the transporting and being displaced from their homes to another place that they weren't familiar with was stressful itself.

To have her here with us, in the element that some of them only knew was more than special. The water moved with Adaliya as she made her way back to the center of the circle. The gold skirt stopped mid-thigh where her tattoo was. The top fitted like one of her bikini swimsuits. It barely covered her full breast with jewels hanging from the thread. I envied how they brushed against her stomach. I envied the way the water caressed her body. Trinity topped it off with a blueish barrette that would bring out the true color of her eyes. The woman looked regale in the sexiest way. I felt myself rising to the occasion, creating that task that she was talking about earlier. I didn't want to be rude and pull her from the children, but I needed her in the worse way. I exhaled deeply with my eyes closed. When I opened them, Adaliya was staring at me with that same look in her eyes. She wanted me just as bad as I wanted her. The thrill of that warmed the water. I held my hand out for her to continue her movement toward me. Adaliya complied and grabbed it. She pressed her body to me, giving me the attention that I always craved from her. Adaliya placed her other hand on my face and brushed her thumb over my lips.

"Are you ready to show me our home?" she asked me.

I nodded my head and kissed her exposed neck. She moaned out my name softly, making it harder to hide my desire for her. I peered at my smiling children. They were amazed at the love that was being displayed in front of them.

"We will get settled to rest, now that our Luna is home. Go. Show her the inside of her home," Trinity announced.

"Okay," I answered with Adaliya at my side.

"Sleep well, Luna," Femi told her.

"I will. You all, too," Adaliya responded. They all spoke back and went to their different sections. We floated to the guarded bridge that led us to the gate of Atlantis. Kamau and Amber were the ones that guarded this gate. Even when we were celebrating Luna's return, they didn't falter their positions. They were standing up with their weapons out and ready for anything. Adaliya seemed confused about it at first. She knew they wanted to meet her like the others. It was the passion of their purpose to want to keep her safe that drove them to stay put. Adaliya heard how much they loved her but didn't feel or see it yet. What they were showing her was a piece of what they felt.

Amber was already on the brink of tears when we approached. Kamau tried to keep his composure by squeezing his lips together. I stepped aside to place Adaliya in front of the two. She dropped my hand and placed both of hers on Kamau and Amber's chest. The hard exterior broke as they released a deep sigh.

"It's okay," Adaliya murmured to them. Amber and Kamau fell to their knees, honoring her in their own way. The tears that Amber was holding hostage, came flowing free with the sound of her voice. Kamau grabbed his sister's hand to rejoice with her at this moment. I shifted forward and tapped them on their shoulder.

"Go and spend time with the others. We will be fine tonight," I instructed. They both nodded their agreement and got to their feet. Amber made eye contact with Adaliya for the first time and was ready to fall on her knees again. Adaliya noticed that and wrapped Amber in her arms. Amber's body shivered with emotions.

"I love you, Luna," she said proudly.

"And, I love you back," Adaliya told her without hesitation. Kamau took his sister's elbow and guided her to their sections. I pushed the gates opened and motioned for Adaliya to go in first. From the sound of her gasp, I knew that this place was everything that she dreamt of.

There were some pretty flowers that didn't belong underwater, blooming like it was home to them. Wildflowers, roses, lilies, and carnations surrounded the castle. What made it more special was the dragonflies that sat on them. They lit up the paths to the entrance. The colorful sand was decorated in circles and different sections of the territory. Harmful fishes were swimming in the area, giving it more of a décor. I knew she had questions when she looked over at the gate and saw the children preparing themselves for bed.

"Why can't they be inside of the gate? There is so much room around the castle for their set up camp or they can just come inside. I don't want them to feel like we are above them," she insisted.

"Not yet," I told her and pointed to the waterfall that was over her new home. The water moved on the roof down, creating a curtain as a front door to the castle. I could feel her mind telling her to reject what she was seeing. If it was anyone else's reality, it would have been easy to deny the sight. She made her way to it and brush her hands through the warmer water. She wanted to know how this was happening but shook her head and answer her doubts.

"Anything is possible."

Adaliya took a deep breath and stepped into the home, almost falling on the floor. I followed behind her, prepared for the dry change of the atmosphere.

I watched her as she consumed everything all at once. The

main attraction was the cerulean blue and vantablack staircase that broke off into multiple directions and floors. The metallic gold stairs added the royalty effect to it. It reached the top, which led to the sight of a crystal glass chandelier. The walls were stained with those same colors with specks of white in them. It was marbleized in a way that reflected against the black floor and the chandelier. It wasn't bright as the outside, but it had just the right amount of light to see the beauty of it. Adaliya's beaming face showed how satisfied she was.

"But... where did the water go?"

"This place was meant for you. They knew you needed air of some sort to survive your extended stay down here. We were preparing for you," I stated.

"For how long, though," she asked while placing her hand on the railing. Adaliya jumped back at the shift that the stairs were making. It moved around to circle the center of the staircase that opened into a secret room. I took her hips in my hands and moved her in that direction.

"Since the beginning of the world," I answered her. Adaliya slowly stepped into the room that was filled with everything that has been lost at sea. Treasure, letters, clothes, and other old artifacts that divers and scientists had been searching for. I knew that wouldn't draw her attention as much as the picture window that was made up of water. It had a view of everything that was underwater. She walked over to it and gave into her emotions.

"This is it. This is what I have always wanted for myself. I could never put it in words because I thought it was a fairytale. I thought what I wanted was beyond the expectations of a regular woman. When all along... I was right. I was right to dream big and not to give up on a love that I have carried with me for so long," she stopped talking and stared.

I made my way behind her and inhaled her scent which drove me crazy. "Do you like it?" I wanted to know.

Adaliya turned slowly around to face me. "I love it. I love

everything about this place. I love the mosogens. I love the younglings. I love Zuri and I... I love you," she said the words that broke me completely. I grabbed her hair and held her still for the attack on her lips. Adaliya held on tight to me, pressing her body to mine. The kiss was demanding and passionate. I squatted and cuffed her legs. Adaliya latched onto my tongue while rotating her hips on the finger that slipped inside her. We both had been anticipating this moment for a long time. I didn't plan on disappointing her and from the wetness of her pussy, neither did she. Her shit was so tight and hot. Imagining my dick being squeezed by her walls had me drooling in her mouth. Adaliya pulled back with all the instructions but made her request still.

"Take me, Amanzi."

Like she had to ask.

I walked us to the opposite wall and placed her body against it. I lifted her above my head with her legs resting on my shoulders. The perfect view and position to take what she was offering vocally. I detached the skirt from her hip and dropped it to the floor. Adaliya stared down at me while undoing the top. Those heavenly breasts fell free of their confinement. Adaliya licked her lips and cupped those bitches, teasing me as she licked her lips. She was daring me to make her lose control. I smirked and proceeded with approaching my newfound obsession. My tongue looped around her precious pearl and tugged.

"Ohh. Oh my god. Amanzi, wait," her hands dropped to my head. She tried to push me away, but I was enjoying the taste of her too much. My arms were wrapped around her thighs and my hands were on her waist. She was locked in this position until I was done with her. Those puny pushes and no's weren't getting her anywhere. I delved deeper into her abyss making her moan with every swipe and tug from my tug. I gave her a slight break but began to kiss her moist lips like a man in love.

"Amanzi," she sang my name in a melody she created herself.

She was close. So fucking close...

I took her hands from my head and placed them both on the wall. Adaliya's head went back, relinquishing herself to me in her final trembles and moans. The sweetest liquid embraced my taste buds. Adaliya's cries of ecstasy spawned another orgasm that almost rocked her off my shoulders.

"Please stop. Please," she whined. I listened that time and placed her on her feet, just so that she could squat in front of me

"What are you doing?" It was my turn to be perplexed.

"Completing one of my many tasks," the vixen kneeling before me said. I was still unsure about her motives until she began to remove my loincloth from my waist. She took my enlarged member and slightly bit the tip. My body jerked back, yet she held me in her hand. Adaliya's head dipped underneath. She licked the underside of my dick with her plush tongue and then came up to insert me into her mouth. I gasped and fell forward with my hands on the wall. Adaliya tested my length by going deeper and deeper with every suction. My hips moved forward on their own accord. She welcomed my thrust by relaxing her throat.

I groaned how much I loved what she was doing in a language that she wasn't familiar with. I went to explain what I was saying when I looked down at her. Adaliya's eyes were the color of the rarest and most dangerous jewel in the water. She pulled me out of her mouth and stuck her tongue out to lick upward against my head.

"मम प्रीतिः मम राजा," she responded in one of the oldest languages in the world.

My pleasure my king. My goddess graced me with her presence in the sultriest way. She growled and snatched my ass down to the floor. The goddess straddled my hips. Her hot pussy hovered over my length, teasing the entrance of what I knew to be home. I didn't move. Her daring eyes prohibited me to do so. She was on the tip of her toes. Adaliya dragged her hand down from my chest to the base of my dick. She stroked it twice before inserting the tip into her room of petals. Adaliya's hiss mixed with my torturing groan, forced my eyes shut. Fuck, she didn't stop. Her ass bounced up and down and rotated her hips, all while her hands were on her knees. She stopped and rocked me back and forth. The juices from her pussy ran down the remaining length that have not yet experienced the contraction of her walls. That shit wasn't fair. I took the back of her thighs and pulled her forward. My entire length was embedded into her tunnel.

"Fuck," I sighed. Adaliya's eyes closed as she got used to the invasion. It didn't take her long. Adaliya grabbed my face and pressed her lips to mine. I pushed up, and she pressed down. The throbbing vein in my dick throbbed harder against the pulse in her walls.

"Mmmm," she moaned biting on her lips. "एतावत् उत्तमं भवति सोल."

"Yes, it does my love. It feels so fucking good," I confirmed what she said. Adaliya's arms went around my neck, and she got wilder.

"मम सोल् न निवारयतु। कृपया न स्थगित करें!" she yelled.

"I will never stop, my Luna. Give it to me," I matched her energy. Adaliya shuddered and screamed as her orgasm took over her body. My shit came from the bottom of my spine up to my dick, releasing my essence inside her empty womb. The sound waves of our lovemaking stopped the water flow. The fishes became immobile and stood still. The world stood still and welcomed back their Goddess of the water.

Adaliya

His love. His protectiveness. His patience. His strength. His soul.

Those traits were what brought me to realize how much I was needed down here. I approached Amanzi intending to ridicule him about how he had been raising our children. I hated that they only knew one way to live when there were many things that all of them could do. I was ready to teach that to them. I wanted to show them the water in a different light. One without all these rules and regulations. They were created to look after the water when it was my and Amanzi's purpose. I dare not put that solely on the children to take care of. Amanzi has done well, but a house is a place where a woman transforms it into a home. Right now, they were renters, still paying mortgages and shit with their lives. I wasn't having that. The intruders had to go, and it was time for me to get to work.

We were resting on old royalty blankets that were stitched between paintings and treasures. I rose from the comfort of Amanzi's chest. His hair was a bit longer than usual, but it was how I liked it. I loved him in his element. The freshness of his style would have brought me to my knees at any time. He could have blessed me over and over with his engorged member. Damn, I have never felt so full in my life. Everything about him filled the empty voids that lived freely in my mind and heart. There was nothing more special about a man that took interest in everything that you loved, and the water was one of them. I kissed his tattooed chest with my soft lips. Amanzi didn't move at all. He slept heavily after the craziness that Qala had put him through. That pissed me off more than anything. *As a matter of fact,...*I thought.

My gaze carried to the water-made window. I felt the difference in it as soon I touched it. The chemicals in it were making my head hurt. I grabbed my clothes and placed them back on while approaching the window. I tripped over a gold chalice that had rolled out of the many piles of golden coins in the room. I picked it up and got a glimpse of myself. My skin was a shimmery gold. I had deep wavy brown hair. I brought the chalice close to my face to look at the reflection in my eyes. They were dark. Darker than the part of the ocean that no one talked about. In this state, I remembered everything. The encounters that I had with

Amanzi and my expectations with the water were front and center memories after I gave into her energy. She was really a part of me, and I was willing to embrace her and the power she had over the water. I placed the chalice on the floor and stuck my hand out of the window to feel the cooler temperature of the water. It was hard and made my skin itch.

"Rrr," I snarled and jumped out of the window and into the water. I swam away from the home where we were safe from all the toxins. It was one of the decisions I agreed to. I didn't need my children getting into any of this mess.

"Luna, where are you going?" Zuri's voice followed me. I stopped and gazed back at the little warrior of mine. I waved him forward to join me. I knew he wasn't going to be that far behind me. He had never let me down, and I understood why now.

"Mother Nature created you to protect me from this?" I nodded to the fog that we were approaching.

"No. She created me to protect you while Father helped his brothers. He was supposed to bring you to the water a long time ago. But, he kept getting caught up. So, I took it upon myself to speed up his exaggerating steps," Zuri answered me.

"You don't think that your actions were a little harsh," I replied.

Zuri shook his head. "I don't. Once you realized where you were you would have come back to us as the Luna that stood before Sol," he stopped and looked ahead of us. "Are you going to do something about this now? It is starting to spread."

"That's what I came out here to do," I admitted. I got to the area where the water was thick with that gooey shit. It didn't look anything like the water of Atlantis. This water was grey and cloudy. I kept my hands bald into fists to my sides, separating the contaminated liquid from the water with. It stirred before making a funnel towards me. I threw my hands up and watched the toxins travel up to the surface. The ocean released a loud burb, putting that bad shit in the air.

Zuri inhaled a deep breath and sighed. "This is so much better," he spoke happily.

It was, but it was far from over. There were parts of the water where those creatures multiplied and killed. It was going to take more than this small act of cleansing to get the water back to how it should be.

"It is. Come. We have more work to do," I turn to move in the other direction and came face to face with something. I didn't know if it was a man or a mixture of one and the creatures that were floating up on the side of him. His eyes were purple, an imitation of what Amanzi and Zuri's were. To produce a copy of something that she made, that told a lot about his creator. He needed more work done, though. This thing in front of me looked like he had seen better days. I knew being underwater supposed to have you wet. But this fool looked like he was out of the water, drenched. His hair was stuck to his face. Water was rolling down his chest and dripping down below. He was just a sad sight. I snarled at his impudence to approach me.

"You have no place here," I started.

"That's what your lover told me. I proceeded to show him why this place," he emphasized with his hands out. "Is the right place for me and he ran off. Pity that he didn't get the help that was needed to win this battle. Instead, he came back with you. Although you display energy that I nor my Gocks can't ignore. I'm not understanding why he would allow you to travel alone in these parts, knowing that I am here." The thing patted his pet pile of shit.

I sighed with frustration. I was pretty sure that he had a very long conversation with Amanzi about why he was here. Me...I didn't give a fuck. I wanted him and his infestation gone. To make that perfectly clear, I swiped my hand downward, killing three of those things that were at his side.

He started laughing. The loud outburst was annoying and

caused another minor attack to three others. The thing started clapping his hands.

"He didn't tell you. You can't kill me or my creatures. They will grow back, twice the size with twice the hunger. We are here to stay," he added.

"You should have let me finish. It would have given you the time you needed to vacate the premises. Your father created you to withstand the attacks of Mother Nature's children," I stated. His laughing fell into an uncertain smirk once his pets kept dropping down to the surface.

It was my turn to laugh, but I allowed Zuri to do it for me. His spike teeth were gleaming like diamonds. The thing screamed at me and sent two more of his critters at me. One came straight at me with its mouth open. I grabbed the critter by his jaws and tore him in half. The other tried to attack me from behind. I turned and held my hand up, bringing up an invisible wall. It ran into the wall and slid down to join the other dead ones.

"This is not right. You can't do this," he was now pissed and wanted answers.

My body expanded with a golden glow. My head went from side to side as my hair grew to my feet. The jewels that were on my skirt, fell and circled themselves on my chest with the vantablack stone in the center. My transformation was swift. I didn't want him to wait for death any longer than he did.

"I am the Goddess of the water. I am here to touch you. I am here to hurt you. I am here to kill you," I stated with my head to the side. I smiled showing him how unhuman I really was with teeth like my children.

"Run," I growled. He didn't need any further instructions. He teleported ten feet away from me. I inhaled and blew icicles out of my mouth. His creatures were too dumb to understand the danger that they were in. They tried to come at me to drain my energy but got stabbed by the icicles that were meant for the coward behind them.

"Uggghh!" he screamed for the others to follow him. I floated forward, like a silent killer. Zuri was at my side moving with me. His arm was his weapon of choice, preparing himself to attack. I reached out and placed my finger on the mark behind his ear. Zuri body's shuddered still. His radiance was brighter and mimicked mine. I gave him a quick wink before attacking the rest of his creatures. Zuri smiled and threw his arm out to release his chain and hook. To his surprise, several of chains and hooks shot from his limb. They wrapped around the offensive mess and squeezed the life out of them. Zuri swung it around and smack them into the creatures that were near me. I swam faster to get to their leader. He zigzagged his way from my attacks, placing his pets in my line of fire. They got punched, jabbed, and tossed behind me to deal with my little warrior, who was tearing shit up. As I got closer to the coward that taunted my king, he teleported in and out of the ocean. I was on his ass until he jumped out of the water and onto Davis beach. The sun was rising, which made it empty. I knew in a few more hours, it was going to be pack with people. Evidently, Qala didn't care. He wanted this interaction with me no matter what it was going to cost him. The half-human-beast monsters were waiting with their father in the center. I detected someone else near, but hopefully, he stayed in his lane. I would hate for Egypt to lose her father over some bullshit.

The water recognized the ambush and produced steps for me. Zuri grabbed my hand and floated to the surface as I climbed out of it. My element didn't drip from my body. It stayed in place, hardening into body armor. Zuri's body became human and had more abilities. They didn't understand how much of a front we were. Qala was too sure of himself when he stepped forward to address me.

"Fighting me will be foolish. If you give me what I want, I will allow the boy to live," his suggestion was more of a threat that I took personally.

"Like I told the one that you birth with an imagination of a four-year-old, I am here to kill you. Not fight," I made clear.

"You and what army?" The bastard countered.

"That's your problem. Thinking that she was going to be alone," Landon appeared with Egypt. Skye fell from the clouds heavy and hard. Lenmon and some piyas that weren't injured were running towards us on the beach. The awe look I received, made them stumble. They wanted to fall to their knees and worship me like the others did, but I shook my head. We had all the time in the world to do that after we eliminate the threat.

"Even without them," I answered him anyway and took the vantablack diamond from my chest. I swung it done, generating the weapon of the water. The black scythe had the handle of ice, and the blade was black. I stomped it into the water where I stood. The water ripples, alarming my family that it was time for battle. "My king has me. Ten toes down," I replied. The small wave moved forward and snatched the wolfmen, starting the brawl off. Landon and Egypt began to attack them from behind half-shifted into the retrospective animals. Skye was killing them with a fire that was almost too hot for me to touch. I walked past the bodies that were being dragged into the deeper part of the sea and came upon my first of many victims. I was going to hold it down until the arrival of my true family.

Egypt

"THAT'S what happen between my mother and Qala. She told me that Nesbate was upset that she didn't want to birth any of his kids. She wanted you to meet him for yourself, though," Landon exposed the truth to me. I tried not to show any emotions to what

I have heard until Landon give me the okay. My lips were trembling to stay shut.

Landon moved his hand forward for me to speak. "How the fuck he thought that shit was okay, though? He dead ass wrong for that. I don't condone your mother's action because Nesbate's mate didn't have anything to do with that."

"She knew everything," Landon fussed with his hands. "It took everything in me to hold my composure."

I frowned, thinking that he was going to go the other way. "For real. I wouldn't think that you would have agreed with her decision."

"It is what it is. They both knew what they were doing and got what they deserved. If I have to fight that nigga every day because of it, so be it," Landon growled. I truly believe that the conversation they had made them closer. All Landon and Amanzi ever wanted to know was what they were fighting for. Mother Nature did good reaching out to Landon first. She was going to need Skye and Landon to explain this to Amanzi. He was going to take this very well. I left that alone and jumped on the real reason he explained this to me.

"So...my dad. He is mad at your Moher because she didn't want him?"

Landon scuffed and shook his head. "It goes deeper than that. Nesbate feels that since he's a God, the world has to bow down to him including my mother. He thought her given name was a hint on what she was supposed to do with him only."

"What?" I asked and Landon opened his mind to me. I replayed Mother's conversation with Landon and got disgusted all over.

"That sick bitch!"

"I fucking know. And with that being said, I don't want you meeting up with him alone," Landon pointed out.

"Wait, Landon," I held my hand up. Landon jumped in my

face immediately. His hand when around my neck, squeezing it with the right pressure to shut up and listen.

"The only way for you to see him is if I go with you or you don't go at all. That is that! That are your only two options! Disagree with that and I will make it to where you never see him again," Landon's sabretooth made it clear the second time, which pissed him off. He tugged my neck closer and pulled it up to his ear. I was on my toes with my hands on his thick ass arms. "What will it be?" he whispered. His hot breath touched that spot on my ear that made my juices flow. I groaned and snaked my tongue in his ear. Landon's hold loosened to drop to my legs. He picked me up and placed me on the table. He fumbled with his jeans as I raised my dress to my waist.

"I'm not playing with you, Egypt. After this, we are going to lie down and you are going to let me hold you, wake up, and fuck you again. No sleeping in the other bedroom and shit," Landon added. I nodded my head, agreeing to everything that was said. I smelled and craved his pre-liquid essences. I laid back and spread my legs for easy entrance. Landon licked his lips now distracted from his original plan. I closed my eyes expecting his thick tongue to lay flat on my clit.

The hair on the back of my neck stood up. Landon's head turned to the side towards the window in our kitchen. He looked down at me and grabbed my outreached hand.

"It feels like a lot of them. Where are they going?" I asked Landon.

"I don't know," he replied and teleported us to Davis beach. "What the fuck?" Landon mumbled as Qala's creations were spread out growling at the lovely being that stood on the water. I loved the way the water coated her body and blew in the wind. Adaliya was gorgeous. The power in her was radiant and on the verge of exploding. Qala asked her about the army she had to go up against her. Landon stepped forward to enlighten him about what she did have. "That's your problem. Thinking that she was going to be alone."

Qala made eye contact with him and smirked. The piyas were running toward the beach. There was a slight pause in their steps when their eyes landed on Adaliya. She shook her head while her eyes remained on Qala and threat. Skye landed from the clouds in a different mood altogether. He searched the crowd looking for someone else in particular. His dragon scales covered his throat and half of his face. Skye looked feral.

"Skye," I whispered. His eyes moved in my direction while the rest of his body stayed still. They were completely white with a small black dot in them. Whatever happened between the time we left Mother Nature's home and now, it had to be bad.

"Even without them, my king has me. Ten toes down," Adaliya spat at Qala. The water that she was standing on, reached out and snatched some of Qala's creatures and dragged them in the water. Landon roared and jumped into the crowd full of half-shifted mutants. I teleported to the back of the group to attack the ones that were still coming. I dodged one swinging arm, spun from a mouth wide open, and ran into a creature that was shifted into a bear. He opened his mouth to roar at me. I stuck my hand in his mouth and grab the bottom of it. I ripped it off and stuffed it back in his throat with a kick to his chest. He dropped to his knees. His buddy behind me threw a punch at me. I sidestepped that, forcing him to the one on his knees. The creature's hand got stuck in his friend's head. I grew my claws and chopped his arm off from the elbow and uppercut his head off.

I dropped to the ground, hearing Skye screech. That meant he was ready to release his fire. Landon rolled next to me and threw his arm over my body. The hot flames went above our bodies and scorched Qala's creation to death. Shaking bodies dropped on us. Landon pushed them away and got to his feet while helping me on mine.

"Look out!" Landon pushed me out of the way to take on another big ass creature.

"How many people did they kidnap for this?" I shouted as more creatures began to filter out the beach.

"I don't know, but we gotta get them off the beach before the humans come through," Landon explained. I turned to see how Adaliya was doing. She was swinging her scythe around like she was cutting weeds. Heads were being tossed around like a fucking soccer ball. Qala and what I assumed was the creature he placed in the water to terrorize Amanzi was staring at Adaliya. Qala nodded his head for him to flank Adaliya with a blade in his hand. Knowing what Qala did me, I knew that there was something on that blade. He was doing too much to kill Adaliya. Landon was shocked that he was at Adaliya's condo.

"That is too personal. He would have sent someone else to take care of Adaliya. He has to have a motive behind this," he stated.

I took that all into consideration with the other mess we found out about him to analyze his behavior right now. He looked just as manic as Skye. "Landon," I called and pointed to Qala. He acknowledged what he was seeing and made his way to him. I teleported near Adaliya to help her with the things that she was fighting. It wasn't that she needed it. The tail of her water outfit batted creatures deeper into the oncoming wave that was rushing towards us and blocking the sun from the beach.

"We have to make sure the humans don't come to the beach" Landon hollered.

"We won't need to," I replied. The alarms started ringing around the beach to alert them that the beach was about to get hit by a big ass wave. Landon turned and saw what had me stunned. I got a closer look at this tsunami of a wave and realized it wasn't only water rushing this way. The wave was in the shape of mosogens. They were running to the beach with Amanzi in the center with his sword above his head.

"This nigga about to drown us all," Landon commented.

"Not you," Adaliya answered. She twirled her scythe with the blade of it stopping at Qala's apprentice's neck. Qala moved into attack Adaliya from the side. Landon got between them and snarled.

"You would be a bitch to attack her while she wasn't looking," Landon spat.

"Get the fuck out of my way," Qala growled as he started shifting into Landon's primary animal.

"How is that possible?" Skye finally spoke.

"We will talk about this later," Landon said and charged at Qala. Qala grabbed Landon's arm and swung his ass to the end of the group of things that started jumping on him. Skye released his wing. He flew towards Qala. Qala fell to his back and kicked Skye in the stomach. Skye tumble weave rolled near the water. Adaliya hit the creature she held captive with the butt of her scythe and addressed an oncoming Qala. The wave hovered over us ready to make landfall. Before the water hit the ground, it fell into pieces as the mosogens landed on two feet to join the fight. Amanzi dropped behind Qala, hitting him with an ice fist. Qala slid across the beach. He flipped over his head back on his feet. Amanzi's body became solid while standing in front of Adaliya. She smiled and rested her forehead on the center of his back. Amanzi's eyes closed and dropped his head back. He told her something in his shared language with his mosogens. I didn't know what she told him, but that fool's eyes opened back hard and unsettling. He charged back at Qala with everything backing him. Four of his mosogens surrounded Adaliya, vowing her protection.

"They can't help you," the thing hissed at Adaliya. Adaliya grunted and placed her weapon in front of her. It materialized back into her.

"That's what you think," Adaliya countered. The mosogen in front of her blocked the swinging knife with his machete. Adaliya stepped forward and punched him in the middle of his forehead.

He tried to hit her again. A shield was moved in front of her. Adaliya reached around the shield connecting a hook to his face. He spun around the first to mosogens and tried to get to her at a different angle. The mosogens with the khopesh appeared in front of him and caught his fist as Adaliya spun with an elbow to his throat The woman mosogens wrapped a water whip around his body. Adaliya took one of the jewels from her clothes and jerked it. She grabbed him by the back of the neck. Adaliya placed the blade at his throat.

"This is for all my children that you murdered," she retorted and slid the blade through the layers of his wrinkled skin. He gurgled for help, but there was no one around to save him. His father was literally getting jumped by the sons of Mother Nature. Landon told me it was the only way for them to beat him.

"And while they are occupied," a voice spoke up. I swirled into a punch that dropped me to the ground. I pressed my hand to my ringing ears and tried to see through my blurry vision. *This nigga really hit me. Our first encounter and he swung on me*, I thought.

The four mosogens ran at him, weapons ready to attack. His eyes flashed, bringing the sun back out to shine on the beach. The water mosogens began to shrivel up and deteriorate into puddles. Zuri rolled in front of her and squatted. His mug was nasty. My father stopped and shook his head. "We have been through this already, boy."

"You will not harm my mother," Zuri promised.

"You said that the first time and failed her. What makes you think you can live up to that vow," my father continued walking toward them. Adaliya didn't look bothered or fearful. She stood behind Zuri, thinking that he was going to be enough. I tried to get to my feet to help them both. The dizziness came on too strong, forcing me to stay on the ground. Zuri released a chained hook at his face. My father caught it and frowned.

"This shit again," he stated and tugged it. Zuri tripped

forward and planted his feet on the He dropped his head to hold the hook from connecting with the back of his neck. Nesbate looked over to Adaliya. Her eyes were shining black with a sparkle to them.

"Are you really going to let your son die for you?" he thought.

"Today, none of my children will die for me," she made clear. The puddles moved to the ocean to regenerate. Adaliya took a step back as Zuri started glowing. His arms weren't trembling as much. His head started to rise with violet bright eyes. Water rushed around him, washing away what used to be the old Zuri. The water fell revealing a mature Zuri in mosogens form. The chain and hook that were in Nesbate's hand dissolved. It reappeared and clocked him in the face. Nesbate reeled back from Zuri, giving him the space, he needed to rise to his feet. Zuri's long dreads reached his waist. He had waves tattooed on his legs up to his neck. He was the perfect younger version of Amanzi.

Nesbate wiped his face and proceeded to attack him with all the god-like power he had to prove a point. Skye's dragon shrieked from their fight with Qala. He flew at him, knocking him down.

"Skye!" Landon called out to him and noticed me on the ground. He teleported to me to help me up. "Are you okay?" he wondered. I nodded my head and followed the flow of water that wrapped around Qala and Amanzi.

"Yes. The nigga sucka punched me but it's all good. That will never happen again," I told him. Landon checked my face and turned to where Skye was. Amanzi came flying over and landed in front of us.

"What the fuck are y'all doing over here?" Amanzi questioned.

"He thinks I am going with him," Adaliya answered for us. Amanzi floated to his feet and got closer to Adaliya to watch Skye go rouge on him. He was hitting him with fire, wind, lighting, and everything else he, as the sky god, could produce. Nesbate's clothes were hanging off him with bruises to the body and face. Skye transformed into himself. Lighting and thunder were striking the sky as their angry leader took calmer steps towards Nesbate.

"You think what you did was funny, nigga. You really out here playing with me, bitch," Skye spoke. In the time that I have known him, he has never displayed this type of behavior. If Landon ever went out to do anything for Mother Nature, Skye would be the brother that I will make sure he was safe. Skye was acting like Amanzi and that wasn't good at all.

Nesbate didn't care enough to mince his words. He spat out blood from his mouth and smirked at Skye. "As you know, I didn't play with you. I played with her and both of you will be playing with my son."

Skye reached back to punch Nesbate with lightning wrapped around his fist. Nesbate laughed and vanished off the beach. Skye shrilled in anger and turned back to where Qala was. He too was also gone. Skye grabbed his dreads and started pacing.

"I'ma kill that bitch. I don't want to hear shit from anybody. I am going to dead this nigga on sight," Skye fumed.

"Alright, Skye. We hear you, but we need you to calm down," Landon told him. Skye glared at Landon and shook his head.

"Fuck calm," he stated. He walked off bumping into Landon's shoulder. Amanzi's eyebrows went up in shock like the rest of us.

"What the hell happened here?" Amanzi asked Landon.

"I don't know. We need to go up and talk to Mother. She probably will have an idea of his behavior," Landon answered.

"Yeah. We need to talk to Mother about what Qala revealed to me when I was in the funnel." Amanzi countered. He pulled Adaliya into his arms and kissed her forehead. Zuri was on her side, in his protective nature. Amanzi touched the mark behind Zuri's ear. "I guess Luna was the one to approve your purpose. I should have known. How are you doing?" he asked Adaliya.

"I'm doing great. We have a lot of work to do, though," she motioned to the mess that we needed to clean up. Amanzi whistled for the water to wash the bodies off the beach. The mosogens that were turned into puddles walked on the beach in water form. The piyas stood next to them to get orders from the father and mother.

"We will celebrate our Luna's return to the water tonight after we meet with my mother," he addressed that to the water mosogens. He turned his attention to Lenmon and smiled. "I would love to meet the families that you all have. It will be an honor to meet my grandchildren." Lenmon nodded his head, sentimental to his father's words.

"Thank you," he mumbled and bowed down to Adaliya. "I can't wait for you both to meet them." Adaliya took it a step further. She reached out to hug him. Lenmon's wide eyes got wider for a minute. He got over the shock long enough to hug her back.

"We will prepare everything for your return, Luna," the woman mosogen spoke.

"That will be great Trinity. We shouldn't be long," she threw that to Amanzi.

"We won't," Amanzi reached his hand out and spoke. She grabbed it to bring to her lips. Amanzi wasn't satisfied with that and took her lips for a soft kiss. He expressed his love for her openly. Adaliya glanced at me and winked her eye. We both had the men that were made for us. I was happy to see her acceptance of him and her element. She was a true goddess.

Amanzi

MY EYES DIDN'T SHOOT *open to the alarming ring of the water. They calmly searched for and harden. I wasn't surprised by her actions. She wasn't going to sit and bathe in me with Ali being a tenant in her home. I melted on that blanket into the element that awaited for me to join her. I flew out of the window and rushed to the top. My mosogens were swimming on my left and right, falling in an alignment that was meant to create a tsunami. We all rose above the water in a huge wave in form of our element form. I was in the middle with a sword over my head, traveling towards the beach. Dafari, Femi, Valin, and Trinity flanked me with their weapons out and ready.*

It was the most proper way to approach that battle. Qala was out here being bold about his shit. Nesbate was fucking Skye's mate and getting her pregnant. He was lucky that we didn't have that information on his ass from the jump. I would have given Qala a pass and rushed Nesbate's ass with that ice shit. He was a true hoe for this mess he started.

Skye was sitting in Mother's family room silent as a quiet storm. His eyes were dull, and he was sweating bricks. I was sitting on the sectional with Landon, Egypt, and Adaliya. Mother was standing behind us with Zuri.

"What can we do about this?" Egypt came out and asked.

"There is nothing we can do at this point. She is pregnant and she will give birth to this child," Mother said. Skye growled and shook his head.

"She is not having this nigga's baby," Skye argued.

"You can't tell her to get an abortion Skye. That is not your place to give that order," Adaliya added.

"Did I say I was going to do that?" he growled. Adaliya hunched her shoulders ignoring the way he responded to her.

"You didn't, but that is the only way she is not going to have that baby," she finished.

"I don't want to talk about this shit no more. You said that Qala told you something while you were in the funnel with him. What that bitch had to say?" Skye brought the subject back to me.

"Skye," Mother tried to reprimand him for his language. Skye rolled his eyes at her and gestured for me to talk.

"Qala told me the reason that you created us. Do you want to share what he said or should I?" I directed to Mother.

"Let's start with who you are and why they want you," Mother rested her hand on Adaliya's shoulder. "You are the true goddess of the water. When you fell into the water as a child, your aura brought on the spirit of Lady Water. She sensed the fight in you about the water and knew you would carry the torch with a standard that outmatched hers. The energy that you have inside you can heal or revive any life. Nesbate wants that because he thinks that the two of you can create a child that could overthrow me as Mother Nature. The same reason he wants Egypt by his side. He feels as if she can run and start another empire, birthing children that will be stronger than mine."

"That is sick," Landon growled.

"It is, but now he doesn't need Egypt anymore," Mother noted. She looked off, out into the window. She walked over to it and sighed. "That brings me to why Qalaneive needs Adaliya. Long ago, I used to mingle with the likes of the humans when I got bored. I envied the fun that they had, sometimes at my expense. I was lonely and for the first time, I wanted to feel what it was like to actually feel something for someone. I began to watch this man from where I'm standing. Qalaneieve Ross was an environmental scientist who wanted to see the world be great. His passion for all life on Earth was intriguing. I wanted to know more about him without the stalking. I decided to do something about it and met him at his favorite spot. He was getting coffee at Urban Grind on Marietta Street in Atlanta, Georgia. He was sitting at a small table reading a book called Earthing that explains the healthiness of the earth. I commented on it and got his attention. He invited me over and we talked about my beliefs and what I wanted from the world. My thoughts matched his, so I thought we were compatible. We started dating and spent more time with each other. When I thought it was safe, I disclosed who I was. He believed me on one hand yet needed some clarification of what I was saying. I showed him and it was like he had fallen in love with me all over again. It was magic. Something that I have never felt or dealt with before. What I knew, was that it needed to last forever. I mean he wanted the same things I wanted. Why not help him achieve these goals? Why can't I share my pedestal with the man that I love? I loved him. I loved him so much that I decided to give him my rib. I implanted a piece of myself into this man to help him be my equal, and that was my fault. I didn't think to accept that he was still a man. I didn't think that he would go out and find a mate. I didn't think that he would have plotted to leave me and take or split what I have watched over for years, like some marriage that he came into with nothing and trying to leave with everything. He had her thinking that she could be me. He had the audacity for him to think that he could hide it from me. He did because I didn't think I had to watch over him like that. But he slipped, and I reacted, killing his girlfriend and their unborn child by swallowing them into an earthquake. Qalanieve threatened the human race along with the Earth. I felt like my presence on Earth has caused too much turmoil, so I created the three of you," she finished and turned to me. "Qalaneieve is who he is because of me. He has all the traits that you guys have in one. I didn't want to create another him, so I divided the elements into three sons."

The room was quiet at first. Landon sat forward with his elbow on his knees staring at me. Egypt's eyes were on me, while Adaliya rubbed my back. Mother was standing near the window waiting for my reaction to her truth. When I didn't say anything, she thought she needed to explain herself more.

"I know that you have been asking me your purpose for centuries. I felt like the only way that you could understand what I was talking about was if you had an idea of what it would feel like to be betrayed like that," Mother added and stopped when I waved my hand.

"I'm not tripping Mother. You did what you had to do. The nigga cheated and tried to take what's yours. It is what it is," he sat back on the sectional.

"Wait, what? You are cool with all this?" Landon inquired.

"Yeah. He was a nobody until he met Mother. Mother made this nigga who he is and now he trying to rise above her after she put him on, fuck that," I replied. I couldn't wait to see that nigga Qalaneive Ross again. Landon patted me on my leg like a proud big brother. Mother's arms snaked around my neck. She kissed me on my cheek and grinned.

"Thank you for understanding," she whispered.

"No problem," I told her and kissed her arm.

Clapping and thunderous laughter shot from the other side of the room. Skye was holding his stomach curled over with it. "You have got to be FUCKING kidding me," Skye blurted.

Mother stood upright scowling at Skye. "I'm sorry."

Skye nodded his head and jumped to his feet. "You are right Mother. You are a sorry indi-fucking-vidual. Why would you think that what you did was okay? Creating fucking people to fight a battle against an ex of yours because you couldn't let go. Are you fucking serious right now? The whole time...the whole damn time... I thought I was created to give life back to the sky. To live and make sure it stays safe for humans. Naw. All this fucking time I've protected the sky over some bullshit," Skye's outburst was felt with anger and something else. He was already looking like somebody done pissed in one of his clouds and called it rain. But, this nigga was standing here foaming blue shit out of his mouth. Adaliya sniffed and leaned forward.

"Skye are you feeling well?" she noticed as well.

"FUCK NO! I am not alright?" He growled. Skye's eyes started flashing white and silver. "You are the reason for all this shit. You!"

"Skye," Landon got to his feet. "What's going on brother? Talk to me," he approached him calmly.

"Did you not hear this filth from her fucking mouth? We were created for nothing. NOTHING! My fucking mate is pregnant with Nesbate's baby behind her and her bullshit," he continued to yell. His eyes started leaking with his ears. Skye opened and closed his mouth, releasing fire and lighting from it.

"He inhaled the toxins from those creatures in the water," Adaliya revealed.

"Shit," I stood next to Landon and held my hands out. "Skye you are sick, brother. Let me heal you."

"I'm not fucking sick," he thought until he bent over and started throwing up fire mixed with the poison. It sparked a fire that could have spread. Egypt gasped and jumped off the couch. Adaliya's hands went out to release water over the flames while Mother stood on to watch. She had never heard Skye speak to her in that manner. I would say that it was the poison, but Skye always thought his purpose was bigger than what Mother put on. I guessed finding out about his mate and this Qala shit had him one.

"Amanzi," Landon called out to me. He snatched a fighting Skye and wrestled his ass to the ground. I placed my hand over his body to pull out the poison, but his heart was going to need a special touch. Sadly, none of us in that room had the power to heal it.

www.ingramcontent.com/pod-product-compliance
Lightning Source LLC
LaVergne TN
LVHW012043160826
845678LV00014B/2690

* 9 7 9 8 8 4 7 8 7 5 4 9 3 *